CARNIVAL MAYHEM

SELENA WINTERS

Carnival Mayhem Copyright © 2024 Selena Winters

All Rights Reserved.
No part of this publication may be reproduced, stored, or transmitted in any form or by any means, electronic, mechanical, photocopying, recording, scanning, or otherwise without written permission from the publisher. It is illegal to copy this book, post it to a website, or distribute it by any other means without permission.

This novel is entirely a work of fiction. The names, characters and incidents portrayed in it are the work of the author's imagination. Any resemblance to actual persons, living or dead, events or localities is entirely coincidental.
Warning: the unauthorized reproduction or distribution of this copyrighted work is illegal. Criminal copyright infringement, including infringement without monetary gain, is investigated by the FBI and is punishable by up to 5 years in prison and a fine of $250,000.

❦ Created with Vellum

CONTENTS

Blurb   v
Playlist   vii
Author's Note   xi

1. Colt   1
2. Nash   7
3. Flora   13
4. Flora   17
5. Colt   23
6. Nash   31
7. Flora   41
8. Colt   49
9. Nash   55
10. Flora   63
11. Nash   75
12. Colt   83
13. Flora   89
14. Nash   103
15. Colt   107
16. Flora   117
17. Colt   133
18. Nash   141
19. Flora   153
20. Colt   161
21. Nash   167
22. Flora   171
23. Colt   177
24. Nash   183
25. Flora   193
26. Colt   201

27. Nash	215
28. Flora	225
29. Colt	241
30. Nash	247
31. Flora	253
32. Colt	261
33. Flora	267
34. Nash	281
35. Colt	289
36. Flora	301
37. Nash	309
38. Colt	319
39. Flora	327
40. Flora	333
41. Nash	339
42. Colt	353
43. Flora	359
44. Nash	371
45. Epilogue	387
About the Author	399

BLURB

When I escaped my broken past, a shell of the woman I wanted to be, I discovered a dazzling carnival that offered a new beginning and a chance to reclaim my power.

The moment I met Colt and Nash, everything changed. No longer scared and alone, I found protectors who saw my scars and vowed to shield me from harm. With their mesmerizing charm and fierce loyalty, they pulled me into their world—a world that thrived on the line between darkness and light.

Colt's fiery intensity and Nash's quiet strength became my anchor as they unraveled the very essence of my being. They offered me a chance to reclaim my sense of self and vengeance against those who'd wronged me. In a vibrant underworld of dark dreams and glittering neon lights, one where the lines too often blur between love, protection, and danger, they showed me how to resurrect myself from the ash I had become.

With these two men at my side, I discovered a new

kind of power—the kind that ignites the soul and demands retribution. They breathed life into instincts I never knew I had, revealing a strength and fearlessness that sparked an insatiable desire for revenge. The question looming: Could I navigate the treacherous path of my newfound empowerment without losing myself—or them—in the chaos?

As the carnival lights flicker and the darkness closes in, I must decide: Do I surrender to the intoxicating pull of our shared madness sending us down a dark path together, or walk away?

PLAYLIST

<u>Carnival Mayhem Playlist</u>

"Luci"— ZAND
"Here come the wolves"—Lola Blanc
"F*ck"—Mandrazo, Sebabrazy, Kiyashqo
Heartbeat"—Isabel LaRosa
"Born for this"—CRMNL
"Devil Knows"—Armen Paul
"MAKEUP"—Chris Grey
"Dark Thoughts"—Skylar Grey
"Fatal Attraction"—Reed Wonder, Aurora Olivias
"Tear you apart"—Daniel Farrant, Nick Kingsley
"Angel"—Camyilo
"Can you love me?"—Croixx
"Bad things"—Nation Haven
"Loveless"—Gothic Zero

You can find the playlist on Spotify here

DEDICATION

COLT & NASH

This one's for the depraved little angels who crave being hunted down, caught between our bodies, and claimed until you're dripping with surrender.
We'll corrupt every inch of your soul while we protect what's ours.
Welcome to our twisted playground.

AUTHOR'S NOTE

Author's Note

This story explores dark romance and contains explicit content that may not be suitable for all readers. It includes themes of dominance, psychotic behavior, possessiveness, and explicit mature scenes presented alongside delicate subject matters that may be distressing or triggering for some individuals.

Please refer to the comprehensive list of warnings on my website for detailed information on this book's triggers.

I advise reader discretion and recommend only proceeding if you're comfortable with the mentioned themes. Rest assured, the story ends in a HEA with no cliffhanger or cheating between the main characters.

1

COLT

I pull the rope taut, testing the tension of the main support line. Nash moves along the opposite beam, his movements fluid even when not performing.

"You're favoring your left side again." Nash doesn't look at me as he speaks, focused on securing his rigging.

"I am not." But I roll my shoulder, knowing he's right. The bastard notices everything.

"Ten years of spotting you, Colt. I know your tells." He swings down from his perch, landing silent as a cat beside me. "Let me see."

I grunt but turn to face him. His fingers find the knot in my muscles with practiced ease.

"You're going to injure yourself if you don't sort this out."

"Since when are you my mother?" I try to pull away, but his grip tightens.

"Since you became a stubborn ass who won't admit

when he's hurt." Nash's other hand braces against my back as he works out the tension. "There. Better?"

I rotate my arm, and the movement is smoother. "Lucky guess."

"Skill." He flashes that rare smile that makes his eyes crinkle at the corners. "Though you're welcome to test it in practice later."

"Only if you promise not to show off with that new sequence you've been working on."

"Me? Show off?" Nash places a hand over his heart in mock offense. "I would never."

"Right, and I'm the King of England."

He laughs, the sound echoing in the empty tent. "Your Majesty." With a flourishing bow, he backs toward the rigging. "Now, stop stalling and help me with these lines. Tyson will have our asses if we're not ready for tonight."

I watch Nash climb back up the rigging, his muscles flexing with graceful precision. The way he moves has always fascinated me—it feels like gravity is optional, like physics bends to his will.

"You're staring." His voice carries down, tinged with amusement.

"Making sure you don't fall and crack that pretty skull of yours." I busy myself with coiling excess rope, ignoring the flutter in my chest.

"Pretty, am I?" He hangs upside down, face level with mine. "Careful there, Colt. People might get ideas."

My breath catches. We've danced this line for years, throwing comments that blur the boundary between joking and something else entirely. Something we never name.

"Let them." The words slip out before I can stop them, rougher than intended.

Nash's eyes darken, and the air between us crackles with tension. Then he swings away, graceful as ever, breaking the spell.

"Speaking of practice..." He rights himself on the platform. "That new sequence needs a spotter. You up for it?"

"Depends. Are you planning to listen if I tell you to slow down?"

"When have I ever not listened to you?"

I bark out a laugh. "You want the full list or just this week's highlights?"

"I resent that implication." He starts removing his shirt, muscles rippling beneath intricate tattoos. "I'm a perfect angel."

"Angel of chaos, maybe." My eyes trace the familiar patterns on his skin. I've memorized every line, every shadow. Not that I'd admit it.

"Takes one to know one." He chalks his hands. "Coming up, or am I practicing solo?"

I grab the chalk bag, ignoring how my skin heats when our fingers brush. "Can't let you have all the fun, can I?"

Nash wraps his hands in the chalky powder. I've watched this ritual a thousand times and memorized how his fingers flex. Every time, I have to force myself to look away.

It's not that I'm ashamed. I've known I was bi since

military school, where stolen kisses behind the gym were as common as bloody noses from fighting. But here? In the carnival? Might as well paint a target on my back.

I watch Lars and Tyson by the entrance, their muscles bulging as they haul equipment. Everything about this place screams testosterone and masculinity. The guys here? They'd sooner break your jaw than look at you if they thought you swung that way.

"Earth to Colt." Nash's voice cuts through my thoughts. "You planning on joining me up here?"

And then there's Nash. Beautiful, straight-as-an-arrow Nash. The way he moves, all grace and power, it's like he's trying to kill me. But I've seen him with women, watched him charm them with that deadly smile. He's naturally fluid and comfortable in his skin in a way I never learned to be.

"Yeah, yeah. Keep your pants on." I chalk up my hands, hoping the routine will steady my nerves.

"Now, where's the fun in that?" He winks, and my heart does that stupid flutter thing it's been doing more often lately.

That's the worst part. The banter, the easy touches. To him, it's just how we are—best friends who've spent years learning to trust each other with our lives. To me? It's torture, sweet and slow.

"You're doing it again." Nash hangs upside down again, his face way too close to mine. "Getting lost in that head of yours."

I step back, maintaining the careful distance I always keep. "Just focused on the routine."

He rights himself with that impossible grace. "Sure

you are. Come on, tough guy. Show me what you've got."

I follow Nash up the rigging, my muscles remembering every handhold. We've done this dance thousands of times, but my heart still races when he catches me mid-flip, his hands strong and sure against my skin.

"Good." His breath hits my neck as we transition into the next move. "Now the blind catch."

I release the bar, twisting my body in the air. For a split second, I'm flying—then his hands lock around my wrists. The momentum swings us in a wide arc.

"See?" Nash's eyes gleam with that wild joy he only gets up here. "Perfect trust."

And it is perfect. We move like one being, reading each other's bodies without words. If only he knew how much I notice—how his chest rises with each breath and his fingers linger just a bit longer than necessary when he steadies me.

We run through the sequence three more times. Each catch, each touch, adding another crack to my careful control. By the fourth run-through, I'm half-hard and grateful for the loose shorts I wear over my leotard.

"Last one," Nash calls out. He's sweating now, skin glistening under the tent lights. "Make it count."

We nail the routine. As we descend, his hand brushes my lower back—probably spotting me, making sure I'm steady. But my skin burns where he touched.

"Not bad." He grabs his water bottle and takes a long drink. A drop escapes, trailing down his neck. "Though you're still favoring that shoulder."

"Thought you weren't my mother?" I start packing the chalk, needing something to do with my hands.

"No." He laughs, and the sound hits me right in the gut. "Definitely not your mother."

I watch him gather his things, all fluid grace and natural beauty. My best friend. My torture. My secret.

If he notices my eyes on him, he doesn't show it. But then, that's our whole relationship—this careful dance of almost something, never quite crossing the line.

2

NASH

The lights dim across the big top, casting long shadows that dance like old friends across the sawdust floor. I adjust my sequined costume, watching Colt stretch his shoulders one last time. His muscles ripple beneath the fabric, and I precisely catalog every movement.

"Ready to give them a show?" I flash my performer's smile, which makes the audience believe I'm just another entertainer chasing applause. If they knew the thoughts that circle my mind while I'm up there, watching them all from above like they're prey...

"Born ready." Colt rolls his neck, and I notice the slight hesitation in his left side.

My fingers twitch with the urge to touch, to correct, to control. Instead, I channel that energy into securing my rigging. Everything must be perfect. I've checked the equipment three times already, but perfection demands dedication.

The crowd murmurs as Tyson's voice booms

through the tent. My pulse doesn't quicken—it never does. While others feel butterflies, I feel only the familiar cold focus settling in my bones.

"Remember," I whisper to Colt as we take our positions, "follow my lead on the third transition. I'll compensate for your shoulder."

He shoots me a look that's equal parts gratitude and defiance. Beautiful. I store that expression away with all I've collected of him over the years.

The spotlight hits us, and I transform. My smile grows wider, and my movements become more fluid. The audience gasps at my apparent joy as I swing through the air, but they don't understand. This height, this control is not about joy. It's about power.

As we launch into our routine, our bodies moving in perfect synchronization, I feel the familiar thrill.

The routine flows through my muscles like muscle memory should. Each flip, catch, and moment of connection with Colt happens without conscious thought. Ten years of practice create that kind of perfection.

I remember the day Tyson brought him in. I'd only been here two months, fresh from another circus and looking for something darker that matched the hollow spaces inside me. Colt showed up with fire in his eyes and demons on his shoulders. Same age as me but carrying different wounds.

We clicked instantly. Two broken pieces that fit together in all the right ways, he became my shadow, my mirror, and my partner in everything that mattered, including the legal and illegal sides of carnival life.

My hands find his in the darkness as we cross paths mid-air. His grip is solid and dependable, like always. The audience gasps below, but I barely hear them. It's just us and the void between earth and sky.

"Third transition," I breathe, and he responds perfectly, compensating for my added force as I take more of his weight to protect that shoulder.

Moments like these highlight a decade of friendship: how we read each other's bodies and anticipate each other's moves. No one else at the carnival understands me like Colt does. No one else sees past my carefully crafted facade to the calculating mind beneath.

We spin through our final sequence, our bodies moving in perfect harmony. The crowd erupts in applause, but I'm already planning tomorrow's practice. We'll need to work on his left side and ensure that shoulder weakness doesn't become a liability.

That's what best friends do—they watch out for each other. They notice every detail, every flaw, every perfect moment. They become essential, like breathing.

The lights dim as we take our final pose. Another flawless performance. Another night of being exactly what we've always been to each other—partners, friends, family.

As we descend from the rigging, I watch Colt's movements with practiced attention. His landing is perfect as it always is, but I catch that slight favor of his right side again.

"Stellar performance," I say, reaching for my water bottle. "Though you nearly gave me a heart attack with that triple."

Colt peels off his costume top, sweat glistening on his chest. "Please. You love it when I improvise."

"I love it when you stick to the choreography." I keep my voice level controlled, though my eyes trace the familiar patterns of his tattoos. "There's beauty in precision."

"There's beauty in surprising people, too." He tosses me a towel, and I catch it without looking.

I begin methodically packing our gear, each piece in its designated spot. The routine soothes me and gives my hands something to do.

"Speaking of surprising people," Colt continues, "did you see Tyson's face during the finale?"

"Saw everything. I always do." I zip up the equipment bag just as Tyson approaches.

"Fucking brilliant, both of you." Tyson claps us each on the shoulder. "That's what I call a show. The crowd ate it up."

"All in a day's work, boss." Colt grins.

I follow Colt back to our trailer, muscles aching in that satisfying way after a perfect performance. The familiar creak of the steps under our feet, the rattle of the door that never quite sits right, is part of the rhythm we've built over the years.

"Grab me one?" Colt calls out, dropping onto our worn leather couch while I head to the mini fridge. The cold beer feels good in my hand as I toss one his way.

"Left side's still bothering you." I settle into my usual spot, noting how he favors his right arm even for something as simple as catching a beer.

"Not starting that again." He flicks on the TV, the

blue light casting shadows across his face. The half-eaten pizza from lunch still sits on the coffee table, and he reaches for a slice.

I take a long pull from my beer, watching him from the corner of my eye.

"Pass the remote." I hold out my hand, knowing he'll give me grief about it.

"What, you don't want to watch Monster Trucks?" He smirks but tosses it over anyway.

The familiar drone of some crime documentary fills our trailer as we fall into our post-show routine. It's comfortable, this space we've carved out together. Safe. Even if sometimes the air feels thick with things we never say.

I grab a slice of pizza, cold but still good. The documentary drones on about serial killers—our usual evening entertainment. Colt knows I prefer the analytical side of crime, while he'd rather watch things blow up. But he never complains, just adds his commentary between bites and sips.

"Think they'll ever catch this one?" he asks, gesturing at the screen with his beer.

"They always make mistakes eventually." I lean back, letting my shoulders relax. "Everyone does."

I watch Colt's chest rise and fall as he drifts into a light doze, the TV casting flickering shadows across his face. The documentary's narrator drones on about DNA evidence, but my mind wanders to our performance tonight.

My fingers tap against the beer bottle as I catalog the day's successes: four perfect run-throughs during practice and a flawless performance. The crowd's energy fed into our routine, their gasps and applause hitting all the right beats. Even Tyson's praise felt earned tonight.

Colt shifts in his sleep, and I notice his shoulder position. Whether he admits it or not, he'll need ice on that tomorrow. That's part of my job as his partner—keeping him in peak condition. We can't afford injuries in this line of work, not with the things Tyson has us doing both in and out of the ring.

Today was good. It was the kind of day that reminded me why I chose this life, why I stay: the control, the precision, the perfect execution of carefully laid plans. And having a partner like Colt—someone who matches my dedication, who understands the importance of every detail—makes it all work seamlessly.

The documentary switches to commercials, and I turn down the volume. No need to wake him. He's earned his rest, and I prefer these quiet moments anyway. They give me time to think, plan, and maintain my world's careful order.

3

FLORA

As I scrub last night's dishes, the kitchen clock ticks past seven a.m. My fingers prune in the tepid water while the scent of bacon wafts through the air—breakfast for everyone but me. My foster mother Janet bustles around, plating food for her precious boys.

"Did you iron Tommy's uniform?" She doesn't look at me.

"Yes." The same answer I give every morning.

The calendar on the wall mocks me with its red circle around today's date: December 1st, my eighteenth birthday. Not that anyone here remembers or cares. But I remember—oh, how I remember. This birthday means freedom—no more mandatory placement, no more state oversight, no more...them.

Heavy footsteps thunder down the stairs as Tommy and Jake storm into the kitchen, shoving past me to grab their plates. Jake's hand lingers too long on my hip as he passes. I step away, my stomach churning.

"Move it, freak." Tommy elbows me aside.

The mail slot creaks and flutters. Janet sighs dramatically. "Get that, will you?"

I dry my hands and retrieve the stack of envelopes. Bills, ads, and then—something different. A bright red flyer catches my eye. Gold lettering sparkles across the top: "CHRISTMAS AT THE CARNIVAL - Magic, Mystery, and Masquerade!"

My heart skips as I read further. The traveling carnival is setting up on the outskirts of Easthollow. They're hiring. Looking for new performers, vendors, anything.

"What's taking so long?" Janet snaps.

I stuff the carnival flyer into my pocket before returning to the kitchen with the rest of the mail. But my mind is already racing with possibilities. A way out. A fresh start. Something entirely different from this hell I've been trapped in.

Seven years of abuse and survival have led to this moment. I'm eighteen now. Adult. Free. And the universe just handed me my ticket to escape.

As I climb the stairs, I clutch the flyer in my pocket, heart racing with newfound hope. The worn carpet muffles my footsteps, but not the heavier ones behind me.

A hand grabs my arm and spins me around. Tommy towers over me, his face twisted in that familiar sneer that makes my blood run cold.

"What's this?" He snatches the paper from my pocket. My stomach drops as his eyes scan the carnival advertisement.

"Give it back." My voice comes out smaller than intended.

He backs me against the wall, one hand pressed beside my head. The hallway shrinks, memories flooding back—being cornered like this before, the pain, the helplessness. The smell of his cologne makes me nauseous.

"Planning your escape, whore?" His free hand slides up my thigh. I try to squirm away but there's nowhere to go. "Bet you want to run off to that carnival, get stuffed full of cock. Is that what you want?"

Tears sting my eyes. I shake my head, unable to speak. His fingers burrow into my hips so hard I know my skin with bruise.

"It's not happening." He leans closer. "You belong to me and Jake. Don't forget that." His hand moves higher, invasively. "Or do you need another reminder?"

The flyer crumples in his fist as he presses against me. I squeeze my eyes shut, willing myself to be anywhere but here.

Tommy's weight disappears as Janet's voice echoes up the stairs. "Tommy! Your father needs help with the truck!"

His footsteps retreat, but the violation of his touch lingers on my skin. I stumble into my room—if you can call this cramped space with its secondhand furniture a room. The door clicks shut behind me, and I collapse onto the narrow bed, burying my face in the thin pillow.

Hot tears spill down my cheeks. My whole body shakes as I try to muffle my sobs. Seven years. Seven years of this torture, of being their plaything, their punching bag, their *property*.

I curl into a tight ball, hugging my knees to my chest. The crumpled carnival flyer lies discarded in the hallway, but its promise burns bright in my mind. A way out. Something different. Anything has to be better than this.

My fingers trace the bruises forming on my hip. Fresh marks layered over old ones, a map of pain and survival etched into my skin. But not anymore. I'm eighteen now.

They can't stop me. Tommy can threaten all he wants, but I won't stay. I won't let them hurt me anymore. The carnival might be my only chance at escape, and I will take it.

I wipe my eyes and sit up, determination replacing fear. I don't care what it takes. I don't care if I have to beg, plead, or work for free. I'm leaving this house and getting away from this family.

My gaze falls on the small backpack tucked under my bed—the one I've kept packed for two years, ready for this moment. It's time to finally use it.

4

FLORA

My hands shake as I ease the window open, wincing at every tiny squeak of the old frame. The December air hits me like a slap, but I welcome it. Anything is better than staying here another night.

The backpack weighs heavy on my shoulders. It is filled with everything I own that matters—which isn't much: some clothes, my birth certificate hidden in a sock, and all the dollars I've saved from working a part-time job at the diner.

Below me, the drainpipe looks more daunting than during my daytime practice runs. But I've mapped this out for months, testing each spot where my feet need to go. I swing one leg out, then the other, clinging to the windowsill.

A noise from down the hall freezes me in place. Footsteps. My heart pounds so hard I'm sure they'll hear it. Please just be Jake going to the bathroom. Please don't check my room.

The footsteps pass. I release the shaky breath I didn't realize I'd been holding and start my descent, trying not to think about how technically I'm still in the system until graduation. Six more months of high school shouldn't matter more than my safety, but breaking the rules still makes my stomach twist.

The drainpipe creaks under my weight. I pause, listening for any sign I've been discovered. Nothing but the distant sound of a car on the highway. Three more feet to go. My muscles strain with the effort of moving slowly, carefully.

My foot touches grass and relief floods through me. I made it. But I'm not safe yet—I must get off this property before anyone notices I'm gone.

I stick to the shadows, avoiding the motion-sensor lights Tommy installed last summer. I walk past the garage where so many horrible things happened, past the front porch where they first welcomed me into their "loving" home. Each step takes me closer to freedom, but my nerves jangle with every tiny sound.

I walk quickly down Oak Street, keeping to the shadows. The sound of carnival music drifts through the crisp night air, growing louder with each block. My heart races, not from exertion but from hope. Real, tangible hope for the first time in years.

The carnival lights paint the sky in bursts of color above the tree line. I pull the mask from my backpack. It's nothing special, just a cheap thing I found at the dollar store last Halloween. But tonight it represents everything: freedom, escape, a chance at a new life.

The entrance looms ahead, strung with twinkling

lights and draped in red and gold fabric. A sign advertises "Christmas Masquerade Night - All Welcome." My fingers tremble as I slip the mask over my face, adjusting the elastic band where it digs into my hair.

I reach into my pocket and touch the crumpled flyer. In bold letters, it promises, "Performers and Vendors Wanted."

The ticket taker barely glances at me as I hand over most of my saved cash. Inside, the carnival thrums with energy. Masked figures weave between the booths and rides, their laughter carrying on the wind. The scent of cotton candy and popcorn fills the air.

For a moment, I stand frozen, overwhelmed by the sensory assault after the quiet of my midnight escape. But there's no time to waste. I have to find the ringmaster before my foster family discovers I'm gone.

The masquerade tent looms before me, music and laughter spilling from its crimson-striped sides. My feet won't move. Everyone inside looks so polished and confident in their elaborate masks and fancy clothes. I tug at my oversized sweater, suddenly aware of how shabby I must appear.

What if they're just like Jake and Tommy? Different faces, same darkness. My throat tightens. The mask suddenly feels suffocating, but I can't risk taking it off. Not here, not where someone might recognize me.

I drift to the side of the entrance, pressing myself against a support pole. People stream past me, their joy a stark contrast to the anxiety churning in my stomach. A group of women sweep by in sequined dresses, their heels clicking against the wooden platform. I shrink further into the shadows.

The tent flap parts and my breath catches. A man emerges, tall and graceful in a way that makes my heart stutter. His mask is simple but elegant, black with silver accents that catch the carnival lights. But it's not the mask that holds my attention—it's how he moves, like every step is part of some intricate dance.

His dark hair falls just right, and even from here I can see the definition in his arms, marked with intricate tattoos that disappear beneath his rolled sleeves. He's beautiful in a way that makes my chest ache.

As if sensing my stare, he turns. Our eyes meet through our masks, and his lips curve into a knowing smile. He winks at me—a simple gesture that sends electricity up my spine.

I press harder against the pole, trying to disappear but can't look away. My cheeks burn beneath my mask, and for a moment I forget about Jake, about Tommy, about everything except those eyes and that smile.

"What are you waiting for, beautiful? It's Christmas—time to have a little fun." As he passes, his voice carries a hint of amusement, disappearing before I can respond.

My heart hammers against my ribs. Beautiful. The endearment feels foreign, dangerous. No one's ever called me that before. Jake and Tommy had other names for me, cruel ones that still echo in my nightmares.

I touch my mask, making sure it's secure. He's right—I came here for a reason. Standing in the shadows won't get me the job I desperately need. But my feet remain rooted to the spot, my fingers digging into the rough wood of the support pole.

The man's words loop in my head.

Have a little fun.

As if it's that simple. As if seven years of survival instincts can be switched off like a light. Despite how baggy it is, my sweater feels too thin and too revealing. I pull the sleeves down over my hands.

But what choice do I have? I can't go back. Not to that house. Not to them. The thought of returning makes bile rise in my throat. At least here, in this sea of masks and music, I have a chance.

I peel myself away from the pole, one small step at a time. The entrance to the tent looms before me, red and gold fabric rippling in the December breeze. Inside, the masquerade ball continues, voices and laughter spilling out into the night.

5

COLT

The winter chill bites through my jacket as I adjust the white skull mask over my face. Our first night in Easthollow is different—there is no show, just the carnival's Christmas masquerade ball. Colored lights dance across the snow, casting shadows between the food stalls and rides.

I scan the crowds, watching families laugh and couples kissing. Then, my eyes snag on a figure standing alone, her thin jacket barely protecting against December's bite. She has a small backpack on her shoulder, which she clutches for dear life.

Her mask is cheap and frayed at the edges, but something about her pulls me in. She holds herself like she's ready to bolt at any moment.

My feet move before my brain catches up. Haven't felt this instant attraction since... well, since Nash.

"That mask's seen better days." I stop beside her, close enough to catch a hint of vanilla. "We've got plenty of spares in the costume tent."

She startles, taking a half-step back. "Oh, I... I'm fine."

"Come on." I gesture toward the back area. "Consider it a Christmas gift. Can't have you wearing that sad thing at our masquerade."

Her fingers trace the edge of her mask. "Why would you—"

"Because you caught my eye." I lean against the carousel's railing. "And I always take care of what interests me."

She shifts her weight, studying me through those mask holes. Even with most of her face hidden, I can tell she's beautiful. But it's more than that—there's something familiar in how she carries herself, her pain almost palpable.

"I'm Colt." I hold out my hand.

She hesitates before placing her smaller one in mine. "Flora."

Her skin is ice cold. Without thinking, I wrap both my hands around hers. "Jesus, you're freezing. Let's get you that mask and maybe some hot chocolate after?"

I guide Flora toward the costume tent, keeping enough distance so she won't feel crowded. With each step, I notice how she tracks my movements from the corner of her eye, like prey watching a predator.

"Here we are." I open the tent flap, letting her choose whether to enter first. She pauses, then slips inside.

The tent smells of dusty fabric and sequins glisten everywhere. Racks of costumes are lined up like soldiers.

I reach for a box of masks on a high shelf, and Flora jumps at my sudden movement.

"These are the good ones." I set the box on a table between us, giving her space. "Take your pick."

Her fingers hover over a delicate white mask with silver accents. When I shift to get a better look, my arm brushes hers. She flinches hard enough to knock into the box.

I catch it before it falls, my jaw clenching. Someone's hurt this girl. Badly.

"Sorry about that." I step back, hands raised. "I'll give you some space to choose."

Relief floods her posture as I move away; her body sighs visibly with relief. She picks up the white mask again, holding it like it might shatter.

"That one suits you," I say softly. " Would you like to try it on?"

She nods, fingers trembling as she unties her old mask. For a split second, I glimpse her face—stunning, but with shadows in her eyes that make my blood boil.

The new mask fits perfectly, transforming her into something ethereal. But I can't shake what I've seen—how she startles at sudden movements, keeps her back to walls, flinches from touch.

I know those signs. I've seen them in others. The carnival has become a refuge for many who are running from their demons.

"Thank you," she whispers, touching the mask's edge. "It's beautiful."

"Keep it." I resist the urge to reach out, to offer comfort she's not ready to accept. "Consider it a gift."

"Do you work here?" Flora asks, her voice delicate, sweet.

"Yeah, I'm one of the performers." I lean against a costume rack, keeping my movements slow and deliberate. "Acrobatics, mainly."

She fidgets with the edge of her sleeve. "I was hoping to talk to someone about... about joining."

And there it is. I've seen it before. Desperate souls looking for sanctuary in our twisted little family. But something about Flora's fear feels different. Raw. Fresh.

"That'd be Tyson you want, our ringmaster." I study her through my mask. "But maybe you could tell me why, first? Not everyone's cut out for carnival life."

Her shoulders tense. "I just... I need to leave. To get away."

"From what?"

"Everything." The word comes out choked. She wraps her arms around herself, and I have to fight the urge to step closer, to offer comfort.

"Listen, angel," I keep my voice gentle, "I'm not trying to pry. But if you're running from something, we need to know. The carnival... we protect our own. But we have to know what we're dealing with."

She shakes her head. "I can't... I shouldn't have..."

"Hey." I raise my hands, palms out. "You don't have to tell me everything. Just enough so I know helping you won't bring trouble down on my family here."

Flora's quiet for a long moment, her breathing unsteady. "My foster family. I can legally leave. But they... they won't let me go easily."

The way she says it, the waiver in her voice as it

almost crackles tells me everything she's not saying. My hands curl into fists, but I force them to relax. "Are they here tonight?"

"No." She glances toward the tent entrance. "But they'll notice I'm gone soon."

"Right. Let's go talk to Tyson." I push off from the costume rack. "He'll want to meet you anyway, and better now before your family starts searching."

Flora's fingers twist in her sleeve. "Is he... what's he like?"

"Fair." I choose my words carefully. "He looks out for his people. And he's got a good sense about who belongs here."

I lead her out of the costume tent, staying close but not touching. The crowd's thickened, and I notice how she shrinks from brushing shoulders with strangers. Without thinking, I position myself to block the worst of it, creating a buffer between her and the thicket of bodies.

"Ty's usually in his office this time of night." I guide her toward the back of the grounds where the trailers are parked. "He will finish the business while everyone else enjoys the masquerade."

We pass the carousel again, its lights painting Flora's white mask in shifting colors. She stumbles on a patch of ice, and my hand steadies her elbow. She goes rigid under my touch.

"Sorry." I drop my hand. "Just didn't want you falling."

She nods, but her breathing's quick and shallow. I curse myself for the slip-up. Every instinct screams to protect her, but that means keeping my distance right now.

"Almost there." I point to Tyson's trailer, its windows glowing warm against the dark. "You ready?"

Flora takes a deep breath, squaring her shoulders. "Yes."

That single word carries more strength than she probably realizes. Whatever's happened to her, she's survived. And now she's choosing to fight.

"Then let's introduce you to your new boss." I climb the trailer steps first, knocking on the door. "Because something tells me you belong here with us."

The porch light catches something in Flora's eyes as she looks up at me—a flicker of something raw that wasn't there before. My breath catches. For the first time since I saw her, that perpetual fear gives way to something else. Desire.

It hits me like a punch to the gut. After years of keeping my urges locked down, this slip of a girl sparks something primal in me. Something that wants to possess, to claim, to mark.

Her lips open as I tower over her on the steps. Despite her terror of touch, she doesn't back away. If anything, she sways closer, like a moth drawn to a flame.

"You're safe here," I murmur, watching her pupils dilate behind that delicate mask. "No one will hurt you again."

A shiver runs through her that has nothing to do with cold. Her tongue darts out to wet her lips, and my control nearly snaps. After so long burning for Nash, drowning in wants I can never voice, this pure shot of desire for someone else is intoxicating.

Maybe this is what I need—someone soft and broken that I can protect, possess, and rebuild. Someone to help me forget how Nash's body moves when we perform, the electricity when our skin touches, the years of denying what I feel.

But even as the thought forms, I know it's a lie. Nothing could make me forget Nash. This pull toward Flora is different—not a replacement, but something new entirely.

She's still staring up at me, breath coming faster, that spark of curiosity clear in her gaze. Before I can stop myself, my hand traces the edge of her mask.

This time, she doesn't flinch.

I pull back from that charged moment, remembering why we're here. "You might want to take the mask off before we go in. Ty likes to see who he's talking to."

The spell breaks. Flora's hand flies to the white mask, fingers trembling slightly as they trace its edges. "Right. Of course."

"Hey." I keep my voice low and gentle. "You've got this. Just be honest with him."

She nods, taking a deep breath before untying the ribbon. The mask comes away, and my chest tightens. Even in the dim porch light, she's stunning—high cheekbones, full lips, eyes that shift between green and gold. The shadows beneath that beauty catch me—the slight tension around her mouth, the wariness in her gaze.

"Better." I take the mask from her shaking hands, careful not to let our fingers brush. "Ready?"

Flora smooths her hair, squaring those delicate shoulders. "Yes. I need to do this."

There's determination in her voice now. Something inside me growls in approval. This one's a survivor.

"Just remember," I say as I grab the door handle, "Tyson might seem intimidating, but he's fair. Tell him what you can and let him make his decision."

She wets her lips, nervous but resolved. "Thank you, Colt. For the mask, for bringing me here... for everything."

The way she says my name sends heat down my spine. I grip the door handle harder, fighting the urge to pull her close, to shelter her with my body.

"Don't thank me yet, angel." I turn the handle. "Let's see what Ty has to say first."

6

NASH

I'm going over contracts with Tyson when the door swings open. Colt's broad frame fills the entrance, but my attention fixes on the small figure behind him. She's stunning—all golden waves and haunted eyes that catch the light like amber. My pulse quickens as I take in her delicate features and the way she shrinks into herself despite her natural grace.

"Who's this?" Tyson asks, leaning back in his chair.

"Found her outside the masquerade," Colt says. "She wants to join us."

I stand, moving closer. "And does our mystery guest have a name?"

"Flora," she says, her voice soft but carrying a hint of steel that intrigues me.

"Pleasure to meet you, Flora." I flash her my most charming smile, which usually has women melting. She meets my gaze briefly before looking away, but that glimpse is enough to see the shadows lurking behind her eyes. "I'm Nash."

"What can you do?" Tyson asks, direct as always.

Flora shifts her weight, hands twisting together. "I was on the gymnastics team at school. Acrobatics mainly. I'm... I'm good at it."

My interest spikes. An acrobat. That puts her squarely in my territory—and Colt's. I circle her slowly, assessing her build. She has the perfect frame for aerial work, light and lithe.

"Is that so?" I stop in front of her. "Any particular specialty?"

"Floor routines. Some aerial work on bars." She straightens, showing a hint of pride. "I won regional championships three years running."

"Impressive." I enjoy the way her cheeks flush at the husky tone of my voice. "We might be able to work with that." I glance at Colt. "Did Colt mention he's an acrobat too?" I keep my voice light, testing her reaction.

She shakes her head, gaze darting between us. The tension in her shoulders speaks volumes.

I reach out, trailing my fingers along her arm. She flinches hard, stumbling back into Colt's chest.

Interesting. My lips curve into a cold smile as I step closer, invading her space.

"That's going to be a problem, isn't it?" I tilt my head to the side. "How do you expect to perform if you can't even handle a simple touch?"

Her breath catches. "I-I can handle it during routines. It's different then."

"Is it?" I step toward her, close enough that she must feel my breath on her face. "Because acrobatics requires absolute trust. Complete surrender to your partner's guidance. Their hands will be all over you, supporting, lifting, catching."

She trembles but holds her ground. "I understand that."

"Do you?" I move to face her again. "Because you look ready to bolt if I brush against you. That won't work here. One moment of hesitation, one flinch at the wrong time, and you could get yourself—or your partner—seriously injured."

Her fingers curl into fists at her sides. "I said I can handle it."

"Prove it." I hold out my hand, palm up. A simple challenge, but her wide eyes suggest it might as well be a mountain to climb.

"Back off, Nash." Colt's voice cuts through the tension, sharp and commanding. His hand settles on Flora's shoulder, and for once, she doesn't flinch away. "She can start with solo routines if that works better."

I raise an eyebrow, studying my partner's face. In all our years together, I've never seen that protective edge in his eyes—not for anyone outside our inner circle. Yet here he stands, practically shielding this girl from me.

"Solo routines?" I keep my voice neutral, though my mind races with this new development. "That's not what brings in the crowds, and you know it."

"She needs time to adjust," Colt argues, his thumb absently stroking her shoulder. He doesn't even seem aware he's doing it. "We can work up to partner acts."

I lean against Tyson's desk, fascinated by this unexpected display. Colt, who barely spares a glance at the women who throw themselves at him after shows, is actually invested in this one. The way his body curves toward her and his eyes track her every subtle movement is all so wonderfully unlike him.

"Whatever you think is best," I concede, more interested in watching this unfold than pushing the issue. "Though I have to wonder why you're so invested in her success."

Colt's jaw tightens, but he doesn't rise to the bait. Instead, he guides Flora closer to Tyson's desk, his hand never leaving her shoulder. "She's got potential. That's all."

That's all, indeed. I hide my smirk, catching Ty's knowing look. We both see right through him. The mighty Colt, undone by a frightened little bird. How deliciously unexpected.

I watch as Ty's eyes flick between us. "You two, outside. Now."

Flora's shoulders tense, but Colt nods reassuringly before we step out into the crisp night air. The moment the door closes, I turn to him with a smirk.

"Well, well. Never thought I'd see the day. The mighty Colt, brought low by a pretty broken doll."

"Don't be an ass," he growls.

"What? It's adorable, really." I lean against the trailer wall. "How you're hovering over her like a mother hen. Though, I have to say, if you're not actually interested…" I let the sentence hang, enjoying the way his jaw clenches. "Because she is fucking hot. Noticed that the moment she walked in."

Colt's hand shoots out, gripping my shirt. "Back off,

Nash. She's been through trauma. I can see it in her eyes."

"And?" I raise an eyebrow, not fighting his grip. "Maybe that's exactly what makes her interesting. All that fear just waiting to be—"

"I said back off." His fingers tighten in my shirt. The muscle in his jaw jumps, and I can feel the tension radiating off him.

I lean into his grip. "Or maybe... I'm exactly what she needs." My voice drops lower, intimate. "Someone who understands that kind of darkness. Someone who knows how to make it beautiful."

Colt's fingers flex in my shirt, but the white-hot rage in his eyes shifts to something else.

"Or better yet," I continue, watching his reaction carefully, "maybe she needs both of us. Your protection..." I let my gaze drift to his mouth. "My control. Think about it, Colt. How perfect she'd be, caught between us."

His nostrils flare subtly, but his grip loosens just slightly. There it is—that flash of desire I've been waiting for. His pupils dilate, and I can practically see the image I've painted playing behind his eyes.

"The three of us. Together."

The rage drains from his face, replaced by something darker, sexier, and hungrier. He doesn't answer, but he doesn't have to. I can read his body's response and how his breathing changes.

"That's what I thought." I reach up, wrapping my fingers around his wrist where he still holds my shirt. His pulse races under my touch.

I let my fingers linger on his wrist. Ten years we've worked together, and I've never missed the way his eyes follow me during practice, how his breath catches when we're spotting each other on the silks. The tension between us has always simmered just below the surface.

I've seen him checking out other guys at the carnival, too—quick glances when he thinks no one's watching.

Sometimes, I wonder if he's afraid—of what others might think, of what it could mean for our partnership. Or maybe he's just not interested in me that way. But the heat in his eyes right now tells a different story.

His grip on my shirt loosens further, but he doesn't step back. I can feel the warmth of his breath and count every freckle scattered across his nose. If I moved just an inch closer...

But I don't. I never do. That's our dance—always on the edge, never crossing the line. Even now, with desire practically radiating off him, I know he'll pull away. He always does.

Right on cue, he releases my shirt and takes a step back. The mask slips back into place, but I catch that flash of want in his eyes. It's enough to keep me hoping, waiting for the day he finally admits what we both know.

"She couldn't handle both of us," Colt says with a forced laugh. "Come on, Nash. Look at her. She's like a scared rabbit."

I push off from the trailer wall, studying his face. "That's where you're wrong." The image of Flora's eyes flashes in my mind—that steel beneath the fear, how she stood her ground even when I pushed. "There's more to her than that."

"You saw how she flinched," he argues.

"I saw a survivor." I step closer, lowering my voice. "Did you notice how she tensed when I mentioned trust? That's not just ordinary stage fright. Someone hurt her, badly." My fingers brush his chest. "But she's still here, isn't she? Still fighting. Still wanting to perform despite everything."

Colt's breath catches. "Nash—"

"And when you touched her?" I continue. "She didn't pull away. She trusted you instantly. That's rare for someone with her kind of trauma."

He swallows hard. "What's your point?"

"My point is that little bird in there?" I gesture toward Tyson's trailer. "She's got fire underneath all that fear. The kind that burns hot enough to consume us if we let it."

"You don't know that."

"No?" I raise an eyebrow. "Then why are you so protective already? You feel it too—that pull. She's not just another pretty face looking for a job. She's something else entirely. Let's give her a chance to get comfortable with us," I suggest, keeping my voice casual. "Invite her to spend the night with both of us."

Colt's eyes narrow. "What are you talking about?"

"Come on, you've seen how she responds to you already." I tap my fingers against the trailer wall. "She's drawn to both of us, whether she admits it or not."

"We've never..." He runs a hand through his hair. "Why her? Why now?"

I shrug. "Why not? She needs somewhere safe to stay anyway. Might as well be with us."

"That's not—" Colt cuts himself off, shaking his head. "You're talking about both of us together."

"Afraid you can't handle sharing?" I smirk, masking the deeper implications of his words.

"That's not it." His jaw clenches. "We work together. Perform together. Adding fucking the same girl into the mix could complicate things."

"Or it could be exactly what we all need." I step closer, noting how he tenses but doesn't back away. "Think about it. She clearly needs protection. Who better than us?"

I can see him wrestling with the idea, probably imagining how it could go wrong. But I also catch that flash of interest in his eyes.

"Fine," he finally says. "But we take it slow. No pushing her."

"Wouldn't dream of it." I push off from the wall. "Now, shall we go see what Tyson's decided?"

She's exactly what we both need—damaged enough to understand us and strong enough to handle us. I saw that flash of defiance beneath the fear in her eyes when she stood her ground. How she leaned into Colt's touch while flinching from everyone else.

My cock stirs just thinking about how she'd look between us. Her small frame caught between my lean muscles and Colt's broader build. Those haunted eyes would go wide as we take turns claiming her. The sounds she'd make when we pushed her limits.

But it's more than just the physical appeal. The thought of sharing her with Colt is intoxicating.

And once we have her, the possibilities are endless. We can protect her, possess her, and shape her into exactly what we need her to be.

Together.

My pulse quickens at the thought. This little broken bird might just be the answer to everything. And judging by the heat in Colt's eyes earlier, he wants it too—even if he's not ready to admit it.

7

FLORA

I grip the edge of my seat as Tyson studies me with those penetrating eyes. My heart threatens to burst from my chest until he finally nods.

"Welcome to the family, then."

Relief floods through me, but it's short-lived as reality crashes back. "Are we not leaving town until just before New Year's?" The thought of staying in town, so close to the Lowleys, makes my skin crawl. Three weeks of looking over my shoulder.

Tyson must see the fear in my eyes. He leans forward, voice dropping to a dangerous growl. "If those fuckers come sniffing around, they'll get what's coming to them. A good fucking beating should teach them to stay away from you."

The door creaks open, and Colt and Nash slip inside. Their presence fills the small space of Tyson's office, making it hard to breathe for entirely different reasons. Nash is the guy who called me beautiful when I stood outside the masquerade, and Colt is so kind and absolutely gorgeous.

"What's the verdict, boss?" Colt's deep voice sends a shiver down my spine. There's something about him—a raw power tempered by unexpected gentleness.

Nash moves like a shadow behind him, all controlled grace and coiled tension. Where Colt radiates heat, Nash exudes an icy darkness that terrifies and intrigues me. His gaze slides over me, calculating and intense.

I shouldn't be attracted to either of them, let alone both. After everything with the Lowleys, I should run screaming from any man who looks at me with hunger in his eyes. But something about them feels different. Maybe it's how Colt positions himself protectively near me, or Nash's watchful presence that makes me feel oddly safe despite his dangerous aura.

"She's in," Tyson tells them. "You two will be responsible for training her."

Nash's smirk sends a ripple of something through me—not fear exactly, though maybe it should be. Darkness in that curve of his lips speaks of carefully controlled danger. Yet, somehow, I find myself more curious than frightened.

"Come on, princess." Colt's hand hovers near my lower back, not quite touching. "Let's get you settled."

I clutch my backpack tighter, following them out of Tyson's office. The cool, crisp night air hits my face, carrying the scent of cotton candy and popcorn. Strings of colorful lights crisscross overhead, casting rainbow shadows across the packed dirt paths between trailers.

"This one's yours." Nash gestures to a small silver

trailer, its exterior weathered but clean. "For now, at least."

Colt produces a key and unlocks the door. "It's basic, but you can make it yours over time."

The inside is sparse—a narrow bed, tiny kitchen area, and bathroom barely big enough to turn around in. But it's mine. No Lowleys. No fear. Just...freedom.

"Get changed," Nash says, passing me. "The masquerade is in full swing. We'll wait outside."

I nod, unable to find my voice as they step out. Through the thin walls, I hear their low murmurs, keeping watch. My hands shake as I unzip my backpack, feeling both anxious and excited at the same time. I grab my leotard and slip it on in case I get the chance to show of my skills tonight and then pull out the simple black dress I'd managed to hide away. It's nothing fancy, but with the mask Colt gave me earlier, maybe I can pretend to be someone else tonight. Someone brave. Someone who deserves this chance.

The dress slips over my head, and I smooth it down. In the tiny mirror above the sink, I barely recognize myself. The mask transforms my features into something mysterious, almost elegant. For the first time in years, I feel like I belong somewhere.

A soft knock sounds at the door. "Ready, angel?" Colt's voice drifts through.

I step out of the trailer, and my breath catches. Colt and Nash stand waiting, transformed by their masks. Nash's black skull mask makes him look like death incarnate, while Colt's white sends a flush of heat through me. My heart pounds as I take them in—Colt's broad shoulders stretching his black shirt, Nash's lean frame coiled with lethal grace.

I shouldn't find them attractive. After what Tommy and Jake did to me with their friends... I squeeze my eyes shut, trying to block out the memories. But my body betrays me, just like it did then. Heat pools low in my belly as I look at the men before me.

What's wrong with me?

The things that excite me now are so dark, so twisted. When Tommy and Jake hurt me the first time, something broke inside. Or maybe they just revealed what was already broken. Now, I crave the dangerous edge of fear mixed with desire. The thought of being at these men's mercy makes me throb with need even as my mind screams to run.

I catch Nash watching me, his calculating gaze visible even through the mask's eye holes. My cheeks burn, wondering if he can read the sick thoughts running through my head. Colt steps closer, and I fight not to lean into his warmth.

"You look beautiful," he murmurs.

I hate myself for wanting them. Hate that after everything I've been through, I still fantasize about being controlled, about being taken. These dark desires feel like a betrayal of myself, yet I can't stop them from consuming me.

I follow the men into the main tent, which has been transformed into a glittering wonderland of lights and decorations. Music pulses through the air as masked figures twirl across the dance floor. My heart races, caught between fear and excitement.

"Here." Nash hands me a glass of something amber. "Dutch courage."

The anxiety flutters in my stomach as I clutch the glass tighter. While I've drank before, especially when I knew Tommy and Jake were going to attack me, I've never quite gotten used to the taste. I adjust my mask to take a drink and knock it back in one gulp, grimacing as it burns my throat. The warmth spreads through my chest, dulling the sharp edges of my anxiety.

Nash extends his hand, a slight bow making him seem almost courtly despite his dangerous aura. "Dance with me?"

A low growl comes from Colt beside me, and Nash's eyes flash through the eyeholes of his mask. He's clearly enjoying needling his friend, though I can't understand why my dancing with Nash would matter to Colt.

I hesitate, memories of unwanted touches threatening to surface. But Nash waits patiently, hand still offered but not demanding.

Okay, deep breath. This is different. Nash isn't like Tommy or Jake. He's offering a hand, not trying to force anything. You get to choose, and right now, you want to dance. Just take his hand. You've got this!

"Okay," I force out, placing my hand in his.

Nash leads me onto the dance floor with surprising gentleness. His touch is light as he positions my hand on his shoulder, his own settling carefully at my waist. We begin to move, and I'm struck by how different this feels. Where I expect roughness, I find control. Where I brace for pain, I discover grace.

"Relax," he murmurs. "I won't hurt you."

I look into his eyes behind his black mask, searching for any sign of deception. But all I find is intensity tempered with something that might be kindness.

My body begins to unwind, and I let Nash lead me through the dance. Over his shoulder, I catch glimpses of Colt watching us, his posture rigid.

My breath catches as Nash leans close, his mask brushing my ear, sending shivers down my spine. "Come to our trailer tonight," he whispers. "Both of us want you. Together."

My heart pounds against my ribs. The implications of his words sink in, and I pull back to search his eyes through the mask. "Both of you? But... we have to work together. Is that really smart?"

His hand tightens fractionally on my waist. "Sex builds trust. Bonds people. What better way for us to connect as a team?" His thumb traces small circles against my hip. "I've seen how you look at us both. The way your breath catches when Colt gets too close. How your pupils dilate when I touch you."

Heat floods my face. He's right. I do want them. The thought of being with them both makes my core clench with need. But memories of that horrible night flash through my mind—Tommy and Jake holding me down while their friends...

I squeeze my eyes shut, trying to block out the images. This is different. Nash and Colt aren't them. Their touches are careful and controlled. When they look at me, I see desire mixed with something deeper—a need to protect rather than harm.

But still... "I don't know," I whisper.

I try to steady my breathing as Nash holds me close, the music swirling around us. His words echo in my head—the invitation to their trailer, the promise of something thrilling and terrifying. But he doesn't know. None of them know what Tommy and Jake did to me.

I feel something different here, in Nash's arms, with Colt's burning gaze following our every move. Something that makes me want to forget, even for a moment.

"I need time," I whisper. "This is all so new."

Nash's hand remains steady at my waist, neither pushing nor pulling away. "Time is something we have plenty of, little bird." His voice carries no judgment.

The song ends, and I step back, needing space. Colt materializes beside us. His presence is both comforting and overwhelming. They flank me like dark guardians, and for a moment, I imagine telling them everything—about the nights I spent crying silently into my pillow, about the bruises I had to hide, about the way Tommy and Jake...

No. Not yet. Maybe not ever.

These men might seem different and might make me feel safe in a way I haven't in years, but some secrets are too heavy to share. Some wounds are too deep to expose to the light.

"Thank you for the dance," I manage. "I think I need some air."

Nash lets me go, but I feel their eyes following me as I weave through the crowd. Neither knows the real reason behind my hesitation and for now, that's how it needs to stay.

8

COLT

*F*lora returns, her shoulders tense but her eyes determined. Something about her vulnerability, maybe it's her inner strength trying to break free that sets my pulse racing.

"You don't have to do anything you're uncomfortable with," I tell her, keeping my voice gentle, knowing Nash has already propositioned her to spend the night with us. "No pressure."

Nash stands beside me. Flora's gaze flicks between us, considering.

"I'm open to seeing where the night takes us," she says, determination blazing in her eyes as the alcohol loosens her up.

The clock on the wall reads eight.

Nash steps forward. "Why don't we head to the training tent? See what you can do with the equipment?" His suggestion breaks the tension, giving us all something concrete to focus on.

Flora's eyes brighten. "That's actually a great idea." Her relief is obvious since training would be familiar to her. "I even put my leotard on beneath my dress, just in case."

I chuckle. "Eager, aren't you, angel?"

She nods in reply, her cheeks turning an endearing pink.

"Come on, let's go," Nash says, nodding at the exit to the tent.

We lead her through the carnival grounds to the training tent, our private space away from prying eyes. The trapeze hangs center stage, ropes and silks draped artfully around it. Practice mats cover the ground, and other equipment lines the walls—everything we need to train safely.

I notice how Flora's eyes light up at the sight of it all, her earlier nervousness melting away as she takes in the professional setup. Nash and I spend most of our time here, perfecting our craft. Now, we'll get to see what our angel can do.

I lean against one of the support poles, arms crossed, as Nash approaches Flora.

"Show us what you remember from your gymnastics days," he tells her. "Basic floor work first. Tumbling, handstands, whatever comes naturally."

Flora nods, rolling her shoulders back despite not being dressed for the occasion, but it doesn't dissuade her. She stands at one end of the mat, bouncing slightly on her toes. Then she's moving, and damn if she isn't impressive. A series of perfect cartwheels flows into a round-off back handspring. Her control is obvious in every movement, each landing precise.

Nash catches my eye, one eyebrow raised. We've seen plenty of newcomers claim skills they don't have. Flora isn't one of them.

She transitions into a split and presses up into a handstand. Her lines are clean, her core steady—no wobbling. When she finally comes down, there's a slight flush to her cheeks, but her breathing is controlled.

"That's just a warm-up," she says, tucking a strand of hair behind her ear.

"Color me impressed," I say. Natural talent is rare enough, but this level of technical skill? Even better.

Nash steps closer, circling slowly. I recognize his analytical gaze—he's already choreographing in his head, envisioning how we could incorporate her into our routines.

"Your form is excellent," he says. His praise makes her stand a little straighter, and something in my chest tightens at the sight.

"We should see what she can do in the air," Nash suggests. "Take her up, Colt."

I shake my head, pushing off from the pole. "Not if she's never been on a trapeze before. Floor work is one thing, but—"

"I have, actually," Flora interrupts. "Not professionally, but we had one at my high school gym. Coach let me practice after hours sometimes."

That catches my attention. I study this girl's face for any sign of false bravado or lies but find only earnest determination. Still, there's a difference between playing around after school and what we do.

"How long ago?" I ask.

"About eight months." She meets my gaze steadily. "I know it's not the same as what you guys do, but I understand the basics. The grip, the swing, the timing."

Nash moves closer to me. "Perfect time to assess her technique then. You can spot from above; I'll watch from below."

He's right, damn him. It's the safest way to gauge her abilities. I run a hand through my hair, considering the risks.

"Alright," I concede. "But we do this my way. Safety harness first, and we start with basic holds."

Flora nods eagerly, already moving toward the equipment rack where we keep the harnesses. I catch her arm gently.

"Listen carefully, angel. Up there, you do exactly what I say, when I say it. No improvising, no showing off. Clear?"

"Crystal." Her voice is steady.

I help her into the harness, checking each buckle twice. Nash watches from below, his presence reassuring, as always. Once satisfied with her gear, I secure my harness and start up the ladder.

"Remember," I call to her, "this isn't about impressing us. It's about showing us where you're starting from so we can train you properly."

From my position on the platform, I watch Flora climb with natural grace. Her movements are precise, with each grip and step calculated.

"We'll start with a simple catch," I tell her, securing my lines. "When I say go, swing out and release on my count."

She nods, adjusting her grip on the bar. Her form is textbook perfect.

The first attempt is shaky—her timing's off, and she releases too early. The harness catches her safely, but I see the frustration flash across her face.

"Again," I call out. "This time, wait for my signal."

Three more tries, and suddenly, everything clicks. Her body arcs through the air, and our hands connect with a satisfying smack. The electricity of skin-on-skin contact shoots through me.

"Beautiful!" Nash shouts from below.

We move through increasingly complex sequences. Each time I touch, guide, and position her body in the air, my pulse quickens. Her natural athleticism shows in every movement. She recovers gracefully when she misses a catch or fumbles a transition.

"Ready to try something more advanced?" I ask after a particularly smooth sequence.

"Yes," she breathes.

I guide her through a split catch, my hands firm on her waist as she extends into perfect form. Her body responds to my touch like she was made for this—for us.

"Look at those lines!" Nash calls appreciatively. "Try it again but add the half-twist on release this time."

Flora nails it on the second attempt, her body spinning through the air before landing securely in my grip. The trust she's showing, the way she surrenders to my lead while maintaining perfect control of her movements—it's intoxicating.

We're moving together like we've done this for years, not minutes. Each catch, release, and touch becomes more natural; intimate even.

9

NASH

Watching Colt guide Flora through their trapeze routine has my body reacting with a hunger that surprises me. It's not just Flora's lithe form twisting and turning through the air nor the graceful way she moves in Colt's hold that has my cock hardening.

It's the thought of sharing her—of taking her with Colt that has my body thrumming with anticipation. I want her lips around my dick while she rides Colt. I want to see her on her knees, pleasing us both. But more than that, I want to feel Colt against me. I want to touch him.

Our friendship has always been intense, but now something more is emerging, almost forcing its way to the surface, something we haven't dared to voice.

Flora completes the half-twist on release, and I see the pride in Colt's eyes. He's drawn to her, and she to him. Their connection is instantaneous and raw. I wonder if they feel the same spark that ignited between Colt and me years ago when we first met.

"Again," I call out, eager to watch them move in unison.

As they fly through the air this time, my gaze lingers on Colt. His body is taut, his eyes fixed on Flora, but I know he feels my stare. I see the subtle shift in his expression, the hint of awareness that I'm watching him as much as I'm watching her.

The routine ends, and they descend, flushed and breathless. I step forward to offer feedback. "Colt, your strength is impressive, as always. We'll continue to work on those shoulder injuries so they don't hold you back. Flora, you're making impressive progress."

Colt wipes his brow with the back of his hand, his chest heaving from exertion. "It's like a furnace in here," he mutters, peeling off his sweat-dampened shirt. My eyes catch Flora's sharp intake of breath, the way her gaze traces over his exposed torso before darting away.

I step closer to demonstrate a correction in her form, my hand settling on her waist. The touch lingers longer than necessary, and I feel her pulse quicken beneath my fingers. "Your alignment here needs adjustment," I murmur, close enough that my breath stirs the hair by her ear.

"Thank you," she replies, her voice slightly unsteady as she meets my gaze. Electricity crackles through the air between us as she licks her bottom lip.

"What now?" She asks, glancing from me to Colt and back again, her eyes darker than before.

"Are you ready to explore a more exciting part of your training with us?"

Flora bites her lip, her gaze flicking between Colt and me. Her cheeks are a pretty shade of pink, and her breath comes in short gasps. The technical precision of our training session has morphed into something more charged, more primal. I can see the need swirling in her eyes, a mirror of the desire raging inside me. "I want to," she murmurs. "But I—I have some conditions."

The challenge in her words spikes my appetite even further. My smile stretches wider, and I hear Colt's sharp intake of breath. I haven't shared this side of myself with him before, but the games I crave are not for the faint of heart. "Name them. We want you to feel safe and satisfied with us."

She takes a steadying breath, her delicate frame straightening. "I want you to chase me. Into the woods." Her eyes dart to Colt, then back to me. "I want you to catch me and..." She swallows, her voice dipping to a whisper. "I want you to take me, even when I ask you to stop."

Colt tenses beside me. I wrap an arm around his shoulders, sensing his barely restrained hunger, confusion, and curiosity. I lean in close to him, my mouth brushing his ear. "Looks like our little bird wants to play a dark game."

His eyes widen. That twisted part of him, which recognizes my twisted nature, stirs. I know he won't deny me or Flora this experience.

"Are you sure, angel?" Colt asks. "This won't be gentle. We won't go easy on you."

"I need it," she whispers. "I want it rough."

Flora's words slam into my chest, her eyes challenging me. This girl knows what she wants, and it thrills me. I glance at Colt, seeing the dark hunger in his eyes and the muscle ticking in his jaw. This is new territory, a new level of trust we're navigating together.

"You want to play rough?" I ask, relishing the idea of chasing her through the woods. "Colt and I will give you what you need."

Her eyes flicker between us, taking in our height, our strength. A flush creeps up her neck, and she swallows hard, licking her lips. "I... yes. But—"

"But what?" Colt prompts.

Flora looks away, her cheeks flaming. "I—I want you to wear your masks."

I smile, stepping closer. "Our masks? Whatever for?"

She wets her lips again, and her eyes dart to the ground as she mumbles. "I want it to feel like I'm with strangers."

The implication of her words is not lost on me. She wants to forget who we are. She wants the fantasy of being taken against her will by strangers, of escaping her past, of losing herself in the anonymity of masked men. My pulse quickens as she's asking us to unleash our darkest selves.

"You want the full experience, don't you?" I ask.

She nods. "Yes. And... and you can't stop until I say the safe word. Not even if I say no."

Colt's fingers tighten on the trapeze bar beside him, and I know he's fighting to maintain control. "What's the safe word, Flora?"

"Bubblegum," she whispers. "And I'll click my fingers if I can't speak."

The air crackles with anticipation, and I feel Colt's gaze on me, questioning, seeking confirmation that I'm willing to push our boundaries this far.

I step closer to him, sliding my hand into his back pocket, squeezing his ass.

Colt immediately tenses and his breathing catches in his throat at my touch. Feeling his ass clench in my hand makes my dick swell.

"Deal," I say, holding Flora's gaze. "But once we start, we won't hold back."

Colt clears his throat and speaks, clearly affected by me grabbing his ass as there's a huskiness in his tone. "Are you sure about this? What about birth control?"

For a moment, I wonder if she'll back out, but then she surprises me. "Yes. I need this. And you don't need to worry I've got an IUD. I want you both to come inside me."

I groan, my dick swelling my pant. "Fuck yeah, sounds good to me."

Colt and I share a glance, both of us wanting it. He grins and turns his attention back to Flora. "Then run, angel. Take a left outside the tent and head into the woods. We'll give you a fifteen-second head start."

She hesitates, but then she turns and bolts, her movements graceful even in her haste.

Colt turns to me and there's hunger in his gaze. "Ready to hunt, Nash?"

I laugh, placing my hand on his shoulder. "Always,

partner." Immediately, his eyes darken and I feel this electricity crackle between us, making my dick hard.

We count to fifteen, giving Flora her head start. As we exit the tent, the cold night air washes over me, raising goosebumps on my skin. I spot Flora's figure as she just heads into the shadows of the woods.

"Come on, let's give her the thrill of her life!" Colt calls out, taking off.

I follow, my heart pounding with excitement. The darkness of the woods closes around us, the moonlight filtering through the bare branches creating an ethereal glow. I hear Flora's breathless laughter up ahead, and I know she's enjoying this game, the thrill of the chase. I lengthen my stride once again, closing the distance between us.

Flora's golden hair catches the moonlight as she ducks behind a tree. She peeks back, her eyes sparkling with mischief.

She dashes to the left, and I quicken my pace. She's fast, her small body nimble as she weaves between the trees. Is her gymnastics background helping her navigate the forest with such agility?

Colt whoops, his deep voice echoing through the woods. "Not so fast, angel! We're coming for you!"

Flora lets out a squeal, and I know she's loving every moment of this. I lengthen my stride toward her. I'm more graceful than Colt. I dart around a cluster of trees, and that's when I see her—up ahead, frozen in place.

She's trapped between us.

Colt roars, running full tilt, and I know he will get to her first. But at the last moment, Flora darts to the right, straight into my waiting arms. Her body collides with mine, and I wrap my arms around her, lifting her off her feet. She shrieks, and I swing her around, my body buzzing.

"Gotcha," I murmur, spinning her until she's facing me. She's breathless, her eyes bright with exhilaration. And now, the game begins.

10

FLORA

"Let me go! Get off me!"

Colt grabs my wrist from behind in one large palm, his other hand snaking around my throat, not enough to hurt, but a clear statement of possession.

"Keep fighting. It only makes my dick harder."

His words send a shiver down my spine. I know I could make it stop. I could say the safe word. I don't want it to end. Despite my protests, I want them to take me, to claim me. It's confusing, exhilarating, and terrifying all at once. Ever since my assault, nothing has made sense. It's like I crave sex all the time.

I kick out, my heel connecting with Nash's shin. He grunts in response but doesn't let up, his lips trailing down my neck.

"You dirty fucker, Colt." Nash's voice is a low growl. "Getting off on her reluctance."

I shouldn't like it, but I do. It's different from what I experienced before, where I had no choice. Now, I have the power to stop it, but I don't want to. I want to play the reluctant captive, surrendering to their demands.

I squirm as Nash's fingers dig into my hips, his eyes dark with hunger. He tears at my leotard, the fabric ripping with a loud shred, and I'm helpless to stop him. My panties soon follow, leaving me exposed and wanting.

"Fucking hell, she's drenched." Nash's voice is hoarse as he rubs his nimble fingers along my wet slit, teasing my lips.

I moan at how good his touch feels, even as I try to cover myself, feeling suddenly shy under the heated gaze of these gorgeous men.

But Colt grabs my wrists, pinning them behind me. For a moment I feel the fabric of his shirt against my bare nipples. I shiver and writhe in excitement. "None of that, angel. You want this as much as we do." His voice in my ear brings out a wanton cry from my lips, surprising myself.

I do want this. All of it. And that realization only makes me struggle more. It's madness. This is madness. I shouldn't want this. I shouldn't be enjoying it. But how they look at me, like I'm their entire world, is too much to resist.

"Colt, get down on your knees and make her come. Nice and slow." Nash's command is firm, his dominance evident.

Colt bristles, his alpha nature clashing with Nash's order. But something passes between them, a silent agreement, and he drops to his knees. I whimper as his warm breath ghosts over my sensitive skin, his tongue tracing patterns on my clit that send shivers through me.

I feel my legs open, my body ready and eager.

"That's it, Colt. Lick that sweet pussy." Nash's fingers tighten in my hair, holding my head still so I can't look away from the sight of Colt on his knees between my thighs. "You like that, don't you? Being told what to do. Being a good boy for us."

Colt's eyes flash with something primal as he looks up at Nash, and his dick grows visibly hard in his tight pants. He growls, the sound vibrating against me, and I can't hold back a desperate moan. This is too much, too intense. But I don't want it to stop.

"Stop, please!" My pleas fall on deaf ears as Colt teases and caresses my clit, his tongue stroking and circling me with practiced precision.

I feel his fingers grasp my ass, and one slides up and down between the soft mounds of flesh there. His finger brushing against my asshole sends a jolt of arousal through my body. I almost forget to fight, it feels so good.

"That's it. Let yourself feel it." Nash's voice is low and rough, filled with need. "You like this, don't you? You like the way he makes you feel." His voice lowers. "You love that I'm watching."

The shame washes over me in waves, clouding my already blurred judgment.

"Enough!" I push at Nash's shoulders, trying to break free. "Let me go!"

Nash laughs, the sound cold and cruel. "I'm sick of

your protests. We both know you're a dirty little slut who can't wait to get her holes filled by our cocks."

The harsh words hit me like a slap, reminding me of the times my foster brothers forced themselves on me, their friends laughing as they held me down. But this is different. This time, I asked for it. I chose this.

"You're so fucking responsive." Nash's voice is a combination of wonder and lust.

My head spins as Nash pulls away, removing the illusion of safety his body provides. The cool night air washes over my heated skin, goosebumps rising along my arms. I feel exposed and vulnerable but also powerful. These men, so strong and in control, have been reduced to primal need because of me.

"I think she needs something in her mouth to keep her quiet." Nash's eyes glitter with amusement as he takes in my flushed face. "Sit on Colt's face while I plug it with my cock."

Before I can protest, he's wrapping my hair around his fist and pushing me to my knees.

Colt lies down so I'm straddling his face and continues to devour me like a starving man. I'm trapped between two men, completely at their mercy.

I struggle initially, not wanting to give in so easily, but Nash is relentless. . I watch as he drops his pants, his cock springing free in the moonlight. I hear Colt's sharp inhale as Nash stands strong and naked from the waist down. I gulp. He's huge.

"Open your mouth for me like a good girl." The head of his cock pushes against my lips. I open my mouth and feel his swollen head rub against my lips. I'm overwhelmed by the sensation of him. He's thick, so much thicker than anything I've ever felt before.

My reluctance melts away as he slides into my mouth, filling me, claiming me. I moan around him, the vibrations eliciting a harsh curse from Nash. His grip on my hair tightens, and he moves slowly at first, then with increasing urgency. I relax my throat, accepting him, wanting to give him pleasure.

I can't get enough of Nash. I suck hard, taking him deeper, and those sexy eyes of his slowly close. He moans, his pleasure evident. I love the way he tastes, the way he feels sliding against my tongue. I want to devour him, to make him lose control.

His fingers tighten in my hair, and his hips stutter.

"Fuck, Flora, I'm gonna come." His voice is a hoarse whisper.

I don't want him to stop, but I can't bring myself to pull away. I want this—need this. His release spills down my throat, and I swallow, my body buzzing with satisfaction. He pulls out slowly, a stray bead of cum escaping the corner of my mouth.

"Fucking hell. I'll be feeling that for days." Nash's voice is filled with wonder, his eyes dark with satisfaction.

I'm vaguely aware of Colt's tongue on me, but my mind is spinning, my body thrumming with need. I want more.

Colt's tongue flicks my clit, as he slides two fingers into my pussy.

"Oh fuck," I cry out, and my eyes roll back in my head. I'm so close, teetering on the edge. His fingers find my G-spot, and he thrusts in time with his tongue. My orgasm hits me like a freight train, overwhelming and intense. I cry out, my body shaking uncontrollably.

"That's it. Let go for us." Nash's voice is a low purr.

Colt laps up my release, his moans vibrating against me. His tongue owns me, drawing out my pleasure until I'm a boneless heap, my mind blissfully blank.

Nash's eyes glint with a dark hunger as he tears his gaze from Colt to meet mine. "I want to watch Colt fuck that pretty little pussy of yours, and then I'm going to breed you too."

I squeak at his harsh words, but there's no denying the excitement that shoots through me at the idea.

Colt growls, a sound that reverberates through me. "Since when are you in charge?"

Nash laughs, the sound sending shivers down my spine. "Since that's exactly what you want."

I bite my lip, unable to deny the truth of his words— I want to be controlled.

"Get your cock out, Colt," Nash demands.

I hold my breath as the sexual tension between them burns like fire, making me wonder if they've ever done this before. Slowly, almost reluctantly, Colt unbuttons his jeans and pushes them down. His eyes never leave Nash's, a silent challenge in his gaze.

My eyes are drawn to Colt's cock, thick and hard, and—I swallow—pierced. I gasp at the sight of the silver ring adorning him. It's stunning and intimidating at the same time.

I watch as he strokes himself slowly, eyes locked on Nash.

"Fuck, he's even thicker than Nash." I blurt out my observation, unable to keep the awe from my voice.

Colt's cock twitches at my words, a drop of pre-cum beading at the tip. "Not quite as long, but I think you'll manage."

His voice is deep and rough, sending a shiver down my spine. I nod, my eyes flicking between the two men. Their rivalry is palpable, the air thick.

Nash's eyes glitter with anticipation as he steps back, motioning for Colt to take his place. "Go on, then. Show her what a real man can do."

Colt's gaze softens as he looks at me, his expression holding a question. "You ready for this?"

My heart hammers in my chest as I nod. I'm terrified and excited, my body buzzing with anticipation. I want both of them and the fact that they want me, too, is almost too much to bear.

Colt throws down his coat. "Lie on your back."

I do as he says, lying down on his jacket. And then, he shifts forward between my thighs, his cock leaking. With one hand, he guides himself to my entrance, teasing me with the tip and the piercing. I whimper at the sensation, wanting more.

"You're so fucking wet," Nash murmurs, his eyes fixed on the sight of Colt's cock pressed against me. "Your pretty little pussy can't wait to be stretched."

I heat at his words, but I can't deny the evidence of my desire. I'm soaked, and the head of Colt's cock slides an inch inside.

"Fuck, she's tight." Colt's voice is strained as he

pushes forward, filling me slowly. "So fucking tight and hot."

His girth stretches me, and I can't suppress a moan as he bottoms out. He stays still for a moment, letting me adjust to his size. His hands rest on my hips, his thumbs stroking my sensitive skin.

"Move, Colt," Nash commands, his voice rough with need. "Fuck her hard."

Colt's eyes darken, and he pulls out almost entirely before thrusting back into me hard. My eyes widen at the new depth of sensation. I bite my lip, savoring the slight sting of pain, and throw my head back, reveling in the feeling of being wanted and possessed.

"You like that, don't you? You like it rough." Colt's words are a statement, not a question.

I whimper in response, unsure if I can form coherent words. My body is on fire, every nerve ending singing with pleasure. I want more, need more.

His hands grip my hips tightly making the bruises from Tommy throb as he pulls me against him. The piercing in his cock rubs against sensitive spots inside me, sending sparks of pleasure through my flesh.

"Fucking hell. Your pussy's milking my cock." His voice is harsh, full of gravel as he pumps into me. "Been a while since I had a tight little slut like you."

His words shouldn't turn me on, but they do. I arch my back, breasts bouncing as I meet his thrusts. I want him to keep going, to never stop. meeting his thrusts. I want him to keep going, to never stop.

"Tell me to stop, Flora." His voice is demanding, his eyes daring me to deny him.

I don't want him to stop, ever. But I can't deny the little girl inside me who needs to play this game and pretend that she has some control, even if it's just an illusion.

"Please, stop," I whisper, my eyes darting to Nash, pleading with him to understand. "It hurts. You're too big."

I don't need to say the safe word. I just need them to know that it's an act, that I'm playing a role, inviting them to take what they want.

Colt's eyes flash with a dangerous light, and his thrusts become more urgent, more forceful. I cry out, my body responding to his roughness, my channel dripping around him.

"That's it, fight me." Colt's voice is harsh, his jaw clenched with the effort of his restraint. "But you can't escape me… escape *us*."

His words strike a chord deep within me. I don't want to escape. I never want this moment to end. I want to be theirs, to surrender completely.

My eyes dart to Nash's and I see the extent of my desire reflected back at me in his dark brown depths.

Colt's pace never falters, his eyes fixed on mine. "You want this. Don't try to deny it."

I can't, not anymore. My eyes lock with Colt's, and I give him a small nod, granting him silent permission to take what he needs from me.

Colt's hand tightens on my hip, his thumb finding the spot that weakens my knees. With each thrust, his piercing rubs against that bundle of nerves, sending shocks of pleasure through me.

"Fuck, Flora, you feel so damn good." Colt's voice is strained, his control slipping. "I'm not gonna last. Gonna coat your walls with my cum."

His words send me over the edge. My orgasm hits me like a tidal wave, and I cry out, my body shaking uncontrollably as pleasure washes over me.

Colt lets out a harsh groan as he follows me, his release pulsing inside me. I cling to him, not wanting this moment to end. I feel branded by their possession, marked as theirs.

Nash's eyes burn with desire, his gaze flicking between Colt and me. His hand moves to his own cock, stroking himself as he takes in the sight before him.

"Your turn, Nash," Colt grunts, his voice still rough. "Take what you want from her."

Nash's eyes glitter with a combination of hunger and something akin to relief. He closes the distance between us, his hand gentling as he cups my cheek.

"Mine now," he whispers, his eyes searching mine. "All mine."

I feel exposed and vulnerable at the intensity of Nash's gaze, like he's seeing through to my very core. I feel the weight of his gaze like a physical touch, sparking something within me.

"Please..." I whisper, looking up at him through my lashes. I'm not sure what I'm asking for. Forgiveness, maybe? Or perhaps I'm begging for something more.

Nash cups my cheek, his thumb brushing my bottom lip. "Shh, little bird. It's okay. I've got you."

His eyes, deep and unreadable, hold mine captive. I

feel like he's looking into my soul, seeing the darkest corners of my mind. It should scare me, but it doesn't. I feel understood in a way I've never experienced before.

11

NASH

"Please..." Flora whispers.

She's beautiful like this, her cheeks flushed, her body trembling in anticipation of what's to come. I step closer, savoring the power I hold over her.

"Please, what, little bird?" I ask softly, my voice husky with need.

She hesitantly bites her lip before whispering, "Please take me."

My breath catches at her words. This power exchange—it's more than physical. She's handing me her trust making herself vulnerable and, somehow it feels like here, now with us, is the first time she's ever done that of her own free will. We're the first to see her like this—completely exposed and wanting.

I know what she asks, but I want to hear her say it. I want her to acknowledge the deeper surrender that's taking place here tonight. "You want me to fuck you?"

She nods, a mix of shame and desire flitting across her face.

"Say it," I coax, my voice gentle but firm. "Use your words, baby."

Her eyes meet mine, and I see not just desire but a deeper need for connection. "I want you to fuck me, Nash. Please."

Hearing my name on her lips sends a bolt of desire straight to my cock. I ache to be inside her, to claim her, but I force myself to take it slow.

I lean in and whisper, "You're doing so well. So fucking brave. But I want to hear you say it again. I want you to tell me exactly what you need."

Her breath catches, and her chest rises and falls rapidly as she processes my request. "I need you to fuck me, Nash. I need you to make me forget."

"Forget what, angel?" Colt asks.

"Everything," she says softly, her eyes not meeting mine. "Make me forget it all."

I rub the head of my dick through her wet pussy, soaking wet with her arousal and Colt's release. I feel my cock throb at the thought of being coated by both of them. "I can do that. I can make you forget. But first, I want you to look at me."

Her eyes lift to meet mine, and I see the hope reflected there. I tilt her chin up with my finger, exposing her slender neck. "That's it. Look at me while I take you. Watch me as I make you mine."

Her body tenses beneath me, a delicate mix of fear and excitement. I reach out and cup her breast with one hand, pinching her tight nipple gently, then harder until she gasps.

I position myself at her entrance, the tip of my cock

teasing her wetness. With my hand, I guide myself into her, inch by inch, savoring the way she clenches around me.

"There you go, little bird," I murmur. "Take it all."

Her breath catches as I sink into her, her eyes flicking to Colt, who watches us with his hand on his still semi-hard cock. I hold her gaze, watching the emotions play across her face: uncertainty, arousal, and something deeper.

I pull out slowly, enjoying the way she whimpers at the loss, then thrust back into her with purpose. I set a relentless pace, her soft body arching with each stroke. Her legs wrap around my waist, pulling me deeper.

I love the shape of her. Those full breasts moving without restraint, that slender waist that widens out into womanly hips. She's soft and sweet, sexy and lithe all at once.

And Colt, for the first time I can let my eyes take him in without stealing a glance and then feeling ashamed about it. His strong legs, narrow hips, and the hint of hair that travels from his belly button down to the base of that cock. I think of all the times I've wanted to… no, I've never let myself go there.

Colt steps closer, his eyes flicking between us, taking in the sight of my cock disappearing into her, over and over. I can see the need in his eyes, and I wonder if it's the sight of my dick or her cunt that gets him going.

"You like that, don't you? Feeling so full."

She nods, her breath coming in short gasps. "Yes... oh God, yes."

I pull out and thrust back into her, my pace increasing. Her body responds to mine, our rhythm perfectly in sync. Colt moves closer, his hand still on his cock, his eyes fixed on the place where we join.

"Look at him, Flora," I command softly. "Look at what you do to him."

Her eyes flicker to Colt, taking in the strain on his face, the way his hand moves faster on his cock. "You make him hard, little bird. He wants you just as much as I do."

I lean down to whisper, "You want to be filled, don't you? Want to be so full you forget your own name."

She whimpers, her head tipping back.

"Tell me what you want."

"I want..." She pauses, her hands gripping my shoulders, her legs tightening around my waist. "I want Colt in my mouth… I want to taste him."

Colt growls, and I know he's imagining it too—her lips wrapped around his shaft, her tongue swirling.

"You want my cock in your mouth?" Colt's voice is rough, strained. "That pretty mouth of yours is watering for it, isn't it? Almost as much as your cunt is dripping for Nash to fuck you."

She nods, her cheeks flushed. "Yes."

Colt drops to his knees by the side of her head, his cock resting on her thick lips. Flora turns her head toward him and wraps those pretty lips around Colt, and I feel her muscles clamp down on me as she focuses on him. She moans while I continue to thrust, slow and deep.

Colt's eyes meet mine, and I don't look away this time. I see the raw hunger in his eyes. We've danced around our desire, but now, with Flora writhing between us, the truth is laid bare.

Colt's eyes darken as he looks at me, and I know he's thinking the same thing. With her haunting beauty and bruised soul, this woman has the power to unravel us. She makes us feel things we've kept buried.

I thrust into Flora, my pace increasing as my need builds. Colt's hand tangles in her hair, guiding her farther down on his shaft. She gags slightly but then relaxes, taking more of him in. He lets out a low groan, his eyes squeezing shut as he savors the sensation.

"That's it, angel. Take it all," he says hoarsely.

Her eyes flutter open, and she meets my gaze. Her walls clench around me, and I know she's close. I find her clit with my thumb and begin to rub circles, my tempo matching my thrusts.

"You're so beautiful like this. So fucking gorgeous," Colt says, his voice strained.

I continue to thumb her clit. "Come for us. Let us see you fall apart."

Her breath hitches, and her eyes squeeze shut as her walls tighten like a vise around me. I feel her release, the wet heat of it, and I thrust through it, wanting to draw out her pleasure.

"I'm close," Colt says hoarsely. "Her mouth is so fucking good."

I pull out of Flora slowly, and she makes a noise of protest, her eyes fluttering open. "Shh, I'm not done with you yet. But first, I want you on all fours, giving him full access to your pretty little throat."

I position her on her hands and knees in front of

Colt. She looks up at him and then takes him into her mouth again.

Colt threads his fingers through her hair, guiding her further onto his length. "Good girl. Take me to the hilt."

As Flora takes Colt's length into her throat, I position myself behind her and sink inside. Her walls clench around me, milking me, and I groan, my hands gripping her hips tightly.

Colt's eyes squeeze shut. "Holy hell, that mouth is perfect, angel. I can't get enough."

She moans, the vibration making his hips jerk in response. Her walls clench around my cock, and I know she's close again. This time, I can't hold back. I thrust into her, and she cries out, the sound muffled by Colt's cock in her mouth.

"You like that, baby? Like being filled from both ends?" I ask.

She nods, her eyes squeezing shut as she loses herself in the pleasure.

Colt's hand moves to her jaw. "Take me deep."

I thrust into her, my pace increasing. "Take everything we give you like a good little slut."

She whimpers, her body trembling. Colt groans, his eyes rolling back.

"Such a good girl," he says hoarsely. "You're making me so hard."

I lean down, my mask brushing her ear. "You're making me hard, too, baby. So fucking hard."

I pull out slowly, and she whimpers, her body begging for more. I snap my hips forward, burying myself back inside her, and she cries out.

"I'm close," he says, his voice strained. "I'm gonna come in your mouth. You ready for that?"

She nods as she sucks him eagerly.

"Keep going, little bird. You can do it," I coax, my movements becoming frantic. "I want to feel you come again."

Her walls clench around me, her body arching as she loses herself in the pleasure. I feel her juices drip down my cock, and I know she's falling apart.

Colt's hand tightens in her hair, and he groans, his hips thrusting forward as he fills her mouth with his release. "Drink every drop. Swallow it all down."

Her throat works as she swallows, her body shaking with the force of her orgasm. I pull out slowly, savoring the sensation of her walls milking me, then thrust back into her, my own release building.

"There you go," I whisper, my voice low. "Drink him down as I bury myself inside you."

She whimpers, her body shaking as she comes again, her mouth still wrapped around Colt's cock. I thrust into her a few more times, burying myself deep inside her and filling her with cum.

"So good," I whisper, kissing her shoulder. "So fucking perfect."

Colt pulls out of her mouth, and she turns her head, her eyes meeting mine. I see the satisfaction in her gaze, the softness that comes after falling apart.

"You did so well, angel," Colt says gently. "So fucking brave."

She smiles softly, her cheeks flushed, her body trembling. "Thank you for… everything."

I lean down, lifting my mask enough to kiss her lips softly. "We're not done with you yet, little bird."

Colt chuckles, his eyes darkening as he looks at me. "Oh no, we're far from done."

I watch Flora's face, memorizing every detail of this moment. Her breath still comes in small catches, and my heart pounds with more than just the physical exertion.

Colt's presence feels different now. The tension between us has shifted into something new, catalyzed by Flora's arrival. I catch his gaze, and neither of us looks away. There's an understanding, a bridge built over the chasm we've maintained.

Flora trembles slightly between us, and I'm struck by how perfectly she fits. Not just physically, but in the space between Colt and me—a space I never knew needed filling until now. She's like a missing piece we didn't realize we were searching for.

12

COLT

I help Nash guide Flora, wrapped in my coat, into our trailer, my hand resting protectively on her lower back. It wasn't lost on me the way Nash looked at me as I stroked myself just minutes before. We've opened doors to a world of new pleasures. It thrills me to no end.

The familiar space of our trailer feels different tonight, charged with an energy I've never experienced here before. We've shared this space as best friends and performance partners for ten years, but something has shifted.

Flora's eyes dart around, taking in our living quarters—the small kitchen area, the worn but comfortable couch, and the two bedroom doors. Nash moves with his usual grace, getting water for all of us while I help Flora settle onto the couch.

"Make yourself comfortable, angel," I murmur, hyper-aware of Nash's presence behind me.

Nash hands Flora a glass of water, his fingers

brushing against hers. We've never shared someone like this.

"You can take my room," Nash offers Flora, but I catch his eye. There's something new there, an intensity I've never allowed myself to acknowledge.

Flora curls up on the couch, clearly exhausted. I drape a blanket over her while Nash dims the lights. We move in perfect sync, just like during our performances. Still, the familiar choreography of our friendship feels charged with new meaning.

"Thank you," Flora whispers, her eyes heavy with sleep. "Both of you."

I settle into the armchair while Nash leans against the wall. The silence between us speaks volumes. We have been sharing this space and knowing each other's every move and mood. But tonight has changed something fundamental between us.

Nash meets my gaze across the darkened room. Neither of us needs to say it aloud—we know this is the beginning of something.

I notice Flora trying to stifle another yawn. "Come on. Let's get you to bed. You need rest after today."

Flora bites her lower lip, a gesture I'm learning means she's nervous. "Could you both... I mean, would you sleep with me?"

Nash's rich laugh fills the trailer. "Well, we can't use my room then. I have a small double bed and wasn't planning on two visitors." He pushes off from the wall, stretching his long frame. "Colt's got the bigger bed anyway."

"My room it is," I say, keeping my voice steady

despite my heart racing. "I've got a king size. Plenty of room for three."

Flora's eyes dart between Nash and me, her cheeks flushing pink in the dim light.

Nash extends his hand to help her up from the couch. "Come on, little bird. Let's get you settled."

My bedroom door has never seemed so significant as it does now, watching Nash guide Flora toward it. This is the first time we'll share a bed—all because of this beautiful, broken angel who's stumbled into our lives tonight. It feels like I've known her just as long as Nash.

"I usually sleep on the right side," I offer, trying to maintain normalcy in this anything-but-normal situation.

"Always gotta be on your right side, don't you?" Nash teases, his eyes dancing with mischief. "Even off the trapeze, you're predictable."

I roll my eyes. "You want to argue about sleeping arrangements all night or get some sleep?"

"Take your precious right side," Nash concedes with an exaggerated bow. "I'm flexible. You know that better than anyone."

I can't keep my eyes from flitting down to his crotch at that statement, damn it. I want to see his legs splayed open in that masculine way, his cock standing tall… for me.

Fuck. I watch Flora drop my coat onto a chair as my blood races in my veins. It's at that moment I notice the bruises on her hips and wrists. Bruises I know we didn't cause. My jaw clenches.

Who hurt her?

I don't mention it, but Nash looks at the same spots. He looks just as pissed as I feel.

The bed dips as Flora crawls into the middle, her movements hesitant. I pause just a second before I drop my pants, leaving on my underwear.

I settle onto my side of the bed, hearing the rustle of fabric as Nash's pants fall gently to the floor. He settles on the left side of the bed. There's a moment of awkward shuffling before Nash curves his body around Flora's smaller frame, fitting against her like a puzzle piece.

Flora lets out a soft sigh and rests her head on my chest. Her hair fans out, tickling my skin, and I catch Nash's knowing look over her head. The familiar scent of his aftershave mingles with Flora's vanilla shampoo.

Nash's arm drapes over Flora's hip. I feel his fingertips barely brushing against my side. The touch, however slight, sends electricity through my body and makes my dick solid. Flora's breathing begins to even out, her body relaxing between us.

"Comfortable, angel?" I whisper.

She makes a sound of contentment, already half-asleep. Nash shifts closer, eliminating the space between them, and I feel the mattress move.

"You need to get that shoulder looked at," Nash whispers, his voice barely audible. "I noticed you favoring it with Flora."

I roll my eyes. "Always the mother hen."

"Someone has to be." His fingers absently trace patterns on Flora's arm. "We've got the Christmas show in three weeks. Can't have you getting injured."

"I'll ice it tomorrow," I concede, knowing he won't let it go. Ten years of friendship have taught me which battles to pick with Nash.

"And see the physio," he adds, raising an eyebrow.

"Fine." I shift, careful not to disturb Flora. "But you need to stop pushing yourself so hard on the triple twist. I saw you wobble on the landing earlier."

Nash's lips quirk into a half-smile. "Noticed that, did you?"

"I notice everything about your performance." The words come out before I can stop them.

"I know you do." His voice is soft. "Just like I notice everything about yours."

Flora stirs, mumbling something in her sleep, and we both fall silent. Nash's hand has stilled on her arm, and I find myself studying the familiar lines of his face in the shadows.

"We should get some sleep," he murmurs after a moment.

"Yeah," I agree, though neither of us closes our eyes. "Goodnight, Nash."

"Goodnight, Colt."

We lie in comfortable silence, both aware of the weight of what remains unsaid between us, yet neither willing to shatter this moment.

13

FLORA

I wake with a jolt, my body stretching across unfamiliar sheets that smell of masculine musk and cedar. The empty spaces beside me hold warmth from where Nash and Colt slept, but they're gone now. Sunlight streams through the trailer's window, casting strange shadows across the rumpled bedding.

A harsh buzz cuts through the peaceful morning. My phone vibrates against the wooden nightstand, the screen lighting up with a number I'd hoped to never see again. My foster family. My heart pounds against my ribs as I snatch the device, my thumb hovering over the decline button.

Tommy's face enters my mind—the cruel twist of his lips when he found me holding the flyer. "Not happening. You belong to me and Jake. Don't forget that. Or do you need another reminder?"

I press decline, but my hands won't stop shaking. The phone slips between my trembling fingers onto the bed. On the outside, no one would think anything was amiss with my foster family. Sure, they overworked me. But that was the least of my worries. Tommy and Jake were the real nightmare, especially two years ago when I turned sixteen.

Looking around Colt's bedroom, I wonder if I've traded one cage for another. But this feels different. Despite their intensity, their possession feels like protection rather than imprisonment. Still, can they keep me safe if Tommy and Jake come looking? They won't let me go easily.

The phone buzzes again. Same number. I decline it faster this time, my breath coming in short gasps. I pull my knees to my chest, making myself small like I used to do in that house. The carnival seemed like a perfect escape, but now I'm unsure. Maybe nowhere is truly safe.

The bedroom door creaks open, and Colt's broad frame fills the doorway. He's gorgeous, his movements strong and sure. He balances a steaming mug of coffee and a plate stacked with golden pancakes. His hair is damp from a shower, a few drops sliding down his neck and into his tight black t-shirt.

"You're awake." His ice-blue eyes scan my huddled position, taking in my phone clutched in my white-knuckled grip. The mattress dips as he sets breakfast on the nightstand. "Everything okay?"

I force my fingers to release the phone, letting it fall onto the sheets. "Just... spam calls." The lie tastes bitter on my tongue, but I can't bring myself to explain. Not yet.

"Here." He hands me the coffee mug, and warmth seeps into my cold hands. The rich aroma helps ground me in the present moment. "Nash is handling some business with Tyson but will return soon. I thought you might be hungry."

The pancakes smell divine, topped with butter and real maple syrup. My stomach growls, reminding me I barely ate yesterday. Colt's lips quirk up at the sound.

"Thank you," I reply, carefully sipping the coffee. It's perfect—just enough cream to cut the bitterness.

Colt settles beside me, close enough that his thigh brushes mine through the blanket. The contact sends a shiver through me, but not from fear. His presence pushes back the darkness that Tommy's call stirred up, replacing it with something warm and safe.

"Eat," he says, his voice gentle but leaving no room for argument. "We've got training later, and you'll need your strength."

I take a bite of the pancakes, savoring the sweetness as Colt shifts beside me.

"About the Christmas show," he says, eyes on my face. "It's our biggest performance of the year. Nash and I have been talking, and we want you in it."

The fork freezes halfway to my mouth. "But I've barely started training."

"You're a natural on the trapeze. Your form is perfect, and you take direction well." His hand finds my knee through the blanket, squeezing gently. "We've got three weeks to get you ready."

"Three weeks?" I set the fork down, my appetite

wavering under the weight of his expectations. "That seems impossible."

"Not impossible. Challenging, yes. But Nash and I will work with you every day." His thumb traces circles on my knee. "The Christmas show is special. We transform the big top into a winter wonderland. Snow machines, ice-themed costumes, the works."

I picture myself suspended above a glittering white floor, wrapped in sparkles and frost. The image is beautiful but terrifying. "What if I fall?"

"You won't." The certainty in his voice makes me look up. His blue eyes lock with mine. "Nash and I won't let that happen. Ever."

"What's the routine?"

"A three-person aerial dance. Nash and I have performed it as a duo before, but with you..." He pauses, something dark and hungry flickering across his face. "It'll be different. Better. You're the missing piece we've been waiting for."

The intensity of his gaze makes my cheeks flush. I take another sip of coffee to hide my reaction, but Colt sees right through it. His hand slides from my knee to my thigh, his palm burning through the blanket.

"Say yes," he murmurs. "Let us show you what we can create together."

I nod, setting my coffee down. "Yes. I want to be part of the show."

Colt's smile transforms his entire face, softening the hard edges. He pulls me into a tight embrace, and I melt against his chest. His warmth envelops me. The scent of his shower-fresh skin fills my senses—clean soap and something uniquely him.

My fingers curl into his t-shirt of their own accord. His heart thunders against my palm, matching the rapid beat of my own. His eyes darken when I tilt my head back to look at him. Time seems to slow as he leans down, giving me plenty of chance to pull away.

I don't.

His lips brush mine, gentle at first, then more insistent. The kiss deepens, and I lose myself in the sensation until we're both breathless.

When we finally break apart, Colt rests his forehead against mine. "We should probably talk about last night." His voice comes out rough. "It wasn't the conventional way to start working together."

I feel the heat rise in my cheeks at the memory. "No, it wasn't."

"Any regrets?" His thumb traces my jawline, his touch feather-light.

"None." The word comes out barely above a whisper, but I mean it. Despite how intense things got with him and Nash, I feel safer here than ever.

Colt's smile is playful, something I haven't seen on him before. "Any questions so far?"

I swallow hard, my gaze darting between him and the closed bedroom door. "I— I mean, yes. I do have a question."

"Go on. Ask me anything." His fingertips trace lazy patterns on my thigh, each touch sending a shiver through me.

I take a steadying breath. "Have you ever, I mean... with Nash. Have you ever shared a woman before?"

For a moment, Colt doesn't answer. His hand stills, but his eyes hold mine. I can see the wheels turning in his head, weighing his response.

"Never," he says, his voice steady. "You're the only one."

My eyes widen. "Really?"

Colt nods, his thumb brushing my cheek. "You're different, Flora. Special. It's like you woke something up in both of us."

"But I felt this... tension between the two of you. Almost like—" I stop, unsure how to put it into words without offending him.

Colt's fingers pause on my cheek, his eyes suddenly guarded. "Go on. Don't hold back."

My pulse quickens, but I forge ahead. "Like there's something between you. Something more than just work colleagues or best friends."

He's quiet for a moment, his thumb stroking my cheekbone. I can see the wheels turning in his head as he weighs his response.

"It's true. There's more to Nash and me than meets the eye." He sighs, his eyes fixed on the window. "I've always been attracted to him, but he's straight."

I frown because I saw the way Nash looked at Colt's dick. "Are you sure about that?"

Colt tilts his head. "Yes, he's always been with women only."

"Have you ever tried anything?" I ask.

"No." He shakes his head. "I've wanted to plenty of

times. But I value his friendship too much to risk losing it." His eyes meet mine again. "It's a weird limbo, wanting someone you can't have."

There's an invisible tether between them that defies explanation, and it draws me in just as much as it confuses me.

"Would you—" My voice falters, uncertain if I should ask.

"What, angel?" His thumb brushes my lower lip, his gaze never wavering.

"Would you want to try?" The words tumble out in a rush. "With Nash, I mean. I think it would be..." My cheeks flame, but I force myself to continue. "I think it would be hot."

Colt's eyes widen, and I worry I've said too much. But then a slow smile curves his lips, making his dimples appear. "You think so, huh?"

I nod, unable to look away from his intense blue eyes. "It's just— you two have an almost tangible connection. And you obviously care about each other deeply. It could be beautiful if you explored that side of things."

"And what about you, angel?" He leans closer, his eyes darkening with desire. "Would you want to be part of that exploration?"

My pulse hammers in my veins, and my breath comes in short gasps. "Yes," I whisper, the word coming out on a breath. "I think I would."

As soon as the words leave my lips, I regret them. But then Colt's mouth crashes down on mine, silencing any apologies. His tongue tangles with mine, kissing me like he means it. His hand grabs my thigh under the blanket, and I squirm against him.

His kiss deepens, and he pulls me tighter against his growing erection. My core throbs with need, remembering what it was like to have him inside me.

"So damn beautiful." His lips trail hot kisses along my jaw. "You like the idea of me and Nash, huh?"

"Mmm." I nod.

"You want to see me suck his cock?" Colt's voice is hoarse as his hand cups my breast through the shirt. "Want to see how much I've wanted him?"

I let out a ragged breath, my body arching against him. His kiss is sloppy and hungry, conveying his own pent-up desires.

"Yeah," I whisper against his lips. "I want to see it."

Colt groans, his hips thrusting against me. "I've dreamed about his mouth on me, his hands... but you... you're what I want most right now."

I tear my mouth from him, panting. "Then take me."

Without breaking eye contact, he shifts me off his lap. His hands find the hem of my shirt and lift, eyes darkening as my skin is revealed. I lift my arms, letting him pull it over my head and toss it aside. He cups my breasts, thumbs brushing my nipples through my bra.

"So fucking perfect." His eyes burn into mine as he leans down to take a nipple into his mouth. The sensation shoots straight between my legs, and I gasp.

While he teases my nipples with his tongue and teeth, his hands move to the band of his sweatpants. He pulls out his thick, pierced cock, the tip already leaking.

My mouth goes dry at the sight of it, but he lies down beside me instead of entering me.

"Sit on my face," he growls, eyes flashing with dark need. "I need to taste you."

I obey, positioning myself above his mouth as he rests on the bed. My core hovers over his face, the anticipation building as he grabs my thighs.

His tongue teases my entrance, making me cry out. Then he pulls me down so his mouth covers me completely, his tongue penetrating deep as he laps at my juices. My hands tangle in his damp hair, holding him to me as my hips rock involuntarily against his mouth.

"Fuck, you taste so good," he mumbles, his hands squeezing my ass as he lifts me away to speak. "I could eat you out all day."

My moans fill the room, my knees bracketing his shoulders as his tongue works magic on my clit. "Please," I pant, unsure what I'm begging for. Release? For more? Both?

Colt chuckles, the vibrations sending shocks of pleasure through me. He pulls me tighter against his mouth, his tongue working me in all the right ways. My hips buck as I teeter on the edge, and suddenly, he stops.

I force my eyes open. "Your fantasy, remember? Tell me," he orders, voice muffled between my legs.

"I want you to fuck me," I gasp, thrusting my hips against his face. "Like last night. Missionary."

His groan vibrates against my core. My eyes roll back as his fingers find my clit, rubbing circles as he sucks and licks from below.

"And Nash?" His voice is strained as he pushes me toward a second peak. "What's he doing?"

"You're sucking his cock." I try to form a coherent sentence, but it's difficult with the way he's eating me. "He's holding your hair while you take him down your throat."

"Good girl." His fingers curl inside me, stretching and filling me. "But how does it feel? Tell me."

"It feels..." I struggle to put words to the image in my mind, the sensation of his fingers fucking me slowly, his tongue dancing across my clit. "It feels filthy. So dirty."

Colt hums his approval, the vibration sending shivers through me. "Anything else?"

I hesitate, uncertain if my fantasy is too much. "I want your cum. Both of you." I bite my lip, hesitating. "Inside me. And then, I want you both to take turns eating it out of my pussy."

"You filthy angel," he growls, withdrawing his fingers and throwing me onto my back beneath him, his thick cock grinding against my soaking wet pussy. "Do you want my cum now?"

"Yes." The word is a plea as he teases my entrance, rubbing the tip of his cock against me. "Claim me."

He plunges inside me with a groan, his thrusts urgent and deep as if to brand me as his own. I moan, clenching around him. He sets a brutal pace, pounding into me relentlessly. I'm dizzy with pleasure, arching my back to meet each thrust.

"Your fantasy, angel. Finish it." Colt's hips snap against mine as he reaches between us, rubbing my clit.

"I want your mouth on him," I pant. "Tasting me on his cock."

"Fuck, yes," he groans, momentarily breaking his rhythm, consumed by the fantasy. "I crave the taste of him, your sweetness lingering on every inch of his cock."

I moan and claw at his shoulders, pulling him down for a kiss.

"Mm, yes." I kiss him hungrily, biting his lip as he thrusts into me. "Then he fucks my mouth while you take me from behind, pumping me full of your cum."

"You're killing me, angel." Colt's voice is thick, strained with the effort of his self-control. His hand slides down to rub my clit in time with his relentless thrusts.

"Tell me your fantasy, Colt," I whisper, my fingers threading through his dark hair as he continues to nibble and suck at my neck. "A fantasy of the three of us."

He pulls back, his eyes glinting with desire. "You sure you want to know?"

I nod, my chest tight with anticipation. "Tell me."

His smile is wicked as he continues to fuck me. "You on your back just like you are now, and I'm fucking you hard and rough."

I arch my back, wanting him deeper. "Go on," I breathe.

"And Nash is behind me, his dick lubed up, and my ass stretched and ready to feel him take me."

"Oh fuck!" I murmur, the image so hot. "You want him to fuck you while you fuck me?"

"Yeah." Colt thrusts into me, each snap of his hips sending shockwaves of pleasure through me. "I want to feel Nash stretch me open while I'm balls deep in your sweet pussy."

My vision blurs as the image takes over my mind. Colt fucking me while Nash takes him—all three of us connected so intimately.

The thought is enough to push me over the edge. I shatter around Colt, my pussy milking him as I cry out his name.

"Just like that. Surrender to me." Colt thrusts through my orgasm, his grunts of pleasure filling the room. His pace becomes erratic, his hips snapping against mine as he chases his own release.

His grip on my hips tightens, fingers digging into my flesh. "My turn to fly." He slams into me, his cock pulsing as he fills me with his cum. "Come with me, baby. Let go again."

I sob against his shoulder as he angles his hips in a way that slams his piercing into my G-spot, and another climax consumes me, this one even more powerful than the first. My body shakes uncontrollably as Colt fills me, his hips jerking as he empties himself inside me.

Gradually, my senses return. Colt's sweat-soaked chest heaves against me as he tries to catch his breath.

"That was..." I trail off, unable to find words.

"Incredible." Colt chuckles, his lips pressing kisses to my shoulder. "I knew you'd be something special, angel. But you've exceeded every fantasy."

I smile. "That's saying something, considering your imagination."

He chuckles, his chest rumbling against my back. "We've only just begun." His voice turns wicked, sending a thrill through me. "We've hardly explored the fantasies I have of you, me, and Nash."

A shiver runs through me at the thought. "I can't wait."

Colt pulls out of me slowly, then tugs me against his chest. I snuggle against him, enjoying the warmth of his arms around me. The safety that this man offers is everything I've ever craved since I was a little girl.

14

NASH

I know he's fucking her.

The words echo in my head as I walk back to the trailer. The sun beats down on me, but it's the heat in my blood that's suffocating. Hell, if I had the chance to stay back with her, I'd be balls deep in her cunt right about now.

When I woke this morning, finding Flora sleeping, I tried to shake off the memory of her flushed cheeks and disheveled hair. The image of them together, naked and tangled in each other's arms, is burned into my mind. It's not just that; there's something more complex bothering me; there's a new thread that ties us all together.

As I near the trailer, the low murmur of voices reaches my ears. Colt's deep tone, rough with desire, shatters my spine. I pause, my hand hovering over the doorknob. I shouldn't eavesdrop, but my body betrays me, needing to hear more as I crack open the door to the trailer.

"Yeah, I want to feel Nash stretch me open while I'm balls deep in your sweet pussy."

My dick hardens at the words, my breath catching in my throat. I know I should walk away and give them privacy. But my feet are rooted to the spot.

I've always been drawn to Colt. His intensity matches my own, his strength complementing my agility. We've performed together for years, and our partnership is seamless. But I never imagined him like this, really. Or am I in denial?

I think back to last night, seeing him naked for the first time. His body, sculpted by years of training, his skin marked with tattoos that tell stories of his past. And his dick, beautiful, pierced, and thick, the sight of it making my mouth water.

I shake my head, trying to clear my thoughts. I've never considered myself to be bisexual, or at least I've never been attracted to guys before. But something about Colt is different. It's not just about sex; it's about the connection we share, the understanding that goes beyond words.

Their passion reaches a climax, and I hear Flora cry out. Moments later, Colt follows, his voice hoarse as he fills her with his release.

I take a step back, my heart pounding. I need to get out of here to clear my head. But even as I turn to walk away from my trailer, my body hums with need, my cock throbbing with unspent desire.

I slump against the wall outside the trailer. The memory of Colt's naked form burns in my mind—those sculpted muscles, the way his tattoos dance across his skin when he moves. My cock strains against my jeans, and I press the heel of my hand against it, trying to will away my arousal.

What the fuck is wrong with me?

I've never looked at another man this way before. But last night, watching him with Flora, seeing the raw power in his movements, the way his ass flexed as he thrust into her... Christ. I imagined dropping to my knees, tasting him. The thought of his thick cock stretching my lips makes me groan.

"Get it together," I mutter, running a hand through my hair.

But the images won't stop. I picture him bending me over, his strong hands gripping my hips. The phantom sensation of him filling me makes my breath catch. Would he be gentle? Or would he claim me with the same intensity he shows in our performances?

Fuck. This could ruin everything. Years of friendship, our perfect partnership in the show. One wrong move or slip of control could bring our world crashing down. The thought of losing Colt or making things awkward between us feels like a knife in my gut.

We've built something special here. Our acts are flawless because we trust each other completely. How many times have I put my life in his hands? How many times has he trusted me to catch him?

I lean my head back against the trailer wall, closing my eyes. Our connection is undeniable—something deeper than physical attraction. When Flora walked into our lives yesterday, it felt like finding our home.

My protective instincts surge whenever I look at her.

A vulnerability in her eyes calls to me, but not in the way I'm used to. Instead of exploiting her weakness, I want to shield her from anyone trying to hurt her.

The way she fits between Colt and me feels natural like she was meant to be there. Her presence soothes something wild in both of us. The shadows that usually haunt me seem less overwhelming when she's near.

I imagine waking up with them every morning, sharing meals, and living our lives intertwined—training, performing, and building something real. The thought makes my chest tight with longing.

We're three broken pieces that somehow make something whole together. The darkness that's always lived inside me, which makes me keep everyone at arm's length, retreats a little when I'm with them.

I've never believed in fate or destiny, but this feels different. Flora's trust in us and her perfect understanding of our dynamic without words can't be a coincidence. Yesterday, she was a stranger. Today, I can't imagine our lives without her.

I leave the trailer, my mind in turmoil, but my body knows what it wants. It's time to face the truth and explore the depths of our desires.

15

COLT

One week.

Seven days that bled together in a blur of pleasure.

Flora is a fucking angel. Eager to please and responsive to every touch.

We have fallen into a comfortable routine. Wake, fuck, repeat. Training in the day, then returning to our shared space to cook dinner, only to lose ourselves in each other's bodies all night. Flora's body was like a canvas; we painted it with our desire, leaving our marks all over her; hickeys and bruises. We need to calm it down before the Christmas show.

But there's still an itch I can't scratch. It's the fantasy that Flora and I discussed. Neither of us can bring it up with Nash, and Flora did mention that I had to do it, not her. I agree, as Nash might do it to please her rather than wanting it for himself.

The thought lingers as I watch Flora and Nash practice their trapeze routine. Nash guides Flora through another aerial sequence, and his muscles ripple as he catches her.

My cock hardens at the sight of them together—the way Nash's hands grip Flora's waist, how she arches into his touch without hesitation now.

What a difference from that first day, when she'd jump at sudden movements. Now, she melts into Nash's hold, trusting him completely. Whatever darkness haunts her past, we're helping her overcome it one touch at a time.

Nash lifts Flora higher, their bodies pressed close. My mind wanders to forbidden territory—imagining myself behind Nash while he takes Flora. The image of my cock buried deep in his ass while he fucks into her makes my breath catch.

Flora catches my eye and gives me a knowing look. We've talked about it—my hidden desires for Nash. She understands and encourages it; she says we should explore it together. But bringing it up with Nash... that's different.

What if it changes everything?

Nash calls out instructions to Flora, his voice deep and commanding. She responds instantly to his direction, her body moving fluidly through the air. There is no trace of that scared girl who first came to us in these moments. Here, suspended above the ground, she's found her freedom.

I adjust myself discreetly, unable to tear my eyes away from them. The way they move together, the trust between them—it's intoxicating. And knowing that later, we'll take that connection to an even deeper level in our bed...

My cock throbs painfully against my zipper. Watching them is pure torture but the sweetest kind.

I watch as Nash helps Flora down from the rigging, his hands lingering on her waist longer than necessary. My mouth goes dry at their casual intimacy.

"Great work today," Nash says, ruffling Flora's hair. "You're picking this up faster than anyone I've seen."

"Lunch?" I suggest rolling my shoulder to work out the stiffness. "I'm starving after watching you two."

Nash's expression shifts, a flash of regret crossing his features. "Can't. Ty needs help with some business." He grabs his bag from the corner. "But I'll meet you both back here before tonight's show."

Flora's face falls slightly at the news, but she brightens as she turns to me. "We could grab lunch together?" She tucks a loose strand of hair behind her ear, a habit I've come to find endearing.

"Yeah, angel. I'd like that." I grab my own bag, slinging it over my good shoulder.

Nash heads for the exit, pausing briefly to squeeze my uninjured shoulder. "Don't forget to ice that before the show tonight. Can't have you dropping me in front of the crowd."

"When have I ever dropped you?" I call after him, but he's already gone, leaving me alone with Flora.

"Ready?" I ask her.

She nods, stepping beside me as we head for the

tent's exit. Crisp and clean winter air hits us, a stark contrast to the warmth of the training space.

I guide Flora to my truck, noting how her shoulders tense as we drive into town. Her fingers twist in her lap, a nervous habit I've picked up on this past week.

"There's a quiet place on the edge of town," I say, taking the long way around to avoid the main streets of Easthollow. "Best burgers you'll ever taste."

Flora's eyes dart between buildings and passing cars. "That sounds perfect."

I pull into Marie's Diner, a weathered building with peeling paint and a flickering neon sign. Only two other cars occupy the lot. Inside, the smell of coffee and grilled onions fills the air. An elderly waitress leads us to a corner booth far from the windows.

"This okay?" I ask as Flora slides into the vinyl seat.

She nods, but her eyes keep tracking the door. I sit opposite her, positioning myself to watch the entrance.

"You know," I say in a low and gentle voice. "If anyone tries to bother you, they'll have to get through me first."

Her hands shake slightly. "I just... I grew up here. There are people I'd rather not run into."

The fear in her voice makes my blood boil. I reach across the table, covering her trembling hands with mine. "Angel, look at me."

She meets my eyes, vulnerability written across her face.

"You're safe now. With me. With Nash. Nobody's going to hurt you anymore."

The tension in her shoulders eases slightly, but her

fingers remain curled tight around the menu. I understand her fear—this town holds her demons. But I'll be damned if I let them touch her again.

The waitress returns with our menus, and Flora orders a cheeseburger with fries. At the same time, I go for the double stack with extra bacon. After the waitress leaves, Flora leans forward, her hazel eyes searching mine.

"You know, despite spending every moment together this past week, I realize I don't know much about you," she says, fidgeting with her straw wrapper. "Where did you come from? How did you end up at the carnival?"

I lean back against the vinyl booth, my shoulder twinging slightly. "Not much to tell, really. Rich dad, absent mom. She..." I pause, the memory still raw after all these years. "She overdosed when I was twelve. Dad shipped me off to military school right after."

Flora's hand reaches across the table, her fingers brushing mine. The simple gesture catches me off guard.

"I got kicked out at sixteen," I continue, trying to keep my voice steady. "Couldn't handle the authority, the rigid structure. Ran away before Dad could find out. Found the carnival a few months later, and Tyson gave me a shot."

Flora's fingers trace patterns on my hand, her touch gentle and understanding. "And Nash? Was he already there when you joined?"

"Yeah." I can't help the small smile that forms. "He'd been with the carnival about two months already.

Tyson paired us up almost immediately—said our heights matched perfectly for the aerial act."

Flora nods, still absently drawing circles on my skin. "You two just... clicked?"

"Not exactly." I chuckle at the memory. "Nash was this perfectionist who couldn't stand my military-style counting during routines. We butted heads for weeks until Tyson threatened to separate us. After that, we figured out how to work together."

The waitress arrives with our food, and Flora withdraws her hand. Steam rises from the perfectly grilled burgers, and the fries smell divine. But my mind is stuck on Nash, on how that initial friction transformed into something deeper.

"He saved my life once," I say quietly, picking up a fry. "About a year after I joined. I was being reckless on the trapeze, showing off without a net. The rope frayed, and I would've fallen if Nash hadn't caught me. He didn't speak to me for three days after that—just kept drilling safety protocols into my head during practice."

"That sounds like him." Flora smiles, taking a bite of her burger. "Always protective."

"Yeah." I roll my shoulder, remembering how he's fussed over my injury. "That's Nash."

I clear my throat, pushing my half-eaten burger aside. "How did you end up in foster care, angel?"

Flora's hand freezes mid-reach for a fry. Her eyes dart to the exit before settling back on her plate. The question hangs heavy between us.

"My parents..." She takes a shaky breath. "They

dropped me off at a care center when I was four. I hardly remember them."

Her voice cracks. I reach across the table, covering her trembling hand with mine. She pulls her hand away, wrapping her arms around herself. "I spent years bouncing between homes before the Lowleys took me in on a more permanent basis when I was eleven."

The way she says their name—like it tastes bitter on her tongue—makes my jaw clench. There's more to that story, but I won't push. Not here, not now.

"Seven years with them," she whispers, more to herself than to me. "Seven years until I turned eighteen last week."

The pieces click into place—why she chose now to run, why she jumped at the chance to join the carnival. Freedom at eighteen, but what happened in those seven years?

I want to ask more, but the haunted look in her eyes stops me. Some wounds need time to heal before they can be exposed.

My fork clatters against the plate. "Wait—eighteen? I thought you were at least twenty."

Flora's eyes drop to her half-eaten burger. "No, I... I turned eighteen the day we met. At the masquerade."

The diner suddenly feels too small, too warm. I run a hand through my hair, my mind racing through the implications. "Your birthday? That was your eighteenth birthday?"

She nods, still not meeting my eyes. "I had to wait until I was legally an adult, but officially, I haven't aged out of the system until I've graduated high school." She shrugs. "I couldn't face staying there another six months."

"Christ." I lean back against the vinyl booth, my appetite gone. "Why didn't you tell us?"

"Would it have mattered?" Her voice is barely above a whisper. "I needed to get away. The carnival was my only chance."

I reach across the table, tilting her chin until she meets my gaze. "Of course, it would've mattered. Nash and I—we should've known."

A tear slides down her cheek, and she quickly wipes it away. "Are you angry?"

"Not at you, angel." Never at her. But at myself? That's a different story. "We should've known so we could have made it special."

Flora's eyes meet mine, a small smile tugging at her lips. "But you did make it special," she says, pushing her plate aside. "You and Nash gave me something I never thought I'd have—freedom."

My chest tightens at her words. She reaches across the table, her fingers brushing against mine.

"It was the best birthday I can remember," she continues, her voice soft but sure. "For the first time in seven years, I felt... safe. Protected. When you found me at the masquerade and helped me meet Tyson—" She pauses, collecting her thoughts. "You gave me a home, Colt. You and Nash both did."

I swallow hard, remembering how terrified she'd looked that first night, hiding behind her mask. Now, here she sits, strong and determined, despite everything she's been through.

"We'll always protect you, angel," I promise, squeezing her hand. "No matter what."

She nods, and I see the trust in her eyes—the trust we've earned over this past week. The same trust she shows when flying through the air, knowing Nash and I will always catch her.

"I know," she says simply, and those two words carry more weight than any lengthy declaration could.

16

FLORA

My hands shake as I stare at the unknown number on my phone screen. Another voicemail. The bathroom's fluorescent lights flicker overhead as I press play, sliding down against the cold tile wall.

"You think you can just leave?" Tommy's voice slithers through the speaker. "You belong to us, Flora. We'll find you."

I end the message, my chest tight and breathing shallow. Jake's texts flood my notifications from yet another number I didn't block. The words blur together—threats, promises of what they'll do when they find me.

The carnival feels far away, even though I can hear the music and laughter outside. My safe haven suddenly seems paper-thin.

I scramble to my feet, needing to escape the suffocating confines of the bathroom stall. My vision tunnels as panic sets in. I throw open the door and bolt forward, slamming straight into someone.

"Oof!" A feminine voice exclaims as we collide.

I stumble back, my phone clattering to the floor. Through tear-blurred eyes, I make out a brunette woman about my age.

"I'm so sorry," I gasp, dropping to retrieve my phone. My hands are trembling so badly I can barely grip them.

"Hey, are you okay?" The woman—Aurora, I think her name is—kneels beside me. Her eyes are filled with genuine concern. "You look like you've seen a ghost."

I try to speak, but my throat closes up. The phone buzzes with another message, making me flinch.

I wipe my eyes, trying to compose myself. Aurora's kind face reminds me of someone I knew in high school—before everything went wrong.

"I'm fine," I manage, though my voice cracks. "Just... family stuff."

Aurora nods, understanding filling her eyes. She doesn't push, doesn't pry. Instead, she helps me up from the bathroom floor, giving me space to steady myself.

"Listen," she says, tucking dark hair behind her ear. "Some of us girls are having a movie night tonight. Nothing fancy—just popcorn, snacks, probably some terrible rom-coms." Her smile is warm and inviting. "You should join us. It's always nice to have fresh faces around."

My instinct is to decline. Being around people I don't know makes me nervous, especially after everything. But something in Aurora's gentle demeanor makes me hesitate.

"I... maybe?" The word comes out as a question. "I'm not sure if—"

"No pressure," Aurora cuts in smoothly. "We're meeting in the main tent at seven. If you feel up to it, great. If not, there's always next time."

She makes it sound so simple, so casual. Like I'm not broken. The thought brings an unexpected lump to my throat.

"Thanks," I whisper. "I'll think about it."

I hesitate at the trailer door, my hand hovering over the handle. Through the window, I can see Nash sitting at the small table, focused on what appears to be paperwork. My earlier conversation with Aurora still echoes, but something about Nash's presence helps steady my nerves.

Taking a deep breath, I push open the door. Nash looks up, a smile crossing his face as he sees me.

"Hey, little bird." He sets down his pen. "Thought you'd be practicing with Colt."

"He had to check something with Tyson." I step inside, closing the door behind me. The trailer feels different with just the two of us—not uncomfortable, just... different. "What are you working on?"

Nash shuffles the papers together. "Schedule planning for the Christmas show. Making sure everyone's routines flow together." He gestures to the empty chair across from him. "Want to join me? I could use a fresh perspective."

I slide into the seat, grateful for the casual invitation. Nash has always been quieter than Colt, more reserved but less intense. "I don't know much about show planning."

"You know more than you think." He pushes a sheet toward me. "See these time slots? Each act needs proper setup and breakdown time. It's like a puzzle."

As Nash explains the intricacies of show planning, I find myself relaxing. He has a way of making complex things seem simple. We discuss different acts, and he asks my opinion on transition times.

"What made you join the carnival?" I ask during a lull in the conversation. "If you don't mind telling me."

Nash leans back, his eyes meeting mine. "Freedom," he says simply. "The chance to create something beautiful and dangerous." He pauses, studying me. "What about you? What brought you to our world?"

"Freedom," I echo his word, watching something flicker in his eyes. A shadow of recognition, maybe understanding. There's darkness in his past, too—I can sense it, like recognizing your own reflection in murky water.

"What about your family?" The question slips out before I can stop it. "Do they—"

"Ah ah," Nash cuts me off, but his tone stays light, playful. His fingers drum against the table. "That's not a road we're going down today." He pushes back his chair slightly, patting his thigh. "Come here instead."

I recognize the deflection for what it is—I've used similar tactics myself often enough. But I like having Nash's full attention without Colt present. Different dynamic, different energy.

Rising from my chair, I move around the table.

Nash's hands find my hips as I straddle his lap. The position is already familiar despite being new with just him.

"Much better topic of conversation," he murmurs, one hand sliding up my back. His other grips my hip, keeping me steady.

"Tell me what you want," Nash murmurs, his lips ghosting along my jawline, up to my ear, his breath hot against my skin. "Tell me exactly what I can do to drive you wild."

My pulse thrums between my legs, my core throbbing with desire as he teases me. I squeeze my thighs together, savoring the delicious pressure. With Colt, things started rough. But with Nash... my body craves something different. Something that makes my skin shiver and my heart pound.

"I want you to take your time." My voice sounds breathless, even to my own ears. "Make me wait for it. Every touch, every kiss, every stroke... I want to feel it building inside me until I can't take it anymore."

His teeth nip at my earlobe, and a shiver runs through me. "And then?" His hand slides down the small of my back, the promise of possession in his touch.

"Then I want you to claim me," I whisper. "Mark me. Make me scream your name."

A low growl rumbles in his throat as his hand squeezes my hip. "I want to hear those cries, little bird. I want to make you feel so good you can't remember anyone else." He nibbles his way down my neck, his tongue tracing a path that makes my breath hitch. "But you have to earn it."

My breath catches as he speaks. Earn it. Those words send a thrill through me, something primal and captivating. I want his marks on my body. I want him to stake his claim.

"How?" I barely recognize the needy tone in my own voice. My hands tangle in his hair, keeping him close.

His hand slides up my back, sending shivers dancing across my skin. "By taking everything I give you. Every kiss, every touch, every stroke..." He punctuates each word with a kiss along my collarbone. "Show me you can take it all, little bird. That you can fly apart for me."

My entire body tingles, every nerve ending coming alive under his lips and hands. His tongue teases the hollow of my throat as his hands grip my hips, urging me to grind against him.

"Yes," I breathe. "God, yes."

"Good girl," he hums, his breath sending goosebumps along my skin. "Now, for your first lesson..."

He kisses a path back to my ear, his lips brushing against the sensitive skin. "I'm going to kiss you, touch you, make you feel so damn good. But you're not allowed to come."

He swirls his tongue in my ear, biting gently on the lobe. "Not until I say so. Understand?"

The challenge in his words pulls a whimper from deep within me. "Ye-yes, I understand."

His hand finds the nape of my neck, tilting my head back to expose my throat. He kisses along my pulse point, his tongue lapping against the rapid beats of my heart. "If you come before I say you can, the lesson starts over."

I bite my lip, a unique thrill coursing through me. "And if I make it through?"

Nash's chuckle sends vibrations through my body. "Then I'll give you what you've been yearning for. Every inch of me, driving into you while you scream my name."

I whimper as he teases my earlobe with his teeth. His fingers tighten on my hips as he slides me forward, grinding me against the unmistakable hardness straining his jeans. My hands fist in his hair, holding him close, needing this connection.

Nash pulls me to my feet, his hand warm against mine. He leads me through the trailer to his room, which I've never been in before. The bright morning light streams through the windows, splashing across the bed, making the moment surreal.

He halts near the bed, holding my hand to his chest. "There's only one rule here, little bird." His eyes hold mine. "You have to do everything I say."

I swallow, my mouth dry. I can feel the weight of his gaze on me. "Okay."

"Strip," he commands, his voice soft but unwavering. "Take it all off and put on a show for me."

My heart rate quickens as I nod, excitement and trepidation flowing through me. I face Nash and slowly lift my shirt over my head, angling my body to give him a better view. I know he can see the desire in my eyes, reflected back at me in his.

With deliberate movements, I unbutton my jeans,

sliding them down my legs, followed by my panties. Stepping out of the circle of denim and lace, I raise my arms to undo my bra. I let the straps fall from my shoulders, dragging the lace slowly down my arms, my eyes never leaving his. I stand before him, completely naked, vulnerable, and undeniably aroused.

A low growl rumbles in his throat, and he steps forward. But he doesn't touch me, not yet. His gaze roams over my body, drinking me in. My nipples pebble in the cool air, and I feel myself getting wetter by the second.

Nash takes his time, savoring the sight of me with an appreciation that shoots straight to my core. "Beautiful," he breathes, reaching out to tuck a lock of hair behind my ear. His fingers skim my cheek and jaw, his thumb grazing my lower lip.

Without warning, he spins me around and pushes me gently toward the bed. "Grab the headboard."

My heart is pounding as I do as he says, gripping the wooden bars of the headboard. I feel the bed dip as he joins me, his body heat warming the air behind me. His hands wrap around my wrists, guiding them to the center of the headboard, and then I feel the soft fabric of a silk tie winding around them.

"Stay just like that." His breath is hot against my shoulder, making me shiver. "Right where I can see you."

The sound of him removing his clothes fills the room—the rustle of fabric, the jangle of his belt buckle. And then I feel the mattress shift as he kneels on it, his lips and hands caressing the backs of my thighs. "So perfect," he murmurs, planting soft kisses up the backs of my legs, making me quiver.

His lips press against a sensitive spot just behind my knee, making me gasp. And then his hands are on my ass, kneading, squeezing, claiming me as his. His tongue traces a path up the crease, making me squirm, and then his lips are on me, his mouth replacing his hands.

His fingers delve into my folds, spreading me open as his tongue swipes and laps. My knees nearly buckle at the sensation, and I cry out, my wrists straining against the restraints. He hums his approval, the vibration sending shocks of pleasure through me. One finger teases my entrance, slipping inside as his tongue dances over my clit. I cry out again, unable to hold back.

Nash's mouth does things to me that make coherent thought impossible. I'm reduced to a quivering mess of need, and I've only been with him a week.

"Please," I beg, my voice muffled by the pillows. "Please, I need to come. Let me come, Nash."

"Not yet." His voice is firm, his breath hot against my ear. His fingers slide out of me, making me whimper, but then he strokes me again, right where I need it, and my body aches uncontrollably. "I want you begging for my cock."

My knuckles are white as I grip the pillow, pressing my face into the softness to muffle my cries. Nash teases my entrance, circling but not entering, his fingers coated in my wetness. I whimper at the loss of contact, my core clenching desperately.

"You like that, don't you?" His tongue swipes against

my earlobe, his lips brushing my ear. "You like being denied."

"Yes," I whimper, my cheeks burning. "Please, Nash, I need you. Please."

He chuckles, the sound sending shivers down my spine. "Not yet. I want you to remember this."

The pressure builds inside me, threatening to overwhelm my senses. Nash continues to stroke and tease, pushing me closer to the edge. I feel like I'm drowning in sensations, and he's the only thing keeping me afloat.

"Please... Nash..." I'm not sure what I'm pleading for anymore—release, more, him. Everything and anything.

His fingers slide out of me again, trailing down to circle my clit lazily. I look over my shoulder, and he delights as I squirm, his dark gaze burning into mine. My hair is tangled, my body covered in a sheen of sweat, and I've never felt more alive.

"Please, what?" His thumb presses against me, slow and purposeful. "Tell me what you want."

The sensation has me seesawing, hovering on the precipice of something all-consuming. "Please... fuck me. God, Nash, I need you inside me."

"You'll take it when I give it to you," he growls, his thumb circling my clit relentlessly. "Not before."

A strangled sound escapes my throat. I don't know how much more I can take. My head falls back as his fingers delve back inside me.

"Don't be shy, little bird," he encourages. "Let me hear how much you crave it."

I can't speak, can't form words. My walls clench

around his fingers, craving more, needing release. "Nash, please... please..."

"Shh." His fingers slip out of me and find my clit again, rubbing slow, teasing circles that make me squirm. "Not until I say so, remember?"

I'm sobbing, begging for more, and Nash is relentless. With every stroke of his fingers, with every caress of his tongue, he pushes me closer to the edge, only to back off at the last moment, letting me tumble back into the abyss. I don't know how much longer I can take this delicious torture, but I don't want it to end.

Nash's touch is everywhere and nowhere, a ghost haunting my most sensitive spots. His tongue dances along my spine as his fingers graze my nipples, teasing me, tormenting me. My skin is alive with sensation, every inch of me singing with need. "Please, Nash..."

In response, he spreads my legs wider, kissing the backs of my thighs, his fingers dipping between my folds but never quite giving me what I crave. "Soon. It's all coming soon." His breath is hot against my skin as his fingers continue their maddening dance.

His mouth travels up my spine, his lips skating along my shoulder blades as he pushes me forward. I cry out as he nips at my neck, my body yearning to be filled. His fingers continue their teasing exploration, circling, stroking, but never entering. I can feel the slickness between my legs, the ache building, threatening to consume me. "Nash, please... I need you. Now."

He chuckles, the sound warm against my ear. "Not yet. Not until I say so." His fingers slide inside me, filling me, only to withdraw again, leaving me empty and wanting. "You have to earn it. Every inch."

"I'll do anything," I moan, my body burning with the need to come. My core clenches uselessly as his fingers tease me, rubbing circles around my clit, dipping into my entrance but never truly claiming me. "Anything you want, just please let me come."

"Tell me what you want," Nash commands, his voice a low purr that sends shivers down my spine. His fingers curl around my hips, guiding me back so I'm flush against his chest.

I whimper as his cock rubs against my core, his length hard and insistent.

"You know what I want." My voice comes out as a needy whisper. I look over my shoulder, meeting his dark gaze. "I want you to fuck me, Nash. I want to feel you inside me."

A cruel smile crosses his lips as he reaches around, his fingers finding my clit. He rubs his cock through my folds, his touch electric, and I can't help but buck against him.

"I know what you want." His voice is a silken thread of temptation. "But do you know what I want to hear?"

My breath comes in short gasps as he teases me relentlessly. He knows what I want, what I crave, and he's torturing me with it. "Please..." The plea escapes my lips before I can stop it. "Please, Nash. I need you."

His thumb rubs circles around my clit, his cock pressed against my entrance but not entering. "Tell me exactly what you want me to do to you."

The words tumble from my lips, fueled by desperation. "I want you to fill me, Nash. I want your big dick pounding into me, claiming me as yours."

A low growl rumbles in his chest, vibrating against my back. "And if I do that, will you come for me? Right here, on my cock?"

I arch my back. "Yes, I'll come for you. I'll scream your name."

He chuckles, his breath hot against my ear. "Not yet. Hold it in until I say so. Understand?"

I bite my lip, my whole body thrumming with need. "Yes, I understand."

"Good girl." His fingers find my hips, guiding me back until the head of his cock is positioned perfectly at my entrance. "Now, tell me again."

Desire makes my voice hoarse as I speak. "I want you to fill me with your big dick, Nash. Please, make me yours."

"As you wish." With one swift, hard stroke, he fills me. The sensation is overwhelming, consuming me from the inside out. I cry out, my body exploding in a rush of pleasure. My core clenches around him, my release washing over me as he claims me.

"God, little bird," Nash's voice is gravelly as he tightens his grip on my hips. "Let go and cover my cock with your release. I want to feel every drop."

Sensation pulses through me in waves, my body shaking uncontrollably. Nash fucks me through it, prolonging the aftershocks of my release. I can feel his cock twitching inside me, his breathing as unsteady as my own.

"You feel so damn good." His lips brush my shoulder, his hips shifting slightly, making me whimper. "But we're not done yet."

I moan as he begins to move, his thrusts slow and controlled. Each stroke fills me, possessing me, branding me as his. My body reacts to his every touch, my walls clenching around him as if they never want to let him go.

You're doing so well," Nash murmurs, his breath hitching. Accept all of me. Take every inch deep inside you."

His hands find my hips, holding me in place as he increases the pace, pounding into me relentlessly.

"Come for me again," he growls. "Come on my cock."

His words ignite something primal inside me, and my body responds, tightening around him as I fall over the edge again. My release washes over me in waves, my screams muffled by the pillow as Nash continues to thrust into me, his own release imminent.

"That's right. I want to hear you scream out my name." His voice is hoarse, his movements becoming frantic as he seeks his own pleasure.

My core clenches uncontrollably, milking his cock as he fills me with his release. Nash groans, his body trembling against mine as he spills himself inside me, marking me irrevocably as his.

We collapse onto the bed, our bodies tangled together, breathing labored. Nash's arms wrap around me, holding me close as our hearts pound in unison. "That was... incredible," he murmurs, his lips pressing against my hair.

I hum my agreement, my eyes drifting closed as I savor the feel of him inside me. "It was."

Nash's fingers draw idle patterns on my back, his breath evening out as he holds me. After a moment, he asks, "Are you okay?"

I nuzzle into his touch, a small smile curving my lips. "Better than okay."

His low chuckle vibrates against my back. "Glad to hear it."

I lie in Nash's arms, feeling his chest's steady rise and fall against my back. His presence wraps around me like a protective cocoon, making me feel safer than ever.

Strangely, someone who initially seemed so intimidating has become my safe harbor. Nash's quiet intensity no longer scares me; instead, it grounds me, anchoring me in moments when I feel like I might drift away. He doesn't try to fix or change me.

I close my eyes, listening to his heartbeat. With Nash, I'm starting to believe I may deserve this kind of care and understanding. Maybe I'm not as broken as I thought.

17

COLT

I'm sprawled on the couch reviewing choreography notes when Flora appears in the bedroom doorway at six-thirty sharp. My jaw drops because she's transformed from her usual casual self into something else. Her hair falls in soft waves, and she's wearing a flowy winter dress and stockings that make her look like she stepped out of a dream.

"Well, well. What's all this about?" I set my notebook aside, raising an eyebrow.

Nash looks up from his spot at the kitchen counter where he's been meal prepping. His eyes widen slightly at the sight of her.

"Aurora invited me to movie night with some of the girls in the main tent," Flora says, smoothing her dress. "Thought I'd make an effort."

"Leaving us all alone?" Nash puts on an exaggerated pout. "That's just cruel."

I clutch my chest dramatically. "The betrayal. We'll waste away from neglect."

"Talk about blue balls," Nash adds with a theatrical sigh.

Flora rolls her eyes, but she's fighting back a smile. "You two are absolutely insatiable, you know that?"

"We prefer to think of it as having healthy appetites," I say with a wink.

"I'm sure we can find time when I get back," she says, kissing us as she heads for the door. "Try not to pine away too much while I'm gone."

"No promises!" Nash calls after her.

I watch her disappear into the evening, counting the minutes until she returns. But I'm glad she's making friends, building her own life here at the carnival. Even if it means sharing her attention sometimes.

Nash and I are alone in our shared space for the first time since Flora came into our lives and changed everything. The silence between us buzzes, our eyes unable to meet. We've always been careful to keep things platonic, no matter how close we've gotten over the years. There are lines we've never considered crossing.

Until now, Flora's presence, her very essence, has awakened something inside both of us. She's like a spark that's ignited a fire, threatening to burn down the careful barriers we've erected.

The tension existed before she entered our lives, simmering quietly beneath the surface. I ignored it, burying it under layers of friendship and shared passion for our art. But now, with her gone for the evening, it's becoming harder to ignore. I can feel it coursing through my veins, making my skin tingle and my heart race.

"Jesus, it's a damn sauna in here," Nash comments, fanning himself with a tea towel.

"You feeling alright? You're flushed." I raise an eyebrow, smirking.

"Oh, I'm feeling fine." His eyes glint with mischievousness. "Just got blue balls thanks to someone abandoning us this evening."

My throat goes dry. "Yeah, she does tend to have that affect on a guy."

"Understatement of the century. The woman's a walking wet dream."

I know what he means. Flora gets under your skin and makes you feel things you've never felt. It's a different kind of longing than I've ever experienced. An itch that only she can scratch.

I shift uncomfortably on the couch, meeting Nash's direct gaze. The air between us crackles with tension.

"We should talk about Flora," Nash says. "About how this works between all of us."

My heart pounds against my ribs. "What do you mean?"

"That first morning after..." Nash pauses, choosing his words carefully. "I know you were with her. And earlier today, when you were helping Ty, she and I..." He lets the implication hang.

I nod slowly. Part of me had wondered if something had happened between them when I was busy. "And you want to know if I'm okay with that?"

"Yeah. We need clear boundaries here. Are we fine with being with her separately? Together seems ideal, but schedules don't always align." Nash runs a hand through his hair. "I don't want any misunderstandings between us."

"Makes sense," I agree, thinking it through. "I'm good with whatever Flora's comfortable with. Together or separate."

Nash relaxes. "Same here. Though I prefer it when we're all involved. It feels more... right that way."

"Yeah, I know what you mean." The connection between the three of us is strongest when we're together. "Should probably talk to Flora about it too, get her thoughts."

"Definitely. She should have equal say in this." Nash pushes off from the counter and joins me on the couch. "We're in uncharted territory here."

"That we are." I glance at him. "But I think we're handling it pretty well so far."

I shift on the couch, hyperaware of Nash's presence beside me. The air feels thick with possibility. His knee brushes against mine, and I fight the urge to pull away or lean in closer. I'm not sure which impulse is stronger.

"Guess we've got a problem on our hands."

"What do you mean?" I ask.

"Blue balls aren't exactly conducive to a restful night. And I can tell you're feeling it, too." He bumps his shoulder against mine. "Might as well be honest about it."

"Yeah, well..." I shift, suddenly very aware of the bulge in my pants.

"We could help ourselves out together," Nash muses, a devious gleam in his eye.

"What are you suggesting?" I ask.

"Mutual relief if you catch my drift." He stretches his legs out, crossing one ankle over the other. "We've never jerked off together, but hell, it might be fun."

I swallow hard. "You sure about that?"

"If it gets the job done, why not? Besides, we've shared a woman. This isn't that different, right?"

He's got a point, and my body is definitely not arguing. But my mind is spinning. It feels like we're standing at the edge of a precipice, about to leap into the unknown.

"That settles it then." Nash's voice is steady, but his eyes glitter with challenge.

I hesitate, my heart suddenly pounding in my chest. "Hold up. Are we really doing this?"

"You chickening out on me now?" He raises an eyebrow.

I glance down at the bulge in my pants and then back up at him. "I'm no chicken."

Nash chuckles. "Didn't think so."

He reaches for the remote and turns on the TV, scrolling through the options until he finds the perfect scene. My eyes widen as I take in the cover image—a guy pounding into another guy's ass while that guy is fucking a girl. It's out of my deepest fantasies, a vision I've only shared with Flora.

"You read my mind," I murmur, my breath catching as the scene unfolds.

Nash shifts closer, our outer thighs touching, and I feel the heat radiating off his body. We both reach for our belts, undoing them with deliberate slowness. I'm surprised he can't hear my heart hammering.

Our hands move in sync, freeing ourselves from the confines of our pants. The cool air washes over my exposed skin, sending a shiver down my spine as I watch the two men on the screen drive each other wild.

Nash leans back on the couch, our arms brushing as we both stroke in time with the scene's rhythm. I glance at him from the corner of my eye, our gazes locking for a heated moment before breaking away.

"You ever done this before?" I ask.

"Not with a guy. You?"

I nod. "When I was younger, yeah."

I up my pace, taking my cue from the relentless rhythm of the scene. Nash groans, his hips bucking involuntarily. I sneak another glance at him, taking in the flush of his cheeks and how his cock looks with his hand wrapped around it.

I bite my lip, gritting my teeth as the tension coils tighter and tighter in my gut. Rubbing my precum over my piercing sends a jolt right to my balls. My breath comes in harsh pants, mingling with Nash's shaky exhales. All I can think about is his beautiful dick plowing into my ass while I'm deep in Flora.

And then we burst, our release spurting over our pants as the two men and one woman on the screen find their own climax. I feel lightheaded, my body electric with sensation, and I realize I'm panting like I've run a marathon.

Nash turns his head, his gaze locking with mine. "Well," he says with a lazy smile, "that was certainly interesting."

I snort, my face getting hot. "Yeah, that's one way to put it."

I bite my lip as I watch Nash lick his hand, his tongue gliding slowly over his skin to lap up his own cum. The seduction in that simple gesture sends a jolt of electricity straight to my dick, which gives another desperate twitch.

But even as the desire thrums through me, something else is building. A nervous tension. An awareness of what just happened between us.

The scene on the TV still plays, the two men and woman moaning in the aftermath of their pleasure, but it's like background noise now. My brain feels fuzzy, my thoughts a jumbled mess.

"You still look a little unsatisfied," Nash comments with a raise of his eyebrow, gesturing to my straining cock.

He's not wrong. I'm not sure anything could fully satisfy this hunger inside me. Not now, with the floodgates of my desires suddenly thrown wide open.

I clear my throat, fumbling for words. "I, uh... think I'm gonna take a shower."

Without waiting for a response, I push myself up from the couch, my heart pounding so loudly I'm sure Nash can hear it. I need to get out of here and clear my head. Put some distance between us before I do something stupid. Or say something that can't be unsaid.

I feel his eyes on me as I cross the room, my steps purpose-driven, almost rushed. We're usually an open book to each other, but this... this is different. Complicated.

I step into the bathroom, closing the door with a quiet click. My hands ball into fists at my sides as I lean back against the door, my breath coming in short, sharp pants. I can feel the pulse pounding in my throat, my whole body thrumming with a confusing mix of desire and apprehension.

Part of me wants to turn around, march straight out of the bathroom, and take Nash in my arms. Explore the possibility of something deeper than friendship between us.

But another part of me is terrified of what this could mean, of what we might lose if we cross that line.

I curse under my breath, stepping into the shower and turning on the water. I crave the release it will bring, the chance to wash away the tension. But I know it won't wash away the nervous fluttering in my chest.

The water cascades over my head, steaming hot, but it does little to erase the image of Nash licking his own cum from his hand.

The tension between us is like a flame that threatens to consume us. We're teetering on the edge between passion and destruction. And I have no idea what the hell to do about it.

18

NASH

Colt's been acting cagey ever since that night we jerked off to porn together. I thought it was obvious what my video selection meant, but he's holding back.

It's not like I didn't know he had those desires. We've been best friends for years, closer than brothers. I know every inch of his body, every quirk and tic. But that night confirmed what I'd always suspected—he wants me. And, while I never really considered it before Flora came along, I want to explore that dynamic with him.

And now, as I lie in bed next to Flora, I can't stop thinking about it. About him. About us.

Flora's soft breathing fills the dim space, her naked body curled up against mine. She's so gorgeous and innocent, yet she embodies a beautiful strength. Our three-way dynamic has become something special, something I never want to let go of. But there's still a missing piece, a void only Colt can fill.

My mind wanders back to that night, the way he

groaned when I put on that porn movie. Two men fucking as they shared a woman. It was hot as hell, and I could see the desire in his eyes. But afterward, he acted like he was ashamed.

I shift, careful not to wake Flora. It's insane, but I want Colt. The idea of him taking me the way he does Flora drives me crazy.

Dammit, why can't he just see? Why can't he accept that we could have it all?

Reaching out, I run my fingers through Flora's soft golden hair. She stirs but doesn't wake, her face relaxed. I glance at the other side of the bed, where Colt lies, his broad chest rising and falling steadily. He's so close, yet so far. My body aches with desire for them both.

Colt's not sleeping, either. His intense blue eyes meet mine, and my heart skips a beat. No doubt he'll be able to see the turmoil in my eyes.

"You okay?" His deep voice rumbles.

I want to tell him how I really feel, how I wish we could just—

"Will you two stop messing about and just kiss already?" Flora's sleepy voice interrupts, her words laced with amusement and frustration.

I freeze, suddenly aware of how close to the line we are.

Colt hesitates. I see the conflict in his eyes. Flora shifts between us, her warm body pressing against mine.

"I—" I start, but my voice trails off.

Colt sits up, the sheets falling away to reveal his naked chest covered in beautiful ink. I know every inch of his body, but he feels like a stranger now.

"Kiss him," Flora murmurs, her voice thick with sleep. She reaches out, her hand resting on Colt's cheek, then trailing down to his shoulder, caressing the spot that always aches after a performance. "Please."

Colt looks at me, his eyes searching for permission.

I lean forward over Flora, my lips hovering just inches from his. "Yes," I whisper. "Kiss me, Colt."

The moment hangs suspended, thick with anticipation. Flora finally breaks the silence, her voice laced with desire. "Kiss him, Colt."

I shift closer to him, wanting to feel the heat of his skin against mine.

"Go on." Flora's voice is firmer now, her hand reaching to stroke his chest. "We both know you want to."

Colt takes a deep breath, his eyes never leaving mine. Slowly, he leans forward, closing the distance between us. Our lips touch, and everything around us fades away.

His mouth is warm and soft, and I taste the hint of mint on his breath. My lips part, inviting him in, and our tongues dance in a slow, languid rhythm.

I thread my fingers through his hair, deepening the kiss. I feel his big, rough hands land on my back, pulling me closer. Our naked chests press together, and I can feel his heart pounding.

We break apart, breathless, our foreheads resting against each other. Flora watches us, her eyes sparkling.

She shifts on the bed, her legs tucked beneath her. "Now I want to see more." Her voice is playful yet demanding. She's fucking sexy when she gets all bossy.

"Both of you, get on your knees facing each other and rub those beautiful dicks together."

Her words echo in the trailer, bold and demanding. We're frozen for a moment, caught between desire and uncertainty. But then, slowly, Colt and I get onto our knees before each other, our dicks already bumping together. His piercing is cold against my skin.

I trace the contours of his face, remembering the first time I laid eyes on him. He was so full of anger and hurt, but I saw the raw vulnerability beneath it all. My fingers skim the intricate tattoos on his chest.

Colt's eyes are dark with desire as they hold mine, his breathing shallow. I shuffle closer, our bodies pressing together as we share our heat.

I lean in, our lips meeting again, hotter and more desperate this time. Colt moans, and I swallow it as our tongues tangle. He slides a hand into my hair, fisting it and pulling me closer. The kiss grows more frantic.

I mirror his movements, our cocks sliding against each other, the friction of his piercing against my skin sending sparks of pleasure through my body. Our hips move in sync like we've been doing this for years. I close my eyes, losing myself in the sensation.

Our lips part, and I trail kisses down his neck, nipping at the sensitive skin. His hands roam over my back, his touch sending shivers down my spine.

Our cocks continue their dance, the friction building to an intense heat. I feel Colt's hands on my hips, guiding me, our bodies moving in a sensual rhythm.

Colt leans into me, our chests flush, and I feel the heat of his skin against mine. His breath tickles my neck, sending a shiver down my spine as he whispers, "You have no idea how long I've wanted this."

"I know," I reply, my voice hoarse with desire.

"Fuck, Nash," Colt groans. "You have no idea how hard I am right now."

I chuckle. "I have a pretty good idea, considering I feel every inch of you."

Flora's voice cuts through the moment, thick with desire. "You guys are so fucking hot together, and I'm so wet."

I glance over at her, taking in the sight of her fingers sliding in and out of her glistening core. Her eyes are dark with lust, fixed on Colt and me as we grind against each other. "Beautiful, aren't you, little bird? You're the reason we're here."

Colt's hands tighten on my hips as he also watches Flora. "She's our missing piece, isn't she? Fucking beautiful."

"So fucking beautiful," I agree. "But she's not the only one who's wet." I fist my dick as precum spills from the tip. "I bet you both want to taste me, don't you?"

Colt's eyes darken. "More than you know."

"Well then," I purr, "how about we take turns tasting each other? No better way to start than with a good, old-fashioned blowjob."

Flora moans at the suggestion, her eyes glittering with excitement. "Fuck yes," she breathes. "I want to see you both go down on each other. And I want to join in."

Colt growls, his hips bucking against mine. "Eager little angel, aren't you?"

Flora bites her lip. "Just imagining it turns me on."

I lean closer to Colt. "You first, Colt. I want to see that mouth of yours wrapped around my cock."

He doesn't hesitate, his eyes burning with desire as he sinks to his hands and knees in front of me. His hot breath ghosts the tip, and then the wet warmth of his mouth engulfs me. I groan, my head falling back as he swirls his tongue around the head of my cock.

Colt's skilled mouth works its magic, his tongue and lips teasing me with just the right amount of pressure. My fingers weave through his hair, guiding his movements, and I moan softly when he hollows his cheeks and takes me deeper.

I open my eyes, my gaze locking with Flora's as she watches us. Her eyes are hooded with lust, her fingers moving faster on her clit as she bites her lip. "God, it's so hot seeing you two like this," she breathes. "Keep going, Colt. Make him come for you."

Colt hums around my length, sending vibrations through me that have my toes curling. I tighten my grip on his hair, thrusting gently as I encourage him to take more. "Fuck, Colt, that feels so damn good."

Colt takes his time, teasing and tasting, driving me crazy. I feel his tongue swirling around the head of my cock, his lips tight around me, and I know I'm not going to last long.

"Fuck," I groan. The trailer is filled with the sounds of our heavy breathing and the wet, filthy noises of his mouth on my cock and Flora plunging her fingers into her cunt. I feel my orgasm building, coiling in my stomach, and I know I'm close.

"That's it, baby," Flora encourages. "Come for him, Nash. Let him swallow every drop."

Her words push me over the edge, and I gasp as I explode into Colt's mouth. My eyes squeeze shut as I ride out the waves of pleasure, my hips bucking as Colt swallows my cum.

Colt sits back on his heels, a satisfied smirk on his face, and I realize I never want to see that smug look disappear. I want to keep that expression on his face for the rest of our lives.

Then, I realize he has my cum in his mouth. He gestures for Flora to move toward him.

Flora licks her lips, her gaze fixed on Colt's mouth. She crawls over to him on her hands and knees, their lips meeting in a passionate kiss. My heart pounds in my chest as I watch them, knowing they're sharing my cum. It's intimate and filthy and drives me fucking crazy.

"Shit," I mutter. "You two better swallow," I growl. "Don't waste a single drop."

Flora pulls back from Colt. "Already done." Her eyes are sparkling with mischief.

Colt smirks at me. We've crossed a line tonight, a threshold neither of us ever thought we'd cross.

"Fuck, Colt," I breathe, unable to contain the rush of emotions coursing through me. "That was—"

"I know," he interrupts. "It was everything I'd imagined and more."

We look at each other momentarily, lost in the intensity of what just happened.

Flora's voice cuts through the moment. "You two are so cute. Now lie down, Colt, and let Nash taste you."

Colt groans, his dick as hard as steel and leaking. I guide Colt onto his back, his broad shoulders tensing as he braces himself against the mattress. And then I kneel between Colt's legs, taking in the sight of his thick, pierced length. My mouth waters at the thought of tasting him and claiming him with my mouth, but first, we can't leave our girl.

"Flora, my sweet little bird," I murmur, reaching out to stroke her thigh. "I want you to sit on Colt's face. Let him taste you."

She bites her lip. "You want me to—"

"Ride his face," I finish for her, my voice low. "Use that gorgeous body to drive him wild. Show him what a beautiful, powerful woman you are."

Flora doesn't need to be told twice. With a sultry smile, she moves into position, her legs straddling Colt's face as she lowers herself onto his waiting mouth. Her eyes squeeze shut as she settles onto him, his tongue already teasing her.

Colt's hands grip her thighs, holding her in place as he feasts on her. His deep groans vibrate against her, and she shifts her hips.

I lean forward, nipping at Colt's inner thigh as he eagerly devours our girl. My mouth hovers over his length, and I lick slowly through the slit, tasting his precum. "You taste amazing," I murmur, my breath ghosting over his swollen flesh. "But I bet you will feel even better deep inside me someday."

Their moans harmonize, stirring the air around us with need. I swirl my tongue, teasing Colt as I play with his piercing. After a few moments, I take him into my mouth. My attempt to take him deep makes me gag immediately. I've never sucked a dick before, and it's going to take a bit of practice.

His hands tighten on Flora's thighs, his thumbs digging into her soft skin. "Fuck, Flora, your pussy—so sweet."

She moans, her body trembling above him. "Don't stop, Colt. Keep licking me just like that."

Colt's back arches as I take him deeper. His hips thrust gently, his length sliding smoothly past my lips.

"Shit, Nash," he groans, his voice muffled by Flora's body. "I'm close, real close."

I hum around him, my eyes locking with Flora's as she rides his face. Her hips move in a steady rhythm. She's close, too, so tantalizingly close.

Colt's mouth falls open, his breath quickening. "I'm gonna come, Nash. Fuck, I'm—"

He bucks his hips, his release hitting the back of my throat. I swallow, relishing the taste of him. He fills me, his essence coating my tongue, and I hum in satisfaction.

"Fuck," he pants, his body tensing beneath Flora as he takes a breather. "That was—intense."

Flora's eyes are closed, her breath quick and shallow as she rides out her pleasure. "Oh God, Colt. Please don't stop." He returns to taste her with even more determination, and soon enough, she's shuddering above him. "Fuck, yes! I'm—" She cries out, her body trembling as she comes, her juices flowing over his tongue. Colt groans, lapping up her release.

I stroke Colt's thigh, his skin warm under my palm. "That was incredible."

Flora shifts onto her side beside Colt and pulls him to face her. "It really was." She kisses his mouth softly, tasting herself on his lips.

He smiles at her, his hand reaching up to tangle in her hair.

I'm struck by the moment's beauty—we've become more than friends and lovers. We've become a unit, a tribe of three bound together by trust and desire.

Flora rests her head on Colt's chest, her fingers tracing idle patterns on his skin. "I feel like I could spend the rest of the night doing that," she murmurs.

Colt chuckles, his hand stroking her hair. "I know the feeling, angel. But we've got a big day tomorrow. We should probably get some rest."

I run my hand through his sweat-dampened hair. "He's right, Flora. We've got a lot to prepare for the Christmas show."

I watch as Flora shifts, stretching like a contented cat. "Middle again?" she asks, already knowing our preferences.

"Always," I murmur, helping her settle between us. Colt takes his usual spot on her right while I claim the left side.

Flora turns on her side facing me, and Colt curls around her from behind, his arm draping over her waist. His fingers brush against my stomach, sending a pleasant warmth through me. I reach out, threading my fingers through Flora's hair while my other hand finds Colt's where it rests on her.

"Perfect," Flora sighs, nuzzling into my chest. Her

breath tickles my skin as she settles, and I feel Colt's grip tighten.

Our bodies align in a way that feels natural. Flora's warmth radiates between us, and Colt's steady breathing creates a rhythm that soothes my racing thoughts.

I gently kiss Flora's forehead, then brush my fingers through Colt's hair. He hums contentedly, the sound vibrating through all three of us.

"Sleep well," I whisper, feeling the day's weight settling over us. Flora's already drifting off, her breathing evening out, while Colt's grip remains steady, anchoring us all together in this moment of peace.

19

FLORA

I steady my hands as I help Aurora arrange the stuffed animals on the carnival game stand, trying to align each one perfectly. The past two weeks have been almost peaceful. After constant threats and messages, my phone finally fell silent.

"These look cute here, don't you think?" Aurora holds up a pink elephant, but her voice fades into background noise as another sound cuts through the carnival chatter.

"Well, well. Look who we found."

My blood turns to ice. I know that voice. Would know it anywhere.

Tommy's sneering face appears between two game stands, Jake right beside him with that predatory smile I've grown to fear. My fingers grip the stuffed animal I hold so tightly my knuckles turn white.

Aurora's eyes dart between me and the two men, her posture shifting. The moment she picks up on my fear, I see how she steps slightly closer to my side.

"Friends of yours?" she asks, but there's an edge to her voice I've never heard before.

I can't speak. Can't move. Can't breathe. They found me. After two weeks, they actually found me.

"Come on, sis," Jake says, stepping closer. "Time to come home. The family is missing you."

Aurora's hand finds my arm. "Flora?" Her tone carries a question, but I can barely hear it over the roaring in my ears.

The stuffed animal slips from my numb fingers, hitting the dirt with a soft thud that seems to echo in the space between us.

"I suggest you both fuck off," Aurora's voice cuts through my panic like a blade. "Pretty clear she doesn't want anything to do with you."

Jake's face twists into an ugly sneer. "Mind your own business, bitch. This is a family matter."

"She doesn't want to speak to you." Aurora's grip on my arm tightens protectively.

Tommy takes another step forward, his hands curling into fists. "Listen here—"

A shadow falls over us, and the temperature drops several degrees. I feel Aurora relax beside me even as Jake and Tommy freeze mid-step.

Gage towers behind us, silent and massive in his skull mask. He doesn't speak. Doesn't move. He just stares at my foster brothers with an intensity that makes even my skin crawl.

Jake swallows hard, his earlier bravado evaporating. Tommy's face drains of color as he takes an instinctive step backward.

"We'll... we'll catch up later," Tommy mumbles, grabbing Jake's arm and practically dragging him away. They disappear into the crowd so fast they might as well have teleported.

My legs give out, and I sink to my knees, the stuffed animal still lying forgotten in the dirt. Aurora crouches beside me while Gage maintains his protective stance, watching the direction my foster brothers fled.

"Thank you," I whisper, my voice shaking. "Both of you."

I wrap my arms around myself, trying to stop the trembling. Aurora's concerned eyes bore into me.

"Flora, who were they? What did they do to you?"

The genuine worry in her voice almost breaks me. For a moment, I consider telling her everything. The years of abuse, the pain, the degradation. But the words stick in my throat, threatening to choke me.

"I..." I shake my head, taking a step back. "I should go. Colt and Nash will be wondering where I am."

"Flora, wait—" Aurora reaches for my arm, her face a mix of frustration and concern. She wants to help; I can see it in her eyes, but I can't. I just can't.

She holds my gaze for a long moment before letting her hand drop. "Okay. But if you need anything..."

I nod quickly, already turning away. "Thanks. For everything."

I hurry through the carnival grounds, weaving between stands and visitors, not stopping until the familiar shape of our trailer comes into view.

I slip into the trailer, my hands still shaking as I close the door. Nash and Colt are lounging on the couch, but their relaxed postures instantly shift when they see my face.

"Little bird?" Nash is on his feet in seconds, crossing the space between us. "What happened?"

Colt follows, his jaw tightening. "Flora?"

The concern in their voices breaks something inside me. The tears I've been holding back spill over, and my legs give out again. Nash catches me before I hit the floor, pulling me against his chest while Colt hovers protectively nearby.

"They found me," I choke out between sobs. "Tommy and Jake. They're here."

"Who the fuck are Tommy and Jake?" Nash growls.

I swallow hard and meet his gaze. "My foster brothers."

Colt's jaw clenches. "Your foster brothers are the ones who hurt you?"

I nod against Nash's chest, my fingers clutching his shirt. The memories I've tried so hard to suppress come rushing back—the first time they cornered me in my bedroom, their friends holding me down, the pain, the shame, the helplessness.

"There's... there's more," I whisper, my voice breaking. "More than what I told you about my foster family being cruel."

Nash's hand stills where it's been stroking my back. "Tell us, little bird."

The words feel like glass in my throat, but I force them out. "They... they didn't just mistreat me. They..." I can't look at either of them as I speak. "They took turns. They and their friends. I was sixteen the first time."

The silence that follows is deafening. Nash's entire body has gone rigid against mine, while Colt's breathing has turned harsh and uneven.

"They gang-raped you?" Colt's voice is barely recognizable, twisted with a rage I've never heard before.

I manage a small nod, fresh tears falling as Nash pulls me closer, his arms like steel bands around me.

"Why didn't you tell us before, little bird?" Nash's voice is gentle.

I pull back, wrapping my arms around myself. "I was ashamed. Especially after..." I swallow hard, unable to meet their eyes. "After that first night in the woods. The way I responded to you both chasing me, catching me. It's pretty messed up, isn't it? Wanting that kind of thing after what they did to me?"

"Flora, look at me," Colt's voice is firm but kind. When I don't move, his finger gently tilts my chin up until I have no choice but to meet his gaze. "You have nothing to be ashamed of. Nothing."

"But—"

"No," Nash cuts me off, his hand finding mine. "What they did to you was abuse. Violence. Terror. What happened between us was trust. Choice. There's a world of difference."

"Your desires aren't broken," Colt adds softly. "And neither are you. Those bastards tried to take your power away. But choosing to give that power to someone? That's strength, angel. That's healing."

The tears start falling again, but for a different reason this time. "I was so scared you'd look at me differently if you knew."

"Never," they say in unison, and despite everything, it makes me smile a little.

Nash wipes away my tears with his thumb. "You're ours now, little bird. Nothing could change how we see you. Nothing."

I look up at Colt through tear-blurred eyes as his jaw clenches, a muscle ticking in his cheek.

"There's no fucking way those pieces of shit are getting away with gang-raping you with their friends," he growls, his hands curling into fists. "We need a plan to make them pay."

Nash's arms tighten around me protectively as Colt paces the length of the trailer, raw fury radiating from every movement. The intensity of their reaction makes my chest tight with something warm and safe despite the darkness of the conversation.

"Colt," Nash's voice warns. "We need to be smart about this."

"Smart?" Colt whirls around, his eyes blazing. "Did you hear what she told us? What those fucking bastards did to her?"

"I heard," Nash's voice is deadly quiet. "Trust me, I heard every word. But we can't rush in without thinking it through. We need a solid plan."

I press closer to Nash's chest, drawing comfort from his steady heartbeat. "They'll be expecting me to tell someone," I whisper. "They always said no one would believe me anyway."

Colt stops his pacing, and his hand finds mine, squeezing gently.

"We believe you, angel. And they will learn exactly what happens to men who hurt what belongs to us."

The possessiveness in his voice should probably frighten me. Instead, it makes me feel protected, loved, and safe.

"Whatever we do," Nash says, his lips brushing my temple, "we do it together. And we do it right."

I sink deeper into Nash's embrace, feeling his chest's steady rise and fall against my back while Colt's thumb traces gentle circles on my palm. The weight I've carried for so long feels lighter somehow, shared between the three of us.

"I never thought I'd be able to tell anyone," I whisper, watching Colt's fingers intertwined with mine. "Every time I tried before, the words would just... stick."

Nash's lips brush my temple. "You're safe now, little bird. No more carrying this alone."

"It's strange," I say, a small laugh bubbling up. "I should feel worse after telling you both, but instead..." I trail off, searching for the right words.

"Instead?" Colt prompts gently.

"Instead, I feel like I can breathe again. Like maybe there's actually a way forward." I squeeze Colt's hand. "For the first time since I was sixteen, I feel light might be at the end of this tunnel."

Nash's arms tighten around me. "There is. We'll make sure of it."

I turn my head to look up at him, then back to Colt. These two men have shown me what it means to be cherished rather than degraded, protected rather than controlled. Who believe me without question and hold my broken pieces like they're precious.

20

COLT

I pace the length of our trailer, my hands clenching and unclenching as the rage burns through my veins. Nash sits at the small dining table, his silence more dangerous than any outburst could be. The cold calculation in his eyes mirrors the ice in my chest.

"They touched her." My voice comes out rough. "They hurt our girl."

Nash's fingers drum against the table surface. "We'll make them wish they'd never laid eyes on her."

I stop pacing and brace my hands on the counter, trying to contain the violent urges coursing through me. The thought of those monsters putting their hands on Flora, hurting her when she was just sixteen... My knuckles turn white from gripping the counter's edge.

"It needs to look like an accident," Nash says, his tone measured but deadly. "We can't have this traced back to the carnival, back to her."

I nod, understanding the necessity for discretion even as every fiber of my being screams to hunt them down right now. "They'll be watching her. Waiting for another chance."

"Then we'll give them one." Nash stands, moving to stand beside me. His presence steadies my rage into something more focused. "We let them think they have an opening. Draw them out."

"And then?"

Nash's eyes meet mine. "Then we show them what happens to anyone who dares hurt what's ours."

I straighten, a cold smile spreading across my face. "We make sure they never hurt another girl again."

"Never," Nash agrees, his hand gripping my shoulder. "We protect our own, Colt. And Flora is ours to protect now."

We stand there in silent agreement, two predators planning the demise of those who dared harm our girl. The rage still burns, but now it has a purpose. Direction. Those bastards won't know what hit them.

"Phoenix could track them," I say, moving to grab my phone from the counter. "He's got ways of monitoring their movements, their messages."

Nash nods, his expression darkening. "He owes me a favor anyway. And he's got all those surveillance toys he never gets to use."

I pull up Phoenix's contact and hit dial. He answers on the second ring, his voice groggy. "This better be important. I was in the middle of coding."

"Need your help, man. We have two targets we need to monitor. Tommy and Jake Lowley." I grip the phone tighter. "They're a threat to Flora."

"Who are they to her?" Phoenix asks.

I clear my throat. "Flora's foster brothers. And they abused her."

There's a pause, followed by the sound of typing. Phoenix's tone shifts from irritated to serious. "Give me everything you've got on them. Phone numbers, social media, addresses."

Nash leans closer to the phone. "We need to know their movements, any messages about Flora or the carnival. They're planning something."

"Consider it done," Phoenix says. "I'll set up alerts for any communication between them, track their phones, monitor their social media. If they sneeze in Flora's direction, you'll know about it."

"Thanks, Phoenix." I share a look with Nash. "We owe you."

"No, you don't. Nobody messes with our family." More typing sounds come through the line. "I'll have everything set up within the hour. Just... whatever you're planning, be careful."

"Aways are," Nash says firmly.

"Right. I'll text you when I've got the surveillance running." Phoenix pauses. "And Colt? Make them regret ever touching her."

"Count on it," I reply, ending the call.

I watch Nash stare at his phone, waiting for Phoenix's updates. Something's off about him—it has been since Flora told us about her past. The tension in his shoulders, the way his jaw keeps clenching.

"You okay?" I ask, keeping my voice low. "You've been quiet since last night."

Nash's fingers are still on his phone screen. He

doesn't look up, but I catch the slight tremor in his hand before he sets the device down.

"Just brings up old ghosts," he says, his voice rough.

I freeze. In all our years together, Nash has never mentioned anything about his past. Not once. He's always been a closed book, deflecting questions with practiced ease or changing the subject entirely.

"You want to talk about it?" I offer, careful to keep my tone neutral. One wrong move and he'll shut down completely.

Nash runs a hand through his hair, still not meeting my eyes. "The foster system's full of monsters."

The implication hits me like a punch to the gut. My hands curl into fists at my sides, rage building for a new reason.

"Nash..." I start, but he shakes his head.

"Don't." His voice is sharp. "It was a long time ago. I dealt with it."

"Did you?"

Finally, he looks up at me, and the raw pain in his eyes makes my chest ache. "Had to. Nobody else was going to."

I want to reach for him and offer comfort, but I know he's not ready. Instead, I lean against the counter, giving him space while letting him know I'm here.

"You're not alone anymore," I tell him quietly. "You know that, right?"

Nash stands abruptly, his chair scraping against the floor. The walls I've seen glimpses behind snap back into place, his expression hardening into that familiar mask of control.

"I need some air." He grabs his jacket from the hook by the door, movements sharp and precise.

I know better than to push. In all our years together, I've learned when Nash needs space. The tightness around his eyes and the rigid set of his shoulders are warnings I've memorized.

"I'll be here," I say simply, giving him the out he needs.

He pauses at the door, one hand on the handle. For a moment, I think he might turn back, might let me in just a fraction more. But then his shoulders straighten, and without another word, he disappears.

The door clicks shut behind him, leaving me alone. I drag a hand down my face, fighting the urge to follow him. Nash will talk when he's ready—if he's ever ready. Pushing him now would only drive him further away.

Still, the glimpse of vulnerability I saw in his eyes haunts me. All these years, I never knew about his abuse. I knew he'd had a shitty childhood bouncing from foster home to foster home, but he never wanted to talk about it.

I sink onto the couch, staring at the door he just walked through. How many nights has he sat here, carrying these secrets alone?

21

NASH

The idea of leaving Flora alone doesn't sit well with me. The memory of witnessing her terror after those pieces of shit made an appearance makes my jaw clench as I head toward Aurora's trailer.

As I climb the metal steps, the morning sun beats down my neck. Before I can knock, the door swings open, and Aurora stands in workout clothes, her dark hair pulled back in a messy bun.

"Hey Nash, what's up?" She wipes sweat from her forehead with a small towel.

"Need a favor." I shift my weight. "Colt and I have to help Ty with something today. Was hoping Flora could hang with you?"

Aurora's expression softens. "Of course. I thought of having a girls' day once my tasks were over. Could invite Tilly, Sofia, Lily, and Alice for movies and snacks."

Relief washes through me. Having Flora surrounded by other women eases my worry. "That would be perfect. Thank you."

"No problem. Flora reminds me of myself when I first joined the carnival." Aurora's knowing look tells me she understands more than she lets on. "Just send her over to me when she's ready."

"I will do that; thanks again." I turn away and stride back toward our trailer. It's ours now. Since Flora joined, she hasn't stepped foot back in her trailer. She belongs with us.

I push open the trailer door to find Flora perched on the small kitchen counter, wearing one of Colt's oversized shirts and sipping coffee. My chest tightens because she looks so at home here now.

"Morning." She holds up her mug in greeting.

"Hey, little bird." I cross to her, pressing a kiss to her temple. "Listen, Colt and I need to handle some business with Ty today."

Her brow furrows. "Everything okay?"

"Yeah, just carnival stuff." The lie tastes bitter on my tongue. I hate keeping secrets from her, especially after what she's been through. But telling her about the drug running could put her in danger. "I talked to Aurora—she's having a girls' day at her trailer. Movies, snacks, the works."

"You don't want me alone because of Tommy and Jake." It's not a question. Flora's too perceptive for her own good.

"Can you blame me?" I brush a strand of hair from her face. "I'd rather know you're safe and having fun than worrying about those bastards showing up again."

She nods, setting down her coffee. "How long will you be gone?"

"Most of the day, probably. But we'll be back for dinner." Another half-truth. These runs usually take exactly as long as we plan, but sometimes things go sideways.

"Okay." She slides off the stool and wraps her arms around my waist. "I'll miss you."

My throat tightens. If she only knew what we were doing, would she still look at me with such trust? "I'll miss you too, little bird."

I hold her close, breathing in her scent, trying to memorize this moment of innocence before stepping back into the darkness that helps keep this carnival running.

Her lips find mine, soft and yielding. The kiss deepens, and I lose myself in her sweetness, in the trust she places in me despite everything.

The bathroom door creaks open, breaking our moment. Colt steps into the kitchen, already dressed in his work clothes, his dark hair slightly damp from a shower.

"Ready?" He asks, his eyes lingering on Flora's bare legs beneath his shirt.

"Yeah, I'm ready." I reluctantly release Flora, but she's already moving toward Colt.

She rises on her tiptoes, pressing her lips to his. Colt's hands immediately find her waist, pulling her flush against him. The kiss intensifies, and a low groan escapes him. Even from here, I can see the bulge forming in his jeans.

The sight stirs desire and need. But there's no time for that now. We have work to do.

I watch Colt's hands on Flora's waist, remembering how those same hands felt on my body that night. The memory of his mouth, his taste, the way he surrendered haunts me. We haven't crossed that line again since, but the desire burns beneath my skin every time I look at him.

Flora knows, she sees how we watch each other, the tension that crackles between us when we're all together. Sometimes, I catch her studying us with those knowing eyes, a small smile on her lips.

My cock hardens as Colt deepens his kiss with Flora. The soft moan she makes shoots straight through me.

We care too much about each other to rush this. What we have—this delicate balance between the three of us—it's precious. Sacred, almost. The way Flora trusts us with her body and heart. The way Colt and I orbit each other, drawing closer with each passing day.

That night changed everything. We crossed a line we can't uncross. And I don't want to uncross it. But we're taking it slow, letting this thing between us develop naturally. No pressure, no expectations.

Just three broken people healing each other.

Colt breaks the kiss, pressing his forehead to Flora's. His eyes meet mine over her shoulder, dark with need. We both want more. But not yet. Not today.

Today, we have work to do. The rest will come in its own time.

22

FLORA

I sink into the plush couch between Aurora and Tilly, still getting used to being around so many women. The movie plays in the background, but no one seems to pay attention anymore. Empty pizza boxes and half-drunk sodas litter the coffee table.

I smile as Sofia tosses popcorn at Phoenix's girlfriend, Tilly, who's ranting about some video game boss she can't beat.

"I swear, it's impossible! The hitbox is totally broken—"

"Girl, you've been stuck on this for days," Aurora says, rolling her eyes. "Just admit you need help and let Phoenix show you how."

"Never." Tilly crosses her arms. "I'll figure it out myself."

Sofia stretches out her curves on the loveseat, looking completely at home. "Speaking of Phoenix, how'd you two even meet? I can't imagine him leaving his tech cave long enough to talk to anyone."

I notice Tilly's posture stiffen at Sofia's question, her earlier playful mood evaporating instantly. She sets down her soda, fingers clenching around the can.

"Trust me, you don't want to know." Tilly's voice comes out tight, strained. "He was literally insane with his pursuit of me. So insane he should be locked in a federal prison."

The room goes quiet. I shift uncomfortably, recognizing that haunted look in her eyes.

Aurora reaches over and squeezes Tilly's hand. The gesture reminds me of how Colt and Nash ground me. I wonder what Phoenix did to put that shadow in Tilly's eyes, even though they seem happy together now.

Sofia looks like she regrets asking, her earlier relaxed pose now rigid with concern. "I'm sorry, I didn't mean to—"

"It's fine." Tilly forces a smile that doesn't reach her eyes. "Ancient history now. But let's just say he took obsession to a new fucking level." She shrugs her shoulders. "I love him, but God, he's not right in the head."

Aurora laughs sharply, running her fingers through her dark hair. "Pretty sure all our guys are a bit fucked up in the head. Have you met Gage? The man's idea of foreplay involves scaring me half to death."

I think of Colt and Nash, their fierce possessiveness, and the darkness beneath their smiles.

I sink deeper into the couch, listening as Lily speaks up. Her voice trembles slightly.

"Cade literally stalked me. Following me home from work, watching my apartment."

Alice nods, leaning forward. "Remember that night

he broke in? Left that creepy note on your kitchen counter with a fucking bullet?"

"God, yes." Lily wraps her arms around herself. "Who does that?"

"That's seriously insane," Tilly agrees, shaking her head.

I stay quiet, processing their words. My situation with Colt and Nash has been entirely different, but hearing about Cade's actions makes me wonder about the line between pursuit and stalking.

Lily's expression suddenly shifts, a flush creeping up her neck. "Though I have to admit... he's absolutely incredible in bed. Like, mind-blowing."

"Oh my God, girl!" Alice fans herself dramatically. "Speaking of amazing sex, Lars is absolutely insatiable."

My cheeks burn hot as the conversation turns explicit. Alice describes her most recent encounter with Lars, which makes me want to sink through the floor. The other women chime in with their own stories, completely uninhibited.

"So then he bent me over his motorcycle and—" Alice's animated description of her latest encounter with Lars burns my cheeks.

"Girl, that man is something else." Sofia fans herself dramatically. "Almost as wild as Tyson."

My eyes widen. I've never heard women talk so openly about their intimate moments. Growing up, sex was either a weapon or a shameful secret. But these women discuss it with such confidence and joy.

"What about you, Flora?" Lily's gentle voice draws

me from my thoughts. "How exactly does it work with Nash and Colt?"

Alice nods. "Yeah, I was wondering. Are you like with both of them?"

I fidget with the hem of my sweater, my heart racing as all eyes turn to me. These women have been nothing but kind, yet old fears die hard. Taking a deep breath, I gather my courage.

"Yes," I whisper, then clear my throat to speak more clearly. "I'm with both of them."

"Both at the same time?" Aurora's eyebrows shoot up with interest.

I nod, a small smile tugging at my lips despite my nervousness. "They're... they're amazing. They make me feel safe."

"And they're okay sharing?" Lily asks softly.

"More than okay." My cheeks warm at the memory of their tender care. "They've been best friends forever. It just... works, somehow."

Sofia leans forward, her expression thoughtful. "That's beautiful, actually. Finding two people who desire you equally."

"It is," I agree, my voice stronger now. The acceptance in their eyes helps ease the knot in my chest. "I never thought I could have something like this. They're teaching me that I deserve good things."

"You absolutely do," Aurora says firmly, squeezing my hand.

Alice grins. "Plus, having two hot guys totally devoted to you? Girl, you're living the dream!"

The room erupts in laughter, and I join in. For the

first time, I feel normal talking about relationships. These women don't judge me for being different; they celebrate it.

"The carnival changes people," Sofia says, reaching for her can of coke. "We're all a little broken here, but we fix each other."

I nod, understanding exactly what she means. These women, with their easy laughter and open hearts, are showing me what friendship really means. It's strange and wonderful, this feeling of belonging.

"Speaking of hot," Alice turns to Aurora with a mischievous grin. "How's tall, dark, and masked treating you?"

Aurora's cheeks flush. "Gage is... different."

"Different as in 'never talks and lurks in shadows' different?" Sofia teases, making spooky gestures with her hands.

"He talks!" Aurora protests, then adds more quietly, "Sometimes."

I lean forward, genuinely curious. "Does he ever take the mask off?"

"When we're alone," Aurora admits, playing with a strand of her hair. "He's actually really handsome underneath."

"I bet he is," Alice waggles her eyebrows. "Why else would you put up with the serial killer vibe?"

"He's not like that," Aurora defends, though she's fighting a smile. "He's sweet in his own way. Yesterday, he left a flower on my pillow."

"Aww," Tilly coos. "That's actually kind of romantic."

"A black rose, probably," Sofia snorts, making everyone laugh.

"You guys are terrible," Aurora rolls her eyes but grins. "At least my man doesn't wear a top hat."

"Hey!" Sofia throws a piece of popcorn at her. "Tyson rocks the top hat, thank you very much."

The easy banter continues, and I relax more with each passing minute. These women have accepted me without question, making me feel like I belong. It's a new feeling, but one I could definitely get used to.

23

COLT

I lean against the warehouse wall, watching Ty negotiate with the Easthollow crew. The dim lighting catches the edge of his smirk as he quotes them prices that make even my eyes water. Nash stands at my shoulder, but I find him distracting after everything between us.

"That's steep," one of the buyers growls.

"Quality costs," Ty shoots back, unfazed. "You won't find better products anywhere else."

Lars snickers from his position by the door, earning a sharp look from the buyers. Cade elbows him, but I catch the grin they share.

"Something funny?" The buyer's hand twitches toward his waistband.

"Just admiring your negotiation skills," Lars drawls, his voice dripping with sarcasm.

Phoenix doesn't even look up from his laptop, his fingers flying over the keys as he monitors security feeds and police channels. The blue glow from his screen catches the edge of Gage's mask, where he looms in the shadows, silent as ever.

"Keep your dogs in check," the buyer snaps at Ty.

Nash tenses beside me. I resist the urge to reach for him, to steady him like I would during our act. Instead, I crack my knuckles, the sound echoing in the warehouse.

"My people aren't the problem here," Ty's voice carries that dangerous edge I've learned to recognize. "The problem is you thinking you can get premium goods at street prices."

Cade shifts his weight, ready for trouble. But the buyer must see something in Ty's expression because he backs down, pulling out a thick envelope.

"Fine. When can we do business again?"

"We'll be in touch," Ty says smoothly, passing the envelope to Phoenix for counting.

The tension bleeds out of the room as the buyers leave. Still, Cade can't help himself: "I've seen better muscle tone in a bowl of spaghetti—they ought to try hitting the gym occasionally."

One of the guys growls, but his boss tells him to leave it. I sigh in relief when the buyers are gone.

"You're going to get yourself shot one day," Nash addresses Cade, but he's fighting a smile.

I watch Cade's face split into that manic grin I know too well. He bounces on his toes like a kid at Christmas, all barely contained energy.

"Did you see that asshole reach for his piece?" Cade's eyes are fever-bright. "Should've let me gut him right there. Would've been poetry."

"Poetry involves less blood usually," I point out, but

I'm grinning too. The rush of a successful deal has us all riding high.

"Speak for yourself." Cade pulls out his knife, spinning it between his fingers. "I write in red ink."

Lars snorts. "That was terrible, even for you."

"Everyone's a critic." Cade feigns offense, but his smile doesn't dim. "Come on, you can't tell me you weren't hoping they'd try something?"

"Some of us prefer not to clean blood off our clothes every night," Nash chimes in.

"That's what dark colors are for," Gage speaks up unexpectedly, making Phoenix jump and curse as his fingers slip on the keyboard.

"Jesus fuck, warn a guy," Phoenix mutters, but there's no heat in it.

Ty counts out shares from the envelope, clearly amused by our banter. "Children, please. Some of us are trying to work."

"All work and no play makes Ty a dull boy," Cade sings, dodging the wadded-up bill Ty throws at his head.

"All play and no sense makes Cade a dead boy," Lars counters, catching the money before it hits the ground. "But he's right about one thing—those suits were tragic."

I watch Remy saunter in late, his dark eyes scanning the room before landing on me with his knowing smirk.

"You missed all the fun," I tell him, adjusting my position against the wall to ease my shoulder.

"Oh?" He runs a hand through his messy black hair. "Let me guess—Cade wanted to stab someone, Lars made fun of their clothes, and Ty closed another deal without bloodshed. How'd I do?"

"Scary accurate," Nash says beside me.

Remy shrugs, a fluid motion that draws attention to his lean muscles. "The classics never get old. However, I'm disappointed that I missed the fashion critique. Nothing brightens my day like watching Lars judge other people's life choices."

"Says the guy wearing yesterday's shirt," Lars fires back.

"Bold of you to assume it's only from yesterday." Remy winks.

Phoenix makes a gagging sound without looking up from his laptop. "I thought something stank."

Remy flips him off. "I smell just fucking fine, thank you."

"Some of us have better things to do than worry about than designer labels."

"Like what?" Cade challenges.

"Wouldn't you like to know?" Remy's smile turns sharp. "A gentleman never kisses and tells. Though I suppose that's never stopped you, has it, Cade?"

Nash stifles a laugh as Cade flips Remy off. The easy banter feels good after the tension of the deal, though I notice Remy's eyes darting to the shadows where Gage stands. Those two have never quite gotten comfortable with each other.

"If you're done with the bullshit," Ty cuts in, "some of us have actual work to finish."

"All work and no play makes Ty a dull boy," Remy quotes, echoing Cade's earlier taunt.

"That's what I said!" Cade exclaims.

"Great minds think alike." Remy grins. "Though in your case, I might be overselling it."

The familiar rhythm of our post-deal comedown fills the warehouse. This is what outsiders don't get about us—we're family. Fucked up, dangerous, and probably all certifiable, but a family, nonetheless.

I shift my weight, glancing at Nash, who's already checking his phone. Flora should be safe with Aurora and the others, but being away from her makes my skin crawl. Especially after Tommy and Jake showed their faces.

"We done here?" I ask Ty, trying to keep the impatience out of my voice.

Nash straightens beside me. "Got that Christmas show to prep for."

"Christmas show, huh?" Cade's grin turns wicked. "That what we're calling it now?"

"Shut it," I growl, but Lars jumps in.

"How's the new trainee working out?" He waggles his eyebrows. "Must be keeping you both real busy."

Heat crawls up my neck. Nash's fingers brush my arm—a warning or reassurance, I'm not sure which.

"Flora's a natural on the trapeze," Nash says smoothly, but something in his tone makes Cade cackle.

"Oh, I bet she is." Cade mimes a swinging motion. "Real flexible, right?"

My hands curl into fists, but Ty steps in before I can react. "Alright, enough. Get out of here, all of you. And try not to kill anyone on your way home."

"No promises," Cade calls out, but I'm already heading for the door, Nash close behind.

"Tell Flora we said hi!" Lars shouts after us.

I flip him off without looking back, but I catch Nash's quiet laugh. The tension in my shoulders eases slightly at the sound.

"They're just jealous," Nash murmurs as we reach the car.

"They should be," I say, and Nash's eyes darken in a way that makes my breath catch.

We need to get back to Flora. Now.

24

NASH

Flora's movements are beautiful as she practices her routine on the silks. Her form has improved dramatically over the past weeks, and I can't help but feel proud of how far she's come. The winter air in the tent is crisp, but we've both worked up enough of a sweat that it doesn't matter.

"Good, now remember to keep that core tight through the transition," I call up to her. "You're dropping your left hip slightly."

Flora adjusts immediately, demonstrating the perfect body control that first caught our attention. The red silk wraps around her as she executes a perfect spiral descent.

"How's Colt doing?" she asks, dabbing her face with a towel.

"Stubborn as ever." I shake my head. "But he finally went to the physio. Should help with that shoulder before the Christmas show."

I spot Flora as she climbs back up the silk, her movements precise and controlled. We've been performing nightly shows, and while Colt won't admit it, I can see the strain in his shoulder getting worse. The Christmas spectacular is too important to risk injury.

"Let's work on your release timing," I suggest, moving to adjust the safety harness. "Remember, this is all about trust. Feel the rhythm in your body."

Flora nods, her face set in concentration. Her rare combination of strength and grace makes aerial work look effortless.

"We'll do three runs, then break for lunch," I tell her, checking her harness one final time. "Colt should be back by then, and we can work on the synchronized elements of your solo for—"

The tent door flaps open, and Colt strides in, his dark mood evident in the set of his jaw. I know that look. The appointment didn't go well.

"She wants me to sit out for two weeks," he growls, throwing his jacket onto a nearby chair. "Two fucking weeks."

Flora glances between us, concern etching her features.

"What exactly did she say?" I ask.

"Small tear in my rotator cuff. Nothing major, but —" Colt runs a hand through his hair in frustration. "They're worried about permanent damage if I don't let it heal."

Flora approaches him, her small hand resting on his uninjured shoulder. The touch drains some tension from his frame. It's fascinating how she knows exactly what he needs without words.

I study Colt's tense posture, calculating the implications. Two weeks of recovery means he'll miss our season's biggest show. The Christmas spectacular pulls in the most revenue, and our aerial act is one of the main attractions.

"We can adapt," I say, keeping my voice steady despite the concern churning in my gut. "Flora's ready to stand in. We'll modify the routine."

Colt's jaw clenches. "Like hell. I'm not sitting out Christmas."

"Don't be stupid," I snap, harsher than intended. "You think I want to watch you permanently damage yourself?"

Flora's hand tightens on his shoulder, and I see him flinch slightly. That small reaction tells me everything I need to know about his pain level. He's been hiding it well, but this isn't something we can power through.

"The physio said two weeks for a reason," I continue, softening my tone. "We need you at full strength, not pushing through an injury that could end your career."

I watch as Flora moves to stand between us, her presence a calming force. Over these past weeks, she's learned our rhythms well and knows when to step in.

"What if we modified the routine?" she suggests. "Something that showcases your strength without straining the shoulder?"

I shake my head. "Too risky. One wrong move..." I let the sentence hang, remembering too many close calls in this business. "The Christmas show isn't worth your long-term health."

The truth weighs on us. Two weeks means restructuring everything we've practiced, letting Flora take center stage, and trusting that our bond is strong enough to weather this setback.

Colt's resistance is visible in every line of his body. When his eyes meet mine, I read his anger. But beneath that, there's understanding. He knows I'm right.

I study Colt's tense posture and know exactly what he needs, even if he's too stubborn to admit it. "Strip down and let us help you relax. Flora and I can work out some of those knots."

"For fuck's sake, Nash. I don't need—" Colt starts to protest, but Flora cuts him off.

"Actually, that's a great idea." She's already gathering towels from our training supplies. "You're wound tighter than the rigging ropes."

"I'm fine," Colt insists.

"Shirt off, face down on the mat," I order. "Flora, grab that muscle balm from my bag."

Colt glares at me, but I hold his gaze steadily. We've been partners long enough that he knows when I won't back down.

"This is ridiculous," he mutters, but his fingers move to the hem of his shirt.

Flora spreads a clean towel over the practice mat as Colt reluctantly removes his shirt. There's some bruising around his shoulder that wasn't there this morning, mottled purple spreading across his skin.

"Take off the rest of your clothes and lie down," Flora says softly, patting the mat. "Let us take care of you for once."

Colt's resistance crumbles at her gentle tone. He settles onto the mat resignedly, turning his head to the side. "Happy now?"

"Ecstatic," I reply dryly, kneeling beside him. "Flora, you take his legs and ass. I'll work on this stubborn shoulder of his."

I kneel beside Colt, my hands warm from the friction of the training Flora and I did. It's been a while since I last massaged him, and I feel him tense beneath my touch—not from discomfort but from the awareness of my proximity.

I start with broad strokes along his shoulders, working the muscle balm into his skin. Despite his protests, his body responds to our touch, and I watch the tension melt from his frame. His breath evens out, and I can feel the knots in his shoulders loosen under my thumbs.

Beside me, Flora works with equal focus on his legs, her hands sure and gentle.

Colt shifts, his body twitching unexpectedly as Flora's hands glide over a particularly sensitive spot. A soft moan escapes him, and I know we've entered dangerous territory.

"Roll over," Flora instructs, her voice throaty. "Let's work on your front now."

Reluctantly, Colt does as she bids, his dick hard and glistening with precum. I catch my breath at the sight, remembering the first time I'd seen him like this.

As Flora and I resume our massage, her hands drift lower, lingering on the crease of his hips, and I see his cock twitch in response.

"Fuck, Flora," he mutters, his voice strained. "You're killing me here."

Flora's hand drifts lower still, and she wraps her fingers around his length, pumping. I watch as she explores, her thumb brushing over the piercing, and his hips buck involuntarily.

"Jesus, that feels good," he pants, his eyes squeezed shut. "But it's not—ah, fuck—it's not gonna help my shoulder any."

I chuckle, even as my body reacts to seeing them.

Flora's thumb circles around the piercing, and Colt's breath catches. "That feels so damn good, baby."

I lean in, my lips close to his ear, and whisper, "Then why don't you let us take care of that for you?"

As I speak, I glance at Flora, my eyes dark with suggestion. She meets my gaze, her eyes heated with desire, and I know we're on the same page.

Colt's chest heaves as he struggles for breath, his eyes wild. "You sure about this?"

I smile, my lips brushing his ear. "We can take care of this tension for you. Let us finish what we started."

His lips part, and he nods silently, his eyes fixed on Flora's hand moving slowly up and down his length.

I lean in, inhaling the scent of him—musk and desire—as my lips brush his earlobe. "So beautiful."

Colt's breath catches, his eyes flicking between us as if he can't decide who to focus on. His chest rises and falls with shallow breaths, his eyes growing darker with each passing second.

"Please," he whispers.

I smile, my lips curving against his skin, and then I

pull back to watch as Flora kneels before him, her hands never stilling their exploration.

Her touch is feather-light as she explores his beautiful cock. She teases him with soft caresses, her thumb brushing over the piercing.

Colt's eyes roll back as he succumbs to the sensations. "Flora, fuck, yes…"

Her lips part, taking him into her mouth, and she begins a slow, torturous dance of tongue and lips. I watch, transfixed, as she takes him deep, her throat muscles contracting rhythmically.

My own cock strains against my pants, but I ignore it, my focus wholly on the beautiful picture they make— Flora on her knees, sucking Colt with expert precision. Colt throws his head back, his entire body bowing to her will.

She pulls back, her lips slick, and I kneel beside her, capturing her mouth in a hungry kiss. My tongue tangles with her, tasting the remnants of his precum.

I descend, capturing his length in my mouth, tasting the saltiness of him as I swirl my tongue around the head. I take my time, savoring the sounds he makes.

Beneath me, his hips buck, seeking more friction, and I accommodate, stroking him with my hand as my mouth bobs in tandem. His hands twist in my hair, guiding me, and I let him take control, surrendering.

Normally, I'm always in control, but during sex with these two, I love how good it feels to let go.

Flora joins me, her lips teasing and nipping at his sensitive skin, and he cries out. Her hands grip the base of his shaft, and I take him deeper until my lips touch her fingers.

We establish a rhythm, working in sync. Her mouth and hands never stray far, always exploring and giving him something to feel and focus on.

Colt's breath quickens, his hips stuttering as he bucks into my mouth, and I know he's close. I pull back, stroking him firmly now, watching as his eyes squeeze shut and his teeth grit.

I lean in to steal another kiss from Flora, our tongues tangling desperately.

"I'm close," he groans, his voice breaking. "So damn close."

We waste no time, both of us knowing what he craves. Flora moves to kneel before him, her eyes dark with desire, and takes him back into her mouth. I move to his side, stroking his chest and his nipples, and then lower, tracing patterns on his skin with my fingers.

He's so close now; I want to push him over the edge. I dip my fingers lower, tracing the muscle of his hip, the V-line leading to his groin, and watch his body tense in anticipation.

His entire body goes rigid, his eyes clenching shut, his teeth biting his lower lip. My eyes are drawn to where he disappears into Flora's mouth. I ache to join her, to taste him, to feel his essence on my tongue.

With a final, tortured groan, he spills himself into her mouth, bucking his hips once, twice.

I kneel beside her, watching as she holds his cum in her mouth, savoring the sight of her full lips before she releases a soft moan, opening her mouth slightly to reveal the evidence of our work.

"Now kiss her, Nash," Colt whispers. "Swallow some of my cum."

My body responds instantly. It's odd how I always need to be in control in daily life, but here in this setting, nothing is more sexy than being told what to do by him. I lean in, capturing Flora's mouth in a deep kiss, swirling my tongue with hers, sharing his cum with her.

She moans into my mouth, surrendering to the moment.

Finally, we part, reluctantly, Colt's cum consumed by the both of us.

The three of us are breathless, our chests rising and falling sharply, the charged air thick between us.

Colt's eyes hold mine, his expression soft, affectionate. I see the love there, unguarded, and my heart stutters in response.

"Now that," he says with a small smile, "is how you take care of me."

I smile back. "Glad to be of service."

Flora giggles, the sound light and carefree, and it warms something in my chest. She rises gracefully, offering her hand to Colt, and pulls him up from the mat. He winces slightly, and she's immediately at his side, her hand on his elbow to support him.

"Let's get you cleaned up," she gestures to the nearby sink. Then we can grab some lunch."

Colt hesitates, his eyes flitting between us, and I sense his uncertainty. Our bodies have spoken what our mouths have not. This is the second time we've crossed that line, and I'm sure it won't be the last.

25

FLORA

I grip the silk tightly, my muscles trembling as I execute the move Nash demonstrated. The fabric whispers against my skin as I twist, wrapping it around my leg exactly as practiced. Sweat trickles down my neck, but I maintain my focus.

"Better," Colt calls from below. "Keep your core tight through the transition."

Nash's hands steady me as I descend, his touch confident and reassuring. "He's right. You're getting smoother, but remember to breathe through each movement."

The Christmas show looms just days away, and we've been practicing relentlessly. Colt's shoulder injury means I'm taking his place in several sequences, which terrifies me.

"Again," Nash says, positioning himself on the adjacent silk. "Follow my lead, match my timing."

We ascend in unison, the familiar burn in my arms

almost comforting. Each repetition makes the routine feel more natural, though I hesitate at crucial moments.

"Stop thinking so much," Colt instructs. "Your body knows what to do. Trust it."

Nash and I move through the sequence, our bodies weaving around each other in an intricate dance. The silk hugs my body as I execute a drop, my heart racing at the controlled fall. Nash's movements mirror mine perfectly, creating the symmetry we need for the show.

"You've got it," Colt encourages. "Now, hold that tension through the split."

I arch my back, extending my leg as practiced. The position strains my muscles, but I maintain it, feeling the strength Nash has helped me build over these weeks of training. It's hard to believe I've found somewhere I fit perfectly with these two men after years of feeling lost and broken.

"Five more minutes," Nash says, "then we'll work on the final sequence."

The final sequence leaves my muscles burning, but I maintain perfect form as Nash and I descend the silks in tandem. His hands find my waist as my feet touch the ground, steadying me. The heat of his palms seeps through my thin practice clothes.

"You're incredible," Nash murmurs. His lips brush my neck, sending shivers down my spine. "So beautiful when you move up there."

I lean into his touch, tilting my head back as his mouth claims mine. The kiss is deep and passionate, making my knees weak. His hands slide lower, gripping my hips.

"Nash," I breathe against his lips, reluctantly breaking the kiss. "I need to go. I promised Aurora I'd help with the cotton candy stand tonight."

He groans softly, pressing his forehead to mine. "Always running off to help someone else."

"You know Aurora's been good to me." I steal one more quick kiss before stepping back. "Besides, I need to shower and change first."

I feel Colt's presence before his hands touch me. He turns me away from Nash, his fingers tangling in my hair as he claims my mouth. The kiss is different from Nash's—rougher, more demanding. My body responds instantly, melting against him.

"You shouldn't have all the fun," Colt murmurs against my lips. His good hand traces down my spine, making me shiver.

Nash clears his throat. "About tonight's show…"

"Right." Colt releases me reluctantly. "The main act's off until my shoulder heals and Flora's ready."

I nod, guilt twisting in my stomach. "I'm sorry I'm not—"

"Don't," Nash cuts me off. "You're progressing faster than anyone could expect. We just need more time to perfect it."

"Nash has been doing some solo routines to fill the gap," Colt adds, his hand resting possessively on my hip. "But since I'm grounded tonight anyway, I thought I'd help out at the cotton candy stand with you."

My heart skips. The idea of working alongside Colt, even at something as simple as selling cotton candy, makes my pulse race. "You don't have to—"

"I want to." His fingers squeeze gently. "Besides, someone needs to keep an eye on you with those bastards still lurking around."

Nash's expression darkens at the mention of Tommy and Jake, but he doesn't comment. We all know they're still out there, watching, waiting. Having Colt nearby tonight will help ease the tension.

"Aurora will be there too," I remind them, though I'm grateful for Colt's offer.

"Even better," Colt says. "I'll meet you there after you shower and change."

I hum softly as I walk back to the trailer, my muscles pleasantly sore from practice. The evening air carries the scent of popcorn and cotton candy, mixing with the metallic tang of the approaching rain. My hair sticks to my neck, damp with sweat, and I can't wait for that hot shower.

The gravel crunches under my feet as I approach our trailer. A hand clamps over my mouth, yanking me backward. My heart stops as Jake's cologne hits my nostrils, that same sickening scent I remember from years of abuse.

"Miss us, little sister?" Tommy's voice sends ice through my veins. His fingers dig into my arm as he drags me behind the trailer.

I try to scream, but Jake's hand muffles any sound. My legs kick out, searching for purchase, for any way to break free. The terror I thought I'd left behind comes rushing back, paralyzing me.

"Thought you could just run away?" Jake's breath is hot against my ear. "You belong to us. Always have."

My body trembles as Tommy's hand slides up my thigh. "No one's going to save you this time. Those circus freaks can't protect you forever."

Tears stream down my face as I struggle against their grip. The strength I've built during aerial training seems useless against their combined force. Jake's hand shifts slightly, and I bite down hard, tasting blood.

He curses, loosening his grip just enough for me to scream. "Nash! Colt!"

Tommy's fist connects with my stomach, driving the air from my lungs. "Shut up, you little bitch."

I gasp for breath, my vision blurring as panic takes hold. The sound of approaching footsteps barely registers through the rushing in my ears. Jake's grip tightens painfully on my arms, and I can feel Tommy's hands pawing at my clothes.

Suddenly, a roar of fury fills the air.

Colt barrels into Jake, ripping him away from me. I stumble forward, gasping for breath as Tommy releases me to face this new threat. My legs give out, and I collapse onto the gravel, watching through tear-blurred vision as Colt launches himself at both of my tormentors.

His fist connects with Jake's jaw, sending him staggering. Tommy tries to grab him from behind, but Colt's elbow snaps back, catching him in the ribs. The sound of flesh hitting flesh fills the air as Colt fights with a savagery I've never seen before.

"I'll fucking kill you both," Colt snarls, his voice thick with rage.

Jake and Tommy circle him, looking for openings.

Blood trickles from Jake's split lip, and Tommy's holding his side where Colt struck him. But there are two of them, and even as Colt lands another crushing blow to Tommy's face, Jake manages to get in a hit to his injured shoulder.

Colt grunts in pain but doesn't back down. He charges forward, tackling Jake to the ground. His fists rain down, but Tommy kicks him hard in the back, forcing him off his brother.

"This isn't over," Jake spits blood as he scrambles to his feet. He and Tommy retreat, disappearing into the darkness between trailers.

Colt moves to pursue them, his body coiled with tension, but stops when he hears my sob. Instantly, he's beside me, gathering me into his arms.

"Fucking cowards," he growls. "I should have ended them both." His hands are strong as they check me for injuries, his touch gentle despite the fury radiating from him. "Are you hurt? Did they..."

I shake my head, clinging to him. "You got here in time."

"Should have been faster. Should have taken them both fucking down." His arms tighten around me protectively. "I'm not leaving you alone again. Not for a second."

I collapse against Colt's chest, my body shaking with sobs. His arms wrap around me tighter, and I breathe in his familiar scent. The contrast between his gentle touch now and the raw violence I witnessed strikes me deep in my chest.

"I've got you," he whispers into my hair. "You're safe now."

The tenderness in his voice breaks something inside me. After years of abuse of being treated like property by Tommy and Jake, the way Colt protects me feels almost surreal. He fought for me without hesitation and put himself at risk despite his injured shoulder.

"Why?" I choke out against his shirt. "Why would you do that for me?"

His hand cups my face, tilting it to meet his intense gaze. "Because you're ours to protect. Mine and Nash's. No one gets to hurt you anymore."

Fresh tears spill down my cheeks. The fierce possession in his voice should frighten me, but instead, it makes me feel cherished and valued. I think of Nash, too—how they have shown me nothing but care and protection since I joined the carnival.

"I never thought..." My voice breaks. "I never thought I'd find people to fight for me. Who would believe me and protect me."

Colt wipes away my tears. "You deserve to be protected, Flora. You deserve to feel safe."

I press closer to him, overwhelmed by the realization that I finally have what I've always craved—people who truly care about me, who see me as something precious rather than something to be used and discarded.

26

COLT

I guide Nash into the living area of our trailer, my blood still boiling from earlier. The memory of those bastards touching Flora makes my fists clench. Through the bedroom door, I can hear her soft breathing—finally peaceful after crying herself to sleep.

"We need to handle this now," I whisper to Nash, keeping my voice low. "Those pieces of shit don't deserve to keep breathing."

Nash's eyes meet mine, that familiar darkness I've always recognized in him rising to the surface. He gives a slight nod, his jaw clenched tight.

"Before we leave this town," I continue, "Tommy and Jake need to disappear. Permanently." My hands are shaking with barely contained rage. "You heard what they did to her. For years."

Nash moves closer, his presence steadying me like it always has. "We protect what's ours," he says. "And she's ours now."

I glance toward the bedroom where Flora sleeps.

"No one will ever hurt her again." The promise comes out like a prayer, but I mean it as a threat. "We do this clean. No traces."

"Will Ty let us use the lockup?" Nash suggests.

I rub a hand across the back of my neck. "Possibly. I'll speak to him."

"That would sort out the where; the real question is when?" Nash asks.

"I'll ask Phoenix to check if they're planning a retaliation, really comb through their communications." I crack my knuckles. "When we do this, we will make them suffer. Make them feel everything they put her through."

Nash's hand finds my shoulder. "Together," he says simply.

"Together," I agree. "For Flora."

Nash's hand on my shoulder sends electricity through my body, and I fight to control my reaction. His touch has always affected me, but since that night—since we crossed that line—everything feels different. More intense. My dick starts to stiffen in my jeans, and I shift uncomfortably, trying to hide my body's response.

"What's up?" His hand hasn't moved from my shoulder, and the warmth of his palm seems to burn through my shirt. "You're tense."

I swallow hard, hyperaware of how close he's standing. We haven't talked about what happened—about how his mouth felt on me twice now.

It was supposed to be about Flora, showing her we could all be together. But now, with just the two of us in this dim light, those memories flood back.

"Nothing," I manage to say, but my voice comes out rougher than intended. "Just worried about Flora."

Nash's fingers tighten slightly on my shoulder. "That's not it," he says, reading me like a book. "Something else is bothering you."

My dick throbs, straining against my zipper, and I know there's no way Nash hasn't noticed. He's too observant, too attuned to my body after years of performing together.

"Colt," he says my name like a question, like a challenge. His thumb moves slightly, stroking my shoulder through my shirt, and this time, I can't hold back the small sound that escapes my throat.

I step back from Nash, my body immediately missing his touch. The air feels too thick, too charged. I need space to think clearly.

"Want a beer?" I move toward our small kitchen, grateful for the excuse to put distance between us. My hands shake slightly as I open the fridge.

"Sure," Nash replies, his voice carrying that dangerous edge I recognize all too well. "But we need to talk about the elephant in the room."

The beer can feels ice cold against my palm as I grab two. My throat tightens, and I have to force myself to swallow. "What elephant?" I keep my back to him, pretending to search for something else in the fridge.

"Cut the bullshit, Colt." Nash's words hit me like a physical blow. "Stop messing about."

I close my eyes, gripping the beer cans tighter. My heart pounds against my ribs, and I can feel sweat beading at the back of my neck.

I take a slow breath and turn around, handing Nash his beer. The tension in the room is thick enough to cut. I crack open my can, taking a long drink to steady my nerves.

"Fine," I say, leaning against the counter. "What do you want to talk about?"

Nash sets his unopened beer on the table, his eyes locked on mine with an intensity that makes my heart race. "We need to talk about the fact we sucked each other's dicks and how we both fucking loved it."

The words hit me like a punch to the gut. I nearly choke on my beer, setting the can down with shaking hands. Trust Nash to be so direct, to strip away all pretense and lay it bare.

"Nash..." I start, but my voice trails off. What can I say? He's right. The memory of that night floods back—his mouth on me, my hands in his hair, the sounds he made when I returned the favor. The way it felt so right.

"Don't," he cuts me off. "Don't try to explain it away or make excuses. I saw your face that night. I felt how hard you were when you rubbed that beautiful cock against my dick. You wanted it as much as I did."

I grip the edge of the counter behind me, knuckles turning white. The truth of his words burns my chest.

Nash takes a step closer, his expression softening. "Listen to me, Colt. What we have—it's special. Not just the friendship or the performances, but everything. And now with Flora..."

I swallow hard, unable to look away from his intense gaze.

"I care about you," Nash continues, his voice gentle

but firm. "Have for years. And I care about Flora, too. She needs us, both of us. Together, we give her everything she needs—protection, understanding, love."

My heart pounds against my ribs. "Nash…"

"Think about it," he urges. "The three of us, supporting each other, caring for each other. No more pretending or holding back. We could be a real family, Colt. All of us together."

His words strike a chord deep within me. The possibility of having both of them, openly and completely, makes my chest tight with longing.

"Flora brings out something in both of us," Nash says. "And what we have—you and me—it's always been there, just waiting. We could build something beautiful, something perfect."

I let out a shaky breath, processing his words. The truth of them resonates in my soul. Flora fits so perfectly between us. How natural it feels when we're all together. And Nash—my best friend, my partner, the man who knows me better than anyone else.

I run a hand through my hair, my heart thundering in my chest. The truth claws its way up my throat, demanding to be heard after years of silence.

"Fuck, Nash. You think I haven't wanted this? Haven't wanted you?" My voice comes out rough. "For years, I've watched you. Every time you move on that silk, every time you spot me during practice. The way your muscles flex, the grace in every motion."

Nash's eyes darken, but he stays silent, letting me continue.

"I've laid awake so many nights, thinking about your

hands on me. Imagined what it would be like to touch and taste you." I let out a shaky breath. "But I couldn't risk what we have. Our friendship, our act—it means everything to me."

Moving closer, I meet his intense gaze. "Then Flora came along. And fuck, Nash, she hit me like a freight train. That same raw need, that desperate connection I've only ever felt with you." My hands clench at my sides. "Watching her with you, seeing how perfectly she fits between us—it's like something clicked into place. Like she was meant to complete this."

The confession hangs in the air between us for a heartbeat. Then Nash surges forward, his mouth crashing into mine. His lips are firm and demanding, and I respond instantly, years of pent-up desire exploding in this moment.

My hands grip his hips, pulling him closer as his fingers tangle in my hair. The kiss deepens, turning desperate and hungry. Nash tastes like mint and something uniquely him.

A groan escapes my throat as his tongue slides against mine. His body presses me back against the counter, hard muscle against hard muscle. This isn't gentle or hesitant—it's raw and primal, filled with years of suppressed want.

I bite his lower lip, drawing a harsh sound from him that shoots straight to my groin. His hands tighten in my hair, tilting my head to deepen the kiss further. Every stroke of his tongue, every press of his lips speaks of possession and need.

My heart pounds against my ribs as Nash consumes

me. His body fits against mine like it was made to be there, like we've been doing this forever instead of just these few explosive moments.

I meet Nash's challenging gaze, my breath heavy from our kiss. The familiar competitive spark ignites between us—the same energy that makes our aerial performances so electric.

"You going to be a good boy for me, Colt?" Nash's voice carries that dangerous edge. "Get on your knees?"

I grip his hips harder, pushing back against his body. "I don't take orders from you," I growl.

Nash's fingers tighten in my hair, testing my resistance. "No? Seems like you want to." His other hand traces down my chest, teasing. "I've seen how you watch me during practice."

"Maybe you're the one who should kneel," I counter, spinning us so he's against the counter. Our bodies press together, neither willing to submit. "You're not the only one who knows how to take control."

Nash's eyes darken with desire, but I see the flash of defiance. He's never backed down from a challenge, especially not from me. His hand slides to my neck, thumb pressing against my pulse point.

"Make me," he whispers against my lips, the words both invitation and challenge.

The push and pull between us crackles with tension—both of us are too stubborn, too dominant to yield easily. Yet there's trust here, too, built over years of catching each other mid-air, knowing exactly how far we can push before we need to pull back.

I lock eyes with Nash, our bodies still pressed against

the counter. Our familiar competitive energy shifts into something deeper, more primal. Years of working together, of reading each other's signals, have taught me exactly who Nash is at his core.

His hand remains firm on my neck, but I notice the subtle tells in his posture—the slight tremor in his fingers, the way his breath catches when I push back against his control. Behind that dominant facade, Nash has always craved something he won't admit.

"You want to prove who's in charge?" I growl, letting my voice drop lower. "Then show me."

Nash's pupils dilate, and I feel the moment his resolve wavers. For all his calculated control and careful manipulation of others, Nash has always yielded to me in crucial moments. It's there in the way he trusts me to catch him during our most dangerous stunts and looks to me for final approval before every performance.

I press my advantage, sliding my hand up to cup his jaw. "You talk big, Nash, but we both know what you want."

His resistance crumbles. Nash slowly sinks to his knees with a shaky exhale, his eyes never leaving mine. The sight of him looking up at me makes my heart race.

"Good boy," I murmur, running my fingers through his hair. The trust in his eyes, the vulnerability he shows only to me, makes something protective surge in my chest.

"Fuck, yes," he swears, his eyes dark with desire. "Say it again."

I lean down, my fingers tightening in his hair. "Good boy," I murmur, relishing my power over him now.

The hard ridge of his cock strains against his sweatpants, visible evidence of the effect I have on him. My blood sings with satisfaction—both at the knowledge that I've gotten him so worked up and at the unfamiliar yet thrilling rush of dominance.

"On your knees, that's a good start," I say, my voice dropping lower, commanding. Nash's eyes flash at the order, but he listens, staying on his knees, his gaze fixed on me. "Now take it out. I want to watch you touch me."

Nash swallows hard, his pupils blown wide. Slowly, his hand reaches for the button of my jeans. His fingers are steady as he undoes the button and pulls down the zipper, revealing the bulge of my cock straining against my boxers.

"Go on," I urge, my voice rough with anticipation. Nash's eyes flicker up to mine, his hand hovering over the waistband of my boxers.

"Touch me," I command. "Take it out."

With a deep exhale, Nash hooks his fingers into the waistband and pulls my boxer briefs down, freeing my cock. My dick springs free, fully hard and aching for his mouth. Nash lets out a small sound, eyes widening at the sight.

"You like that, don't you?" I ask, my voice hardening with authority. "You like seeing me like this for you."

"Yes," Nash breathes, his eyes glued to my cock. "God, yes."

I step closer, my jeans pooling at my ankles, as I give him a slight nudge with my foot. "Then show me how much. Show me what a good boy you are."

Nash's breath quickens as he leans forward, his tongue darting out to swipe the tip of my cock. I grip his hair, guiding him as he takes the head of my dick into his mouth.

"Mmhmm, fuck," I groan at the sensation of his wet heat surrounding me. Nash's mouth is hot and wet, his lips soft against my skin. His tongue teases the sensitive tip of my cock, and I feel him hum in appreciation.

The sound vibrates through my shaft, straight to my balls, and I let out a harsh curse. Nash's eyes glint with pleasure at my reaction. He hollows his cheeks, sucking harder as he takes more of my length into his mouth.

"Ah, fuck." The sight of Nash on his knees is enough to steal my breath, but the feel of his warm mouth surrounding me, his tongue swirling around the pierced head of my cock—it's enough to make my knees weak. I reach down, tangling my fingers in his hair, and he meets my eyes as he sucks me deeper.

His eyes—those deep, dark pools that have always drawn me in—they're hazy now with lust, fixed on me with an intensity that ignites a wildfire in my gut. His lips stretch around my girth, full and perfect, the sight of them wrapped around my cock sending a jolt straight to my balls.

Nash's hand moves to his own cock, pulling it from his sweatpants, and he begins to jerk himself in time with his mouth's rhythm. I feel a rush of liquid heat in my veins at the sight of his hard length in his hand. He moans softly as his fist pumps up and down, the sound vibrating against my shaft and making my toes curl.

I've fantasized about this a hundred times. Still, the

reality is so much better—the feel of his full lips on my cock, the way he tongues the sensitive spot around my piercing, his free hand now reaching up to grip my thigh.

The sight of him taking what's mine—it's too much, and I'm overcome with this unbearable need to brand him, to claim every part of him as mine. My hands tighten in his hair, and I start to thrust my hips, fucking his mouth slowly, helpless to hold back.

Nash's eyes flutter closed at the first shallow thrusts, his breath escaping in a soft moan. The sound vibrates through my shaft, straight to my balls.

"Fuck, Nash," I groan, my hips moving on their own now, my cock sliding deeper into his mouth. "Suck it; take it all."

Nash's hands clutch at my thighs, his knuckles white as he tries to ground himself. His mouth is magic, every swirl of his tongue, every bob of his head driving me closer to the edge.

"Take every inch," I grit out, my hands tightening in his hair. "Gonna fuck that pretty throat until you're gagging on my cock."

His hands grip my thighs harder, holding on as I thrust into his mouth.

"Fuck, you're such a good boy," I praise. "Suck my cock, Nash. Show me how much you love it."

His throat relaxes around me, and I slide deeper, finally reaching the back. I groan at the wet, tight heat engulfing me, my hips stuttering.

"You like that, baby?" I ask. "My dick in that pretty throat, making you gag."

Nash moans again in response, his eyes now hazy with lust.

"That's right," I grit out. "I'm gonna make such a mess in that slutty mouth of yours."

Nash's throat works around me as he tries to swallow my length, his eyes fluttering shut, lost in the sensations. His hands move from my thighs to grip my ass, pulling me even deeper into his mouth.

"Yeah, you love that, don't you?" I tease, holding him in place as I thrust. "Sucking my cock like a good little slut."

The dirty words spill from my mouth, fueled by the sight of Nash on his knees, worshipping my cock. It's too much, and I feel my balls draw tight with the need to come.

"Fuck, I'm close," I warn, my hips stuttering as I thrust into his mouth. "Gonna paint that pretty mouth with my cum, cover those lips with my load."

Nash moans again, the sound vibrating through my cock. His throat convulses as he gags, and the sensation sends me over the edge. I spill into his mouth with a harsh groan, my hips moving frantically as I fill him with my release.

Nash swallows every drop, his hands gripping my ass tighter. I feel his throat working as he takes my load, his eyes squeezed shut, his cheeks hollowed around my dick still.

I pull out slowly, my cock finally softening as I catch my breath. Nash keeps his eyes closed, sucking in deep breaths, his hand still wrapped around his own cock. I can see the precum beading at the tip, his heavy length straining for release.

"Look at me, Nash." My voice is low and commanding, and his eyes slowly blink open, hazy with pleasure. "Finish what you started, baby. Come for me."

His pupils are blown wide with lust, his full lips swollen from sucking my cock. I lean down, wrapping my hand around his length, stroking him firmly.

Nash moans, his head falling back as I fist his cock. I stroke him hard and fast, needing to see him lose control.

"That's my good boy," I encourage, my voice soothing. "Come for me, let it go."

It only takes a few more tugs on his cock before his body goes rigid, his release painting my hand and his stomach. His hips stutter as he rides out his orgasm, a string of curses spilling from his mouth.

I keep stroking him through his release, drawing out every last drop until he finally goes limp, completely spent. He remains on the floor, chest heaving as he tries to catch his breath. I step back, letting him recover.

"Fuck, that was hot," Flora says, drawing my attention to our pretty angel, who is sitting on the sofa with her fingers in her cunt. And I know this night is going to be a very long one.

27

NASH

"Did we wake you?" My voice cuts through the heavy silence.

Flora stretches languidly on the sofa, her fingers still buried between her legs, her flushed skin damp with desire. "You did. All that grunting was hard to ignore. Don't worry, I'm glad I caught the show." A mischievous smile plays on her lips as her eyes flick between Colt and me. "I can't wait until you two finally fuck each other in the ass."

Colt's eyes spark with heat, his gaze lingering on me momentarily. I know he wants it, too.

"Is this silly pretense that you don't want each other over?" Flora's question hangs in the air.

I glance at Colt. It's time to stop hiding, to give in. I approach him, reaching out to trace his jawline with my fingertip. "It's over," I murmur. "We both want you, Flora. And we want each other, too."

Colt's eyes darken as he pulls me toward him, his mouth crashing against mine. It's a kiss laden with pent-up desire, the taste of him familiar and yet indescribably intoxicating. Our lips move in sync, our tongues tangling in a desperate dance.

Flora watches us. "I knew it," she breathes, her fingers again moving between her legs. "I want to watch you take each other."

I knew this moment would come. And now, with Flora's eyes on us, eager and gleaming with anticipation, it's time to give her what she wants—what *we* want.

I pull Colt toward me, not breaking eye contact for a second. He resists at first, his gaze questioning, searching my eyes as if to confirm that this is happening. I give him a slight nod, and he relaxes into my touch, his lips crashing hungrily against mine.

His mouth is warm and insistent, his tongue demanding entry. Our kiss is urgent. Our hands are everywhere, tearing at clothes, exploring bare skin.

Flora's eyes are bright as she watches us. Her fingers move feverishly between her legs, her breath coming in sharp gasps. "Fuck, yes," she whispers, her voice hoarse with desire. "I can't wait to see Nash's cock buried deep in your ass, Colt. I want to see you take it all."

Colt moans at her words, his eyes darkening even further. "You want to see that?" he asks, his voice rough. "You want to watch Nash fuck me?"

"More than anything," she replies, her fingers working faster. "I want to see you both lose control. I want to hear you cry out, Colt. I want to know that it's Nash who finally makes you let go."

I can see the desire and conflict flashing in Colt's eyes. We've both always been in control. Colt is naturally dominant, though, especially in the bedroom. But now, with me, he's ready to surrender. "Then that's what I'll give you, angel," he growls. "I'll let Nash fuck me while I'm buried deep inside your sweet cunt."

I swallow hard, my cock throbbing at the image his words evoke. I've often fantasized about this moment, dreaming of the feel of Colt's body yielding to mine. Now, it's finally within reach.

I push Colt toward the sofa, urging him to bend over the armrest. He complies, his breath coming in sharp pants. "Do it, Nash," he grits out. "Fuck me."

I glance at Flora, who is pretty and flushed. "You ready for this, Flora?" I ask. "Ready to watch me sink into Colt's tight hole while he pounds that pretty cunt of yours?"

She whimpers, her eyes rolling back as her fingers work feverishly. "Yes," she breathes. "I need to feel Colt inside me while you're inside him, knowing we're all connected in the most intimate way possible."

Colt's body is taut as a bowstring as he bends over the armrest of the couch, his powerful muscles rippling with restrained need. There's a challenge in his eyes, daring me to take what I want. I step forward, my heart pounding with anticipation.

Flora is already by his side, her delicate hands reaching out to stroke his leaking cock, which is already fully hard again. She's eager, her eyes sparkling with curiosity. I can see the lust building in her, mirroring the ache in my own body.

I press a kiss to Colt's broad shoulder. "Relax," I murmur against his skin. "Let us take care of you."

Flora lets out a soft sigh, her fingers tightening around his length. I know she's imagining what it will be like to have this man inside her, even as she helps prepare him for me.

I head into my bedroom and grab some lube, coating my fingers generously before trailing a slick fingertip down the furrow of his ass. He hisses at the sensation, his body tensing momentarily before he relaxes into my touch. I know how to prepare him, having fucked women in the ass on countless occasions.

I scavenge in the kitchen and retrieve a tapered candle to stretch him open. Coating it generously with lube, my heart pounds with anticipation.

I press the tip of the candle to his entrance, watching as his body swallows it greedily. He lets out a low groan, his head falling forward. "Fuck, yes," he grits out.

I push the candle deeper, my own breath coming in short pants. "You like that, don't you, Colt?" I ask, my voice husky with need. "You like the feel of being stretched open, filled up."

"Do it harder, Nash. I can take it," he growls, his hips pushing back.

I smile, my eyes flicking briefly to Flora, who bites her lip as she watches, her own pleasure forgotten for the moment as she's drawn to the erotic display before her. "As you wish," I murmur, my voice laced with amusement. I begin to thrust the candle in and out of him, setting a steady rhythm, watching as his body accepts the intrusion, craving more.

"You've prepared yourself like this before, haven't

you?" I ask, my fingers tightening around the base of the candle. "You like to fuck your own ass, don't you, Colt?"

He grunts, his eyes squeezed shut as he struggles to maintain his dominant facade. "Maybe," he grunts. "Once you've felt a cock in your ass, it's hard to stop. I've got a few dildos I like to ride, jacking off simultaneously. Always wishing it was your cock pounding into me."

"Fuck," I groan, my dick straining to be inside him.

Flora's voice snaps me back to the moment, her breathless words pulling a smirk to my lips. "You two are so fucking sexy. I can't wait any longer."

Colt's eyes glitter with desire as he stands. "Lie back," he commands, his voice rough with need. "I'm going to sink into this tight cunt while Nash takes what he wants from my ass."

Flora doesn't hesitate, her eyes sparkling with curiosity and lust as she settles back onto the sofa. Her legs fall open, inviting Colt to take what he craves. He positions himself between her thighs, his cock hovering at her entrance as he reaches down to guide himself into her wet heat.

The sight of his thick length disappearing inside her makes my breath catch. I want to be buried deep inside him at the same moment he fills her, our bodies connected in the most primal way possible.

Colt starts to move, his hips snapping forward as he thrusts into Flora's welcoming body. She moans, her hands reaching up to grip his biceps as he sets a relentless pace. "Fuck, yes," she gasps, her eyes squeezed shut as she takes him deep. "God, your cock feels so good."

I move behind Colt, lining up the tip of my lubed-up cock with his waiting hole. I can feel his anticipation, his body trembling with need. "Are you ready for me, Colt?" I whisper, my lips close to his ear. "Ready for my cock inside your ass while I watch you fuck our girl?"

"Yes," he growls, his voice strained with desire. "Do it, Nash. Take me while I take her."

My cock pulses with need as I begin to push into him, feeling the resistance of his body before he relaxes, welcoming my intrusion. I groan at the tight heat surrounding me, the sight of my cock disappearing inside him almost too much to bear.

Colt's hips stutter for a moment as he adjusts to the sensation. He continues his thrusts into Flora, his pace never faltering. I begin to move in time with him, setting up a rhythm with us moving.

Grunts and groans fill the room, a symphony of desire and need. I can feel the connection between us, our bodies moving in unison, driven by the same lust. It's everything I've fantasized about and more.

Colt's body moves in perfect time with mine, his hips snapping forward as he sinks deep into Flora, even as I bury myself deeper into him. "Fuck, yes," he growls, his eyes squeezed shut, a sheen of sweat covering his skin. "This is what you want, angel. You want to be filled up, don't you? Want to feel Nash pounding into me while I split your pretty cunt wide open."

I moan at his words, the filthy image only fueling my desire. I've always been the one in control, the one calling the shots, but now, with Colt's body yielding to mine, I find myself surrendering to the moment, to the raw, carnal lust that courses through my veins.

"You like that, don't you, Colt?" I murmur, my lips close to his ear, my breath hot against his skin. "You like the feel of my cock inside you." I pull back slightly, only to snap my hips forward, driving into him with forceful thrusts. "I'm going to fuck you so good, make you come apart around my cock."

"God, yes," he grits out, his hands tightening on Flora's thighs as he holds her in place, his powerful body working tirelessly to pleasure her even as he submits to me. "Do it, Nash. Make me come. Make me forget everything but your cock and her cunt."

I glance down, watching as my cock disappears into his body, the stretch of his hole tight and perfect around me. His ass clenches around me, milking my cock, and I groan, my head falling back as I savor the sensation.

"Look at me, Flora," Colt commands. "Look at me as I fuck you. As I make you come."

Her eyes fly open, her breath catching at the intensity of his gaze. "Yes, Colt," she breathes, her fingers digging into his arms. "I'm looking at you."

"Good girl. Keep your eyes on me as you come. I want you to see me when you fall apart."

Her chest heaves as she succumbs to his command, her eyes never wavering from his as her body surges toward its peak. "Oh, God," she whimpers, her body tensing.

Colt's hips never stop moving, his thrusts relentless as he drives into her, even as I continue to pound into him, claiming his body as my own. "Come for us, angel," he growls, his voice rough. "Come all over my cock."

Her eyes squeeze shut for a moment, her body arching as she surrenders to the pleasure. "Yes!" she cries, her voice echoing in the room. "I'm coming, Colt. I'm—" Her words devolve into a series of incoherent moans as her orgasm washes over her, her body trembling in the aftermath.

Colt's release is approaching, his body tensing, his breath coming in short, sharp gasps. "Look at her, Nash," he grits out. "Look at her as I fill her cunt with my cum."

My own body responds to his words; the image of his thick length buried inside her, pumping into her, pushing me closer to the edge. "Fuck, Colt," I breathe, my hips snapping forward, driving into him with urgent thrusts. "I'm not going to last much longer either."

"Good," he growls, his eyes narrowing. "Come inside me, Nash. Mark me as yours at the same time as I fill her with my seed."

The mere demand pushes me over the edge. "Fuck!" I cry, my body tensing as my release surges through me, jet after jet of hot cum filling him, branding him as mine.

Colt comes at exactly the same moment, his body stiffening as he empties himself into Flora, his eyes squeezed shut, his teeth gritted as he rides out his orgasm. "Fuck," he grunts, his hips giving a few final, shallow thrusts as he buries himself deep inside her.

The room is filled with the sound of our harsh breathing, our bodies slick with sweat, sated from the intense release. I lean forward, pressing a kiss to the curve of Colt's shoulder, savoring the taste of his skin, salty with our exertion. He shifts slightly, turning his head to meet my lips in a tender and passionate kiss. Our tongues tangle momentarily before he pulls away, a soft smile on his lips.

I glance down at Flora, who watches us, her eyes sparkling with curiosity and something akin to wonder. "What are you thinking?" I ask, my fingers gently brushing the damp hair from her forehead. "Did we meet your expectations?"

She smiles, her face soft and dreamy. "More than I could have ever imagined," she breathes, her hand reaching up to stroke Colt's cheek. I knew it would be intense, but the connection..." She trails off, shaking her head slightly, unable to find the words.

I know exactly what Flora means. Watching her eyes sparkle with contentment, feeling Colt's steady breathing against me—it's a connection I never thought possible. Not just physical, but something deeper that binds us together.

"You're everything to me," I murmur, running my fingers through Flora's hair. Her smile brightens the room, chasing away the shadows of our pasts. Beside me, Colt's hand finds mine, squeezing gently.

"We protect our own," Colt says, his voice rough with emotion. The words carry weight—a promise we've all made to each other. After everything Flora's been through and all the years Colt and I spent dancing around our feelings, we finally found our place.

Flora reaches up, touching both our faces. "I feel

safe with you both," she whispers. "Like I finally belong somewhere."

My heart swells at her words. That's all we've ever wanted—to give her the security she deserves, to show her what real love feels like. In doing so, Colt and I discovered something in ourselves, too.

"You'll always have us," I promise, kissing her forehead. "Both of us."

Colt nods in agreement, his eyes meeting mine over Flora's head. There's understanding there and something more—a depth of feeling that no longer needs to hide in shadows.

We stay like that for a while, wrapped in each other's warmth, savoring the quiet moment. This connection we share is perfect.

28

FLORA

*T*he silk ribbons flow through my fingers as I practice the final sequences for tonight's show. The empty tent feels peaceful in the early morning light filtering through the canvas. My muscles remember each movement now, flowing from one position to the next with practiced grace.

I catch my reflection in one of the mirrors positioned around the tent—my hair pulled back in a tight bun, practice leotard hugging my frame. Three weeks of intensive training have built my confidence. However, butterflies still flutter in my stomach when I think about performing in front of the Christmas crowd tomorrow night.

The tent flap rustles, and I spot Colt and Nash entering. Something seems off about their expressions. There's an intensity in their eyes I haven't seen before. They stand watching me, neither speaking right away.

"Morning," I call out, unwinding myself from the

silk to face them. "I was just running through the finale sequence again."

Nash's jaw is tight, while Colt's hands are clenched at his sides.

"Everything okay?" I ask.

Did something happen?

Are they having second thoughts about letting me perform?

They exchange a look between them before Nash takes a step forward. "We need to talk, little bird."

Colt follows, his ice-blue eyes locked on mine. "There's been a development we must discuss before the show tonight."

I grip the silk tighter, trying to ground myself against the anxiety building in my chest. Whatever news they have, their expressions tell me it's serious.

"What's wrong?" I force the words past my dry throat, watching their faces for any hint of what's troubling them.

Nash runs a hand through his dark hair. "Phoenix intercepted some messages between Tommy and Jake. They're planning to take you after the show tomorrow night."

My knees buckle, and Colt steadies me with his strong hands. The silk ribbons slip from my grasp as memories of their abuse flash through my mind.

"But we're going to flip their plan," Colt's voice is steel. "We'll be ready. Phoenix is tracking them. Instead of them taking you, we're taking them."

I look between them, seeing the cold determination

in their eyes. "What... what are you going to do to them?"

"You don't need to know the details, little bird." Nash steps closer. "And you don't have to be there. We can handle this."

"It's going to get bloody," Colt adds, his fingers tightening slightly on my shoulders. "We want you far away when we're dealing with them."

My heart pounds against my ribs as I process their words. These two men, who've shown me nothing but protection and care, plan to avenge the years of torment I survived on my behalf.

"Tell me what you're going to do to them," I insist, my voice stronger than expected. "I need to know."

"They won't leave breathing," Nash states.

Colt nods in agreement, and I search their faces, seeing the darkness I've always sensed lurking beneath their well-crafted masks.

"I want to help," I say. "I need this. I need my revenge, too."

Nash's dark eyes study me. "Are you sure? This isn't revenge for us. It's avenging the depravity forced on you. This isn't something you can take back."

"It will change you," Colt adds, his ice-blue gaze piercing me. "Once you cross this line, there's no returning to who you were before."

I lift my chin, meeting their stares with unwavering determination. "I'm already changed. They took that innocence from me." My hands clench into fists at my sides. "This isn't about becoming something different.

It's about healing. About taking back the power they ripped from me."

Nash and Colt exchange a look, their debate requiring no words. I've seen them do this before, but this time, it seems to weigh heavier than anything I've seen before between them.

"I need to be part of this," I continue. "I've spent years being helpless, being their victim. I won't be a victim anymore." My voice grows stronger with each word. "I want to see the light leave their eyes. I need them to know I'm not that scared little girl anymore."

The darkness in their expressions shifts, morphing into something I've not seen since before I lost my parents, pride, maybe? They understand. Of course, they do. These two men who harbor their demons have protected me since I stepped into their world.

"If you're sure," Nash says, brushing a strand of hair from my face. "We'll make sure you get your closure."

Colt groans. "You're fucking sexy when you say things like that," he growls, making me giggle, then captures my lips with an intensity that makes my knees weak.

Nash moves behind me, his strong hands gripping my hips. His lips find my shoulder, trailing gentle kisses across my skin in contrast to his firm hold. The dual sensations of their touch ground me, reminding me I'm safe between them.

I reach back, tangling my fingers in Nash's hair as Colt continues to kiss me. They surround me completely—my protectors, my salvation, my home.

Colt breaks our kiss, resting his forehead against mine as we catch our breath.

"We should focus on making plans," I murmur, trying to keep my thoughts clear despite their distracting touches.

"Tomorrow," Colt says firmly. "Tonight is about us." He pulls back, his eyes searching mine with an intensity that makes my breath catch. "We've been wanting to talk to you about something else. Something that's been on our minds."

Nash's grip tightens possessively as he adds, "Something we think you might be ready for soon with a little preparation."

The shift in their tone makes my stomach flutter with nervousness and anticipation. "What is it?" I ask.

Nash steps forward, his eyes filled with concern. "Little bird, we want to start preparing you and explore something wilder tonight. It's been building between us for a while, and we think you might be ready to prepare for the next step."

My stomach drops. "What do you mean?"

Colt's gaze is unwavering. "We want to be inside you at the same time. We've both fantasized about it, but only if you're comfortable with trying to work up to it."

My breath catches in my throat as the implications of their words sink in.

"Are you sure?" I ask, my voice shaking slightly. "I... I don't know if I can handle both of you."

Colt's eyes soften. "You can do it, angel. We'll go slow. Make sure you're ready. But we want to give you that pleasure."

My cheeks flame with heat, and I can't meet their eyes. The idea of it both thrills and scares me.

"Have you ever..." Colt trails off, his voice gentle. "Have you ever had anal sex before?"

The question snaps me back to reality, my nervousness fading as the memories rush in.

"Once," I whisper, my gaze fixed on the floor. "The night they both... the night they first raped me." The words tumble out, and I wince, hating the lingering shame. "They both took turns. It was rough, and I... I bled."

Silence falls as the weight of my admission hangs between us. I feel Colt's hands on my shoulders, his thumbs gently rubbing.

"Fuck, I'm sorry," Nash's voice is thick with anger. "We didn't know. We would never—"

"No," I interrupt, shaking my head. "No, I want to. I really do. But..." I bite my lip, hesitating to voice my deepest fantasy.

"But what?" Colt prompts, his thumbs pausing as he waits for my answer.

"I want the masks," I blurt out, rushing the words out before I can change my mind. "I want it like that first night, except with you both."

They're silent momentarily, and I peek up to see their reactions. Nash's eyes are hooded, while Colt's expression is unreadable.

Colt shakes his head. "I'm not sure that's a good idea. At least not tonight. We need to play with your ass a little, get it prepared, make sure there's no pain. And see how you feel afterward. This isn't something we can rush, especially not with your past experience with anal."

Tears fill my eyes as I've never had anyone who cares about me like Colt and Nash. The way they want to protect me, cherish me. I nod. "Okay, but can you wear the masks but keep it light? I love it when you wear them."

"If that's what you want." Nash kisses me softly. "We're going to help you heal. One step at a time."

"You sure about this, angel?" Colt's eyes are soft, but his voice is edged with hunger. "We don't want to push you too far."

My chest tightens at the thought. "I need it," I confess, even as my pulse pounds in my ears. "It's twisted, I know, wanting you to wear the masks. But it's what I want."

Colt nods. "Then it's what you'll get. We'll give you what you need."

Nash steps forward, his eyes burning. "We'll make you ours in every way that matters."

My knees weaken at his words, my body already preparing for what's to come. "Take the masks," I whisper, my voice husky with anticipation.

They don't need to be told twice. With practiced ease, they stride to one of the equipment boxes and retrieve the same masks from that first night I gave myself to them.

Colt turns to me, the mask dangling from his fingers. "Are you ready?" His eyes hold mine, searching for any hint of uncertainty.

I give a small nod, unable to speak past the dryness in my throat. I swallow, my eyes flitting to Nash.

He's looking at Colt. "I love seeing you in a mask, Colt," he admits, his voice tight. "Makes me wish my ass was ready to be fucked." His words shock me even as a coil of need tightens low in my belly.

Colt's eyes darken with need, and I see the same hungry spark ignite in Nash's gaze. "If your ass was ready, I'd bend you over right now and fuck you so hard, you'd still feel me tomorrow." His voice is a low rumble, and I shiver at the image his words evoke.

"Fuck," Nash breathes, his eyes half-lidded.

Colt's eyes burn into mine, and he steps toward me. "Would you like that? Watching us go at it in masks?"

The image sends a thrill through my body. I gulp, feeling lightheaded as a heat I've never known pools between my legs. "Yes," I whisper, the admission ripped from someplace deep inside.

Colt's eyes darken further.

I crave that darkness, the same darkness that seems to lurk inside me. They understand this about me. They know my needs and desires and never shame me for them.

"Get ready, little bird." Nash's voice is rough as he pulls the mask over his face.

I swallow, my pulse racing as Colt approaches, his eyes full of fiery intention.

Colt's eyes burn with a possessiveness that weakens my knees, but I know I can trust him and Nash. I know they'd never hurt me. Gently, he pulls down the straps of my leotard and pulls it down with my panties until they pool at my ankles. I step out of them, waiting for his next instruction.

"Get on your back like a good girl," Colt demands, his voice softer than usual.

I swallow hard and then lie on the practice mat as he says.

They both stare at me with fire in their eyes, Colt palming his growing erection in his pants.

"What are you waiting for?" I ask

Nash growls and approaches, dropping to his knees before me. "I'm going to fucking devour you," he murmurs.

Nash kneels between my legs, and I gaze up at him, his dark eyes flicking up to meet mine as he settles over my core. And then, he lifts his mask enough so his lips can access me. I moan softly as his tongue begins a slow exploration, drinking in my essence, igniting me from the inside out.

Colt drops to his knees beside me, his expression hungry as he watches his best friend feast on me. I reach up, tangling my fingers in Colt's hair, pulling him down for a kiss even as my hips undulate under Nash's skilled mouth.

Nash pulls back with a growl, his eyes full of hunger and something else. "You taste so sweet, little bird."

Colt releases my lips, his eyes on Nash. "I want to taste her, too."

My breath hitches as Nash nods.

Colt lifts his mask higher so his lips are free, and I cry out as their tongues touch, duel, and dance together over my clit.

I thread my fingers through their hair, moaning as they consume me. Their mouths work in tandem, sucking, licking, and nibbling as I writhe beneath them. My hips buck as a coil of pleasure tightens in my core.

Nash's fingers slide into my entrance, and I cry out, overwhelmed by the sensation. Colt pulls back, his eyes searching mine as Nash finger fucks me. I'm already so wet, so ready, and his ministrations have me trembling on the edge.

"Give in to us, angel." Colt's voice roughens. "Let us watch as you break."

I cry out, my back arching as pleasure erupts within me. Nash laps at my essence, his digits working in and out, while Colt kisses me, swallowing my cries.

As my tremors subside, they pull away. My chest heaves as I soak in the afterglow, my mind floating in a haze of pleasure.

"Are you up for it?" Colt queries, his eyes burning into mine, reflecting deep desire and serious worry. "We'll ease into this, and I'll be right here with you. If it feels off, you just say the word, and we'll hit pause."

My heart hammers against my ribs. I know this will be different than those horrific nights when Tommy and Jake forced themselves on me. I trust Colt and Nash to guide me through this. Their touch has brought me only pleasure and healing.

"I'm ready," I whisper, giving a small nod to reinforce my words.

Colt cups my cheek gently.

"It's okay to change your mind," Nash adds, his voice soft. "We can do this another time."

I shake my head more adamantly, meeting Colt's gaze. "I want this. I want to heal with you both."

Their eyes soften, and a silent communication passes between them.

"Okay, let's get you on your hands and knees." Colt helps me turn over, and I lie facedown, grateful for the soft padding underneath me. "Nash, why don't you talk her through it? I'll take charge of stretching her slowly."

I suck in a sharp breath as I feel Colt's fingers trace the crease of my ass, sending a shiver of anticipation through me.

"Just relax, little bird," Nash murmurs. "Focus on taking long, slow breaths. You're safe with us, and we won't go any faster than you can handle."

I nod mutely, feeling Colt's fingers caress my hole.

"That's good, angel," Colt says, his voice a low rumble. "Now, I'm just going to rub some lube between your cheeks." I feel the slick sensation as he coats his fingers. "This might feel cold."

"Empty your mind, Flora," Nash encourages. "Focus on my voice. Breathe with me."

I try to relax as Colt's lubed fingers make gentle circles, teasing my hole. I bite my lip, tensing slightly.

"Just like that, angel," Colt murmurs, his tone soothing. "Breathe for me, and I'll gently slide one finger inside."

The pad of his finger teases my entrance, and I suck in a breath, my body momentarily tensing.

"Easy," Nash says, his fingers stroking my hair. "You're doing so well. Relax and let him in."

I nod, breathing more rapidly now, and Colt's finger

slips inside me. I gasp, my body adjusting to the intrusion. It's different entirely from what I experienced before. It's not unpleasant at all.

Colt's finger moves in and out gently. "You're so tight, baby."

"You're handling this beautifully," Nash praises, his fingers continuing gentle strokes through my hair. "Feel Colt's finger inside you. It doesn't hurt, does it?"

I shake my head, moaning softly as the discomfort gives way to pleasure. "No, it feels good."

"Good girl," Colt rumbles, his deep voice reverberating through me. "Now I'm going to add a second finger."

Colt applies more lube, and I sense another slick finger brushing against me. "Just ease into it and give me a slight pushback," Colt instructs. "You're handling this beautifully.

I do as he says, pushing back slightly, and he slides another finger into me, stretching me further.

"Just like that, angel," he admires, his fingers gliding smoothly. "You're taking both of my fingers effortlessly."

I moan, my body surrendering to the unusual but not unpleasant sensation. Their voices wash over me, guiding me through it. I feel so safe with them, so treasured. It's the complete opposite of anything I experienced before.

"You ready for more, little bird?" Nash asks, his voice full of anticipation. "Ready for a small dildo next?"

The words send a jolt of excitement through me,

and I nod eagerly, my body humming with desire. "Yes," I breathe. "I think so."

Colt gently pulls out his fingers, leaving me feeling empty, and retrieves something from the drawer behind. I hear the sound of lube squirting, and then Colt passes something to Nash.

"Look at this beauty," Nash says. I turn my head slightly to see he's holding a dildo which is half the girth of either of their cocks and much shorter. Not intimidating at all.

"You sure about this, Flora?" Nash asks gently, holding up the toy.

"I'm sure," I breathe, my heart pounding.

Colt moves behind me as I stay on my hands and knees, his hand ghosting over my clit, teasing and bringing me back to the edge of desire. His other hand slides the well-lubed tip of the dildo back to my hole, using just the very tip to tease my rim.

"Just like this," he whispers. "We'll go slower than slow."

"You're doing amazing," Nash praises, kneeling beside me. "Absolutely perfect."

I tense slightly as Colt pushes harder, the tip stretching my rim wider. My body clenches involuntarily around the intrusion, and he holds still, waiting for me to adjust.

"Just let yourself unwind," Nash reassures. "There's no need to rush. We can take as long as we want."

My body relaxes at Nash's encouragement and how patient they are. Colt begins to tease the dildo in and out, just breaching the tight ring of muscle each time.

My breath comes in gasps, my focus narrowing to the sensations.

"Good girl," Colt says softly, his fingers caressing my clit. "You're handling the toy like a dream."

Nash's lips find mine, his mouth moving urgently against my own as the dildo pushes into me further. I moan into his mouth, my body welcoming the slight burn.

Colt's finger drags through my pussy lips. "God, you're so wet," he groans, his voice thick with need. "So fucking responsive."

Nash kisses his way along my jaw, his tongue tracing the shell of my ear. "It's true, Flora," he breathes. "You have no idea how good it feels to watch you being such a good girl." His lips brush against mine, his mouth hovering just over mine as he speaks. "Knowing that you trust us like this to make you feel good."

I whimper as Colt's fingers slip inside my pussy, curling to find that special spot. "You're dripping, angel. So perfect just for us."

Nash kisses me deeply, his tongue plundering my mouth even as Colt's dexterous fingers stoke my pleasure higher. "Tell us what you want, Flora," Nash urges.

"I want Colt to fuck my pussy while keeping that dildo in my ass," I murmur, my clit throbbing at the thought. "And I want Nash's dick in my mouth."

"You're doing so good, baby," Colt croons, his words like a caress even as he continues to work his fingers deep into my soaked core, stroking that special spot that has me arching and mewling.

I cry out, my walls clenching around his fingers as pleasure spirals through me.

"God, she's amazing," Nash breathes his mouth still against mine, capturing my groans with his lips.

Their praise fuels the flame of my desire, and I groan as Colt's fingers continue to play with my clit. "Please," I whimper, caught between need and a slight discomfort from the dildo.

This time will be different. I'm exploring this with men who would never hurt me.

29

COLT

Flora is a vision. Completely and utterly surrendering to us despite all she's been through. Slowly, I ease the dildo out of her ass.

She whimpers. "No, don't stop."

I chuckle softly. "Don't worry, I will put it back in. I just need to make sure you've got loads of lube in your ass with the dildo before I enter your pussy." I squirt copious amounts of lube onto the dildo and her hole.

I admire Flora's exquisite frame while slowly pushing the dildo back inside her ass, watching her delicate muscles submit with each small movement. She's so fucking responsive, and damn, she looks perfect like this. Her hair tumbles over her shoulders, and her back arches delicately.

"You ready, angel?" My voice is low and rough, and I can't hide the edge of my own need.

"I want you, Colt. I want to feel you inside me. Please." Flora's words send a shot of desire straight to my dick.

Slowly, carefully, I position myself at her entrance. Nash kneels in front of her, stroking himself as he watches our every move. He's breathing heavily, his eyes burning with need.

I trail my hand down her spine, feeling the graceful slope of her back, before curling my fingers around her hip. She's trembling slightly, and I wish I could erase the fear that lingers within her.

"Take a breath and relax, Flora. We're gonna go slow. Remember, you're safe with me." Leaning forward, I kiss her shoulder softly, and her skin is warm beneath my lips. "Trust me."

She nods and takes a steadying breath. "Okay. I'm ready."

Guiding myself with my hand, I push into her slowly, feeling her tightness stretch around me with the dildo in her ass. "That's it, angel. So fucking perfect."

Easing in, I take my time to watch her reactions, not wanting to hurt her. "You doing good? Tell me if I need to stop."

"No, don't stop. It's okay."

Hearing that, I push further, letting her adjust to my length. Pulling my hand from her hip, I move it down, rubbing slow circles around her clit. "You feel so damn tight with that dildo in your ass, Flora. Taking me so perfectly."

I begin to move, slowly at first, dragging my length almost all the way out before pushing back in, finding a rhythm that has her rocking back into me.

Nash's voice is deep and rough as he leans closer.

"That's right, little bird. Embrace what he's offering. It feels amazing, doesn't it?"

She whimpers, nodding. "Yes."

Nash kneels, his dick hard and straining. A rush of desire shoots through me, seeing him like that.

"Can I?" Her voice is hesitant. "Can I suck your cock, Nash?"

Jesus, the words coming out of her mouth drive me crazy.

"Are you sure, little bird?" His voice is hoarse, and he reaches out, tucking a strand of hair behind her ear. "We don't want to overwhelm you."

Flora nods, her eyes dropping to his cock and then back up to meet his gaze. "I want to."

Nash's breath hitches. "Fuck."

Then he's shifting forward to rest his dick against her lips. "Take it slow, okay? If it's too much, just use your hand to push me away."

"Mmm," she hums, leaning toward him.

Nash groans as her lips wrap around him, and he threads his fingers into her hair, holding her gently.

Fuck, the sight of Flora taking Nash into her mouth has my cock twitching inside her. I don't think I'll ever get used to this—the heat of needing her mixed with the rush of letting go of control.

I curl my hand around the nape of her neck as I thrust into her, watching Nash's face. Every emotion I feel is mirrored in his expression. He watches her mouth on his cock, like he can't get enough. Every time she moves, his eyes flutter closed, and small sounds escape his throat.

"You're doing so good, Flora. So fucking amazing." I groan, my voice harsh in the room, and my hips stutter as I fight the urge to be rougher.

Nash's eyes lift to meet mine, and I see my need reflected in his rich brown eyes.

"Damn, Flora. Your mouth was made to suck cock." Nash's voice is gruff as he holds her head, guiding her.

I laugh harshly, my hips stilling as I fight to stay in control. "No shit. She was fucking made to take us both in all holes."

Flora whimpers around Nash's length. Everything about her response is pure perfection. Every single muscle in her body is designed to take us. I wish I could erase every bad thing that happened to her in her past.

Nash's eyes are on me and that same need, that longing between us. Our connection is like a live wire crackling with electricity.

I find a steady rhythm that has her rocking back, meeting my every thrust.

The drag of the dildo against my dick feels good as it moves in her ass with the rhythm of my thrusts, the way her back arches to take more of me. All of it is perfect.

"Jesus, Flora." Nash's voice is wrecked, his fingers tightening in her hair. "Gonna come if you keep that up, little bird."

She moans around him, sucking him deeper. I grip her hip tighter, my other hand sliding to her clit as I start to pound into her, driving us both toward the edge. "So fucking tight. Come for us, angel. Let us feel every wave of your pleasure."

She whimpers, and Nash's hand tightens in her hair as he pushes her down, his hips stuttering as he spills down her throat with a guttural groan. The sound sends Flora off the edge as she spasms around me. Her pussy so fucking tight with the dildo in her ass. I can only imagine how good it will feel with Nash beside me. One more thrust into her, and I come hard, my cock twitching as I mark her, claim her as mine.

We're both spent, breathing heavily and slowly. I withdraw from her body, my cock still semi-hard. I trail the tips of my fingers along her ass cheek affectionately before withdrawing the dildo.

Nash slides his cock from her mouth, looking at her with a mix of awe and hunger. He pushes her hair back behind her ear, and she meets his gaze, her eyes clear and full of need.

"You're incredible, Flora. Fucking beautiful." Nash's voice is raspy, and he kisses her forehead softly.

She's smiling at him, her eyes half-lidded as she drops onto her back on the practice mat. I lie down beside her, and she turns to me, her eyes bright and soft, and my chest aches. Her smile is warm as she reaches out, caressing my face softly.

"Thank you," she whispers. "Both of you." A stray tear rolls down her cheek.

Nash mirrors my position on her other side. I glance at him, knowing he's feeling the same mix of emotions that I am. It's not just sex anymore; there's an emotional bond that's formed.

We lie there for a while, the three of us enjoying the afterglow. I run my fingers through Flora's hair, brushing it back from her face, and she hums softly, nuzzling into my touch. I glance at Nash, seeing the same tenderness in his eyes that I feel, and I know we're all exactly where we belong.

30

NASH

I adjust Flora's costume again, ensuring every strap is secure. The Christmas lights twinkle throughout the big top, creating a magical atmosphere for tonight's show. My hands tremble slightly as I check her rigging—not because of the performance but what comes after.

"Your form is perfect, little bird," I whisper, watching her stretch. Her grace in the air has become flawless over these past weeks of training. Even with Colt sidelined by his injury, we've created something beautiful.

The tent fills with excited chatter as the audience files in. I catch sight of Colt in the wings, his shoulder wrapped but healing well. He gives us both a subtle nod, signaling everything is in place.

Flora's breath catches as she spots movement near the back entrance. I squeeze her hand, reminding her she's safe. We've planned this carefully. Tommy and Jake won't know what hit them when they try their ambush after the show.

"Focus on the performance," I remind her, though my heart races. "Nothing else exists except you and me in the air."

The music starts to swell as Tyson's voice booms through the tent, introducing our act. Flora takes her position on the platform, her sequined costume catching the spotlight. Despite everything weighing on us, her smile remains genuine as she gazes down at the crowd.

I climb up beside her, checking our rigging one last time. Years of experience tell me everything is secure, but tonight, I take no chances. Not with Flora's safety on the line.

The familiar pre-show tension coils in my muscles, but it's different tonight. Usually, I'm only thinking about nailing every move, every transition. My mind keeps drifting to what awaits us after the final bow.

Tyson finishes his introduction. The spotlight finds us. Flora's hand finds mine as we prepare for our first synchronized drop. Whatever happens later, right now, we have a show to perform.

The music swells as Flora and I move through our first sequence. Her movements mirror mine perfectly—each twist and turn executed with a grace that makes my chest swell with pride at her accomplishment in such a short time with us, though somehow it still feels incomplete.

My eyes drift to Colt on the ground below. He's watching us intently, his good arm crossed over his chest, the injured one held close to his body. This isn't right.

He should be up here with us, not relegated to spectator, and he will be as soon as he is fully healed.

Flora releases into a perfect split as I catch her wrists. The audience gasps, but I barely notice. I can only focus on how different this feels without Colt's steady presence. We've worked out a beautiful routine, Flora and me, but it's like performing with only two-thirds of my soul.

The three of us belong together—in the air, on the ground, everywhere. I see it in the way Colt's free hand clenches by his side, fighting the urge to grab the ropes. I feel it in the slight hesitation before each of Flora's releases, knowing Colt isn't there to catch her.

I guide Flora through another sequence, but my mind keeps drifting to what comes after the show. They think they're the hunters tonight, but Colt and I have prepared. We'll turn their planned ambush into their worst nightmare. Tommy and Jake won't know what hit them.

My muscles tense with anticipation as Flora executes another perfect split. Soon enough, those bastards will pay for every mark they left on her, every nightmare. Colt and I have discussed this for weeks, planning each detail. The tools are at the ready in the back of my truck.

Flora transitions into her next pose, trusting me completely. The irony isn't lost on me—while she performs up here, her tormentors lurk below, thinking they'll catch her vulnerable after the show.

Once we've dealt with them, we can be together without these shadows hanging over us. No more looking over our shoulders, no more fear in Flora's eyes when she spots a familiar face in the crowd. Just us, whole and complete, how we're meant to be.

I help Flora down from the rigging, my heart still racing from the performance. The applause thunders through the tent as Ty wraps up the show with his signature flair. His approving nod tells me everything I need to know—we nailed it, even without Colt up there with us.

I guide Flora through the back curtain, where Colt waits for us. His face is lit up with pride. My skin tingles when I see him, still not used to acknowledging these feelings openly.

"You were incredible up there, angel." Colt pulls Flora into his arms, capturing her lips in a deep kiss that catches my breath. "Every move was perfect."

"She's a natural," I agree, scanning the area to ensure we're alone.

"Couldn't have done it without Nash's guidance and all the hours of rehearsal we put in." Flora's cheeks flush from Colt's praise.

After one final check that no one's around, Colt turns to me. His good arm slides around my waist, pulling me close as his lips find mine. The kiss is hungry, passionate—everything we've held back for years.

Flora watches us with darkened eyes as we break apart. I can't resist pulling her in, tasting Colt on her lips as I kiss her. Soon, we're trading kisses between the three of us, hands roaming, breath quickening in the shadows.

Colt groans against my mouth. "We need to stop."

He pulls back, though his hand lingers on my hip. "We have work to do first and can't afford to get distracted."

I nod, forcing myself to focus despite the heat coursing through my veins. He's right—we have more pressing matters before properly celebrating tonight's performance.

31

FLORA

Walking steadily toward our trailer, my heart hammers against my ribs with each step. The gravel crunches beneath my feet, echoing in the quiet night air. Every shadow makes me flinch, but I keep moving forward.

The texts from Tommy and Jake flash through my mind. Their threats. Their plans. I know they're waiting, thinking they'll catch me alone.

My hands tremble as I clutch my bag closer to my body, the familiar weight of it offers no comfort.

The carnival's usual vibrant atmosphere feels muted now, most workers having retired for the night. Only a few distant lights illuminate my path. The space between trailers creates dark pockets perfect for an ambush, but I continue forward. Each step brings me closer to where they plan to grab me.

A twig snaps somewhere behind me. I jump but don't run. Instead, I lift my chin higher and keep walking, remembering Nash and Colt's words about being strong and trusting them.

The wind rustles through the trees, carrying the faint scent of cotton candy and popcorn from the shuttered concession stands. Our trailer comes into view; its familiar outline is a beacon of safety and the designated spot for their attack. My pulse quickens as I approach the location they mentioned in their messages.

Movement flickers at the edge of my vision. Footsteps crunch behind me, getting closer. I feel their presence before I see them, the same suffocating dread I lived with for years creeping up my spine. But this time is different. This time, I'm not their helpless victim.

Putting one foot before the other, I fight every instinct to run. The footsteps grow louder, more deliberate. They're close now—so close I can hear their breathing.

A hand clamps over my mouth, muffling my scream as strong arms wrap around my body from behind. Panic surges through me, freezing me in place. The scent of sweat and cheap cologne assaults my senses, and I know instantly who has grabbed me.

Jake. My foster brother. My abuser.

Jake drags me backward, his grip bruising. I thrash against him, trying to break free, but he's too strong. Fear chokes me even though I know Colt and Nash are waiting nearby.

"Thought you could get away from us, you little slut?" Tommy hisses. "You belong to us. Always have, always will."

Tears sting my eyes, but I blink them back. I won't

let them see me cry. Not again. My heart pounds as they haul me further into the shadows.

Jake laughs, cruel and cold. "We're going to remind you of your place, Flora. Remind you what happens when you try to escape us."

Their words make me want to vomit. Memories of pain and humiliation flood my mind. Years of abuse, of being treated as their personal sex slave with no say in what happened. I want to scream, to fight, but terror has me frozen in its grip.

Suddenly, they stop. I hear the approaching footsteps. Jake's hand tightens over my mouth, cutting off my air. Tommy grabs me around the waist.

"Well, well, well," a familiar voice drawls. "What do we have here?"

Colt's voice cuts through the darkness. Relief floods me, even as Tommy and Jake's grips tighten painfully. Even though I knew he was there, hearing his voice immediately eases my terror.

"Let her go," Nash commands, stepping out of the shadows beside Colt. They both have tranquilizer guns trained on my captors.

Tommy snarls, yanking me back like a human shield. "Back off! She's ours."

Colt's eyes narrow. "Wrong answer."

Two darts fly through the air, finding their marks with deadly accuracy. Tommy and Jake jerk as the tranquilizers hit, their hold on me loosening. I break free, rushing forward into Nash's waiting arms.

He catches me, holding me close as Tommy and

Jake crumple to the ground behind me. "I've got you, little bird. You're safe now."

I cling to him, my body shaking from the adrenaline. Colt moves to stand guard over my unconscious abusers, his expression deadly.

"It's okay, Flora," Nash murmurs, stroking my hair. "They'll never hurt you again. We promise once we deal with them, this will all be over. Forever."

I bury my face against his chest, letting his strength and warmth anchor me. The night's chill seeps into my bones, but Nash's embrace keeps it at bay.

Colt zip-ties Tommy and Jake's wrists and ankles before turning to us. "Let's get out of here so we don't end up with any witnesses. We have some trash to dispose of."

Nash nods, guiding me away from the scene. I lean on him heavily, my legs unsteady as the adrenaline crash sets in. He supports my weight without complaint, half-carrying me toward the truck.

As he helps me into the passenger seat, I catch a glimpse of Colt hoisting Tommy's limp body over his shoulder. A tiny part of me feels like I should be horrified, but all I can muster is grim satisfaction. They deserve what is coming to them, and I can't wait to be part of it.

Nash slides into the driver's seat beside me, reaching over to gently buckle my seatbelt. "Are you sure you want to be a part of this, little bird?"

I stare straight ahead as Nash's question hangs in the air. My fingers clench into fists on my thighs, knuckles white with determination. The memories of years of abuse flood my mind—every violation, any sense of security ripped from me—leaving me helpless against them, fodder for their disgusting debauchery.

"Yes," I say. "I need to be there."

Nash's hand covers mine. "It won't be pretty."

"Nothing about what they did to me was pretty either; they don't deserve pretty." The words come out sharp and bitter. "They took everything from me. My innocence, my trust, my sense of safety. For two years, I lived in terror of their footsteps outside my door at night."

I turn to face Nash, meeting his dark gaze. "I need to see the fear in their eyes. I need them to know what it feels like to be powerless. To understand that they chose the wrong girl to break."

"They'll suffer," Nash promises, his thumb stroking over my knuckles. "Colt and I will make sure of that."

"Good." I lean back against the seat, a strange calm settling over me. "I don't just want to watch—I need to participate. They need to see me strong, not as their victim anymore."

Nash studies my face for a long moment. "You understand what that means? There's no going back from this."

"Going back became impossible the moment they first raped me," I say quietly. "This isn't about going back. It's about moving forward. About taking my power back."

Colt climbs into the passenger's side. "Ready to go. Let's get this show on the road."

Nash clears his throat. "Flora wants to be involved in dealing with these pieces of shit."

Colt raises a brow. "Is that true, angel?"

I nod. "I need to make them pay. I want to see the fear in their eyes when they realize we've taken their power away."

"You're so fucking sexy when you talk like that," he growls, his eyes glittering with hunger. Colt kisses me with a fervor that takes my breath away. His lips crush mine. This kiss differs from the others, fueled by the darkness we're about to enter. It's a claim, a promise of what's to come. The kiss leaves me dazed, my body thrumming with need.

I meet his gaze, no longer afraid of the desire burning there. Colt's thumb strokes my bottom lip. His touch is searing. "And we will, angel. We'll ensure they know what it feels like to be powerless."

He kisses me again, his mouth slanting over mine. My lips part against his, inviting him in. His tongue tangles with mine.

Breaking the kiss, he trails his lips along my jaw, moving down to my neck. I tilt my head to the side, granting him better access.

Nash starts the engine. "We should get going." Nash's voice is calm, but I sense the steel underlying his words.

"Yeah." Colt's lips linger on my pulse point, his warm breath tickling my skin. "Time to go teach those bastards a lesson."

I turn to Nash. "Let's get the show on the road."

His eyes search mine, his thumb brushing my knuckles. "Just know, you don't have to prove anything to us."

I squeeze his hand, gratitude washing over me. "I'm doing this for me."

The drive to the lockup is no more than ten minutes, but it stretches like an eternity. When we finally pull into the abandoned parking lot, Nash reverses the truck to a unit's doors.

"Colt and I will get the trash into the unit. You just get inside and keep warm," Nash says, jumping out of the truck and opening the trunk. Colt pulls Jake out, and Nash pulls Tommy out, both rough with them already. They're not conscious yet, but the game will begin once they are. Time to exact my revenge alongside my two guardian angels of death.

32

COLT

I stand in the doorway of our makeshift prison, watching Tommy and Jake struggle against their bonds. The dim light catches their faces, illuminating the fear that replaces their usual arrogance.

"Ready?" Nash's voice comes from behind me.

Flora stands between us, her chin high, eyes fixed on her former tormentors.

The lockup smells of metal and dust. With Ty's blessing, we've prepared this space carefully, although I didn't exactly detail what I had planned for it.

I flex my fingers, remembering every detail Flora shared about their abuse. The rage burns hot in my chest, but I keep it controlled. This isn't about losing control—it's about justice.

Nash has laid out our tools on a small table. Everything is neat and organized. That's his way. He is always methodical, even in vengeance.

Flora steps forward first, her strength showing in

every movement. She's not their victim anymore. She's become something they should fear.

Tommy tries to speak through his gag, but I shake my head. "You lost your right to words long ago."

Jake's eyes dart between the three of us, finally understanding the gravity of their situation. This lockup has seen its share of justice served, but tonight feels different. It feels special.

I catch Nash's eye, and we share a silent moment of understanding. These men hurt our girl, and now they'll learn the true meaning of the consequences of their actions.

Flora's hands tremble as she pulls on the latex gloves we've offered her. She has every right to vengeance. Nash and I intend to give her that power. We stand in solidarity, ready to follow her lead.

"How do you want to start?" I ask. I want to lay into these bastards, but this moment belongs to Flora.

Her gaze flicks to me, and she bites her lip. "I have something in mind."

Nash nods, his eyes never leaving Flora's face. "Whatever you want, we'll make it happen."

She takes a deep breath, and her hands stop trembling as her resolve strengthens. "They hurt me. They thought it was fun to use me like an object." Her eyes harden. "But I'm not an object. I'm a fucking person, and they took away my power."

I step forward, drawing closer to the men who dared to touch her. "This is where you take that power back. We'll make them sorry they ever laid a finger on you."

Her chin lifts, and her eyes glint with determination.

"I want to shove the handle of those hammers into their asses. Show them the kind of pain they inflicted on me."

My jaw clenches, but I nod, respecting her choice. "Then that's what we'll do." I hand her the hammer, and Nash passes her the lube. "Make them feel it."

She doesn't hesitate; she's thought about this moment. I understand that need. As Nash grabs Tommy down first, he starts to squeal as he's positioned on all fours. She presses the handle against Tommy's anus, and I see the memories flashing in her eyes. Her body shakes, but she doesn't back down. Her fingers wrap tighter around the hammer's grip, and she pushes.

Tommy screams, the sound muffled by his gag. Flora's gaze never leaves his face as she works the handle inside him, centimeter by centimeter. She has the satisfaction of watching him squirm, his eyes widening with shock and pain.

"That's it, angel," I murmur. "Take your time."

Flora's breath comes in shallow pants, and her eyes burn with a fierce light. The hammer slides deeper, eliciting more desperate noises from Tommy. When she finally stops, his body is trembling, and the fear in his eyes matches what Flora must have felt.

"Your turn, Jake," she says. "Let's see how much you can take."

They sob, begging for mercy behind the gags, but Flora isn't done. She's prepared to mete out the same treatment they gave her, and even this is only a fraction of what she felt. Nash and I stand sentinel, ready to support her to carry out her vengeance. We each have our ghosts, and Flora is facing her head-on.

I reach out, squeezing her shoulder. "You're doing great."

Her eyes find mine, shimmering with unshed tears. "Thank you," she mouths.

I step back, giving her space to finish what she started.

My chest is tight with a mix of emotions while I watch her. This woman, this beautiful, fierce angel, has endured so much, and now she's taking back her power. The rage inside me burns at the sight of her abusers. These men thought their actions had no consequences. They were somehow entitled to their evil depravity simply because they *wanted* it.

Her eyes shine with a wild light as she stares down at the men, sobbing at her feet. Jake and Tommy, the monsters who thought they could play their sick games without paying a price. The hammer still in her hand, she leans down, her face close to theirs, and begins to speak.

"You pieces of shit," she snarls, each word dripping with contempt. "Did you think you could get away with what you did to me? Did you think I'd stay quiet forever?"

Their eyes widen in fear as they hear her voice, strong and steady despite the tears streaking her cheeks. She's claimed her power, and she's not giving it back.

"You used me, hurt me, and thought it was funny. Well, how does it feel now, huh?" She digs the hammer's handle deeper into Jake, ignoring his whimpers. "Do you like it? Do you like being the ones on the receiving end?"

The man's eyes dart back and forth, desperate, pleading. But Flora doesn't show them mercy. They never gave her any, and she's not about to start a kindness campaign now. Her words slash at them, sharp and biting.

"Sluts," she growls, spitting the word like an insult. "Whores. You thought I was yours to play with, but look at you now. Pathetic, begging for mercy. You don't deserve it."

Their eyes plead with me, but I offer no comfort. Flora continues her verbal assault.

"No one's going to save you now," she whispers, her lips curved in a cruel smile. "You're mine, just like I was yours. And I plan to make you suffer, just like you made me suffer."

Their struggle intensifies, their eyes wild. Flora has become more than our angel; she's become the avenging angel who sets her demons free. Seeing her like this fuels the fire in my veins. She'll never again be a victim; the proof is her standing tall, holding their fate in her hands.

"Look at these hard dicks," she says, contempt in her voice. "Even now, you're getting off on this. You sick fucks."

Her words strike at the heart of their weakness, and they squirm, unable to deny the truth. I hold their gaze, letting them see the steel in my eyes. No pity. No escape.

"You're right, Flora," I murmur. "They're getting off on this."

With that, I reach down and grab their dicks,

pumping them hard, rough, as Flora watches, her eyes gleaming with dark desire.

"That's it, sluts," she breathes. "Get off on your own pain for a change. But remember, it's us who control this now. We hold the power."

And as their hips buck against my hands, their eyes pleading, I know that we've finally given Flora what she needs—a chance to rewrite her story and become the author of theirs.

33

FLORA

My fingers tighten around the handle of the hammer. I could have handled this in many ways, but this is best. The perfect punishment, an ass for an ass, if you will.

I couldn't have asked for more fitting instruments of revenge than Colt and Nash. Revenge is a sweet dish best served cold, and they're cold as ice.

I watch as Colt strokes their cocks, the muscles in his arms bunching. Tommy and Jake are bound and helpless on all fours.

"Don't let them come, Colt. They don't deserve it—I never did." My voice is steady despite the storm of emotions inside me. "This isn't about pleasure; it's about pain."

Nash arches one of his brows at me as my eyes meet his. I nod, and he understands. Time to stop playing and get serious. They've had their fun; now it's my turn. I yank the hammer carelessly out of Jake's ass and bring it down on Tommy's back with a satisfying thud. He screams, his voice echoing in the confined space.

"Let's see how tough you really are, Tommy. Let's see how you like a little pain." I bring the hammer down again and again. It's cathartic, freeing. Every swing of the hammer releases more of the weight I've carried since I turned sixteen.

I pause, looking at Jake, who is whimpering and struggling against his binds. "Your turn, Jake. Let's see how you like it." I stride over to him and slam the hammer into his back, relishing the sound of flesh meeting metal. "You both deserve this and so much more."

Nash moves to stand behind me, his chest pressing against my back. His arms wrap around me, holding me close as we survey the destruction we've wrought.

I don't want this to end. I want to stay in this moment, feeling powerful and in control. Nash's lips brush my ear as he whispers, "Trade me?" He takes the hammer from my hand, replacing it with a knife.

"Let's slow things down a bit, angel. We want to savor this, don't we?" He slides the knife into Jake's ass cheek, twisting it slightly. Jake screams, his voice piercing the silence. "That's it, scream for us. Let us feast on your fear for a change. After all, it's only fair, right?"

I wield the knife, my hands trembling. I want to draw this out, too, and make them pay for every moment of pain they inflicted on me. I bring it to Tommy's back, running it across his flesh hard. "I'll give you something to scream about."

Colt leans against the wall, a satisfied smile on his

face. "She's got a talent for this, Nash. I think she might be a natural."

Nash winks at me, his dimples flashing. "Oh, I know she is. Our little bird has been hiding her sharp edges." He pulls another knife from his pocket and slices the knife across Jake's back. "Beautiful, Flora. Keep going."

I step forward, the knife in my hand feeling like an extension of myself. Something inside me has shifted, and I feel powerful beyond measure.

"That's it, angel. No need to rush," Colt says, his voice a low rumble. "Take your time and enjoy it."

I turn back to Tommy, digging the knife in a little deeper, a spark of satisfaction igniting within me as he cries out.

"Please," he begs through his gag, his voice breaking. "Stop, please."

Colt laughs; the sound is cruel and void of any compassion. "Not a chance, Tommy boy. You've only just begun to suffer."

I work the knife across Tommy's back, creating a crisscross pattern that mirrors Nash's handiwork on Jake. The blade slices flesh like a warm knife through butter, and I feel a rush of heady power.

"That's perfect, Flora," Nash says, his voice steady. "You were made for this."

I smile, feeling a sense of pride. Cutting them is almost like cutting away the pain they inflicted on me, slicing through the scars they left on my soul.

Colt moves to stand behind me, his body a solid presence at my back. His arms come around me, guiding my hand, making the cuts deeper. "That's it, angel. Let it all out."

I lean into him, relishing his strength. Together, we cut, marking their flesh, our rhythmic movements in sync. Jake and Tommy's pleas and screams fill the room, music to my ears.

"You thought you could get away with it," Nash says. "You thought you could hurt her, and there would be no consequences."

"But you were wrong," Colt continues. "We're here now, and we're not going to stop until she's satisfied that she has gotten her pound of flesh."

I'm covered in blood, and I've never felt more alive. I glance down at Tommy and Jake. Their bodies are broken, bleeding, and bruised, but they're still breathing.

Nash's hand on my arm startles me, and I stop. My chest rises and falls with the effort of catching my breath, my hands clutching the knife tightly. I glance at him, then at Colt, and I see the blood that spatters their clothes and skin. They're splattered with my revenge.

"That's enough, angel," Nash says, his voice quiet. He must see a wild look in my eyes. Something has changed within me; something has clicked into place, and I want more.

But Nash's words bring me back to the present. I blink, looking down at the knife in my hand. I don't want to stop. I feel powerful, untouchable.

Nash and Colt have a primal hunger in their eyes. A dark desire that I can feel rolling off of them in waves, fueling my own desires. I want—no, I need—to touch them, to feel their skin against mine. But more than that, I want to own them, possess them, the way they've possessed me.

I step forward, driven by an impulse I don't fully understand. My hands reach for them, drawn by the fierce protectiveness they inspire.

Colt's eyes meet mine. "You've got fire in your eyes, angel. Put it somewhere useful." His hands palm the bulge in his jeans, and a wicked smile plays on his lips. "You look so fucking sexy like this. You were made for blood and darkness."

My breath catches in my throat at his words. I've never felt so alive, so in control. Hearing him say those words to seeing the raw desire in his eyes sets my blood on fire.

Nash steps closer, and I meet his gaze. "We're yours, Flora, like you are ours. Do with us as you will." He, too, palms himself through his jeans, the bulge straining against the denim.

I want to taste them, mark them as mine. My hands reach for their shirts, tugging them off, revealing their sculpted chests. I run my hands over their skin, feeling their warmth, their strength. I step closer, my body fitting perfectly between theirs.

Their lips find mine, mouths colliding in hunger and need. Our tongues tangle, dueling for dominance, each trying to take control. I kiss them both, my lips moving from one to the other.

Their hands are on me, palming my ass, pulling me closer. I can feel their cocks pressing into me, their desire matching my own. We move as a tangle of limbs and mouths, each seeking to satisfy the other.

Nash's lips leave mine, trailing kisses down my neck as Colt takes his turn, his mouth claiming mine in a passionate kiss. Their hands roam my body, setting my skin on fire and leaving trails of flame in their wake.

Colt's hands move to the button of my pants, popping it open with a feral urgency.

I pull away, gasping for breath. "Together," I rasp, my voice thick with desire. "I want you both at the same time."

"Are you sure you're ready for that, angel?" Colt asks.

Nash clears his throat. "Yeah, we only started prepping you yesterday."

I nod, knowing without a doubt that this is the perfect moment. Standing amidst the carnage of my vengeance, my heart pounding with primal exhilaration, our clothes are stained, but I don't care about the blood on my skin or the destruction around me. I can only focus on the two men before me, their eyes burning with the same fierce hunger within me.

"I need this," I utter, holding Colt's gaze. "I know you won't hurt me."

Colt steps forward, his hands reaching for the hem of my shirt. I let him pull it over my head.

Nash moves behind me, his hands already working to rid me of my bra. I arch my back, offering myself to him a silent invitation. Once I'm naked, both Colt and Nash step in front of me and start to undress each other, their eyes never leaving mine.

I want to touch, taste, and feel their skin against mine.

But Colt's hands are on me first, his lips close to my ear. "You like the sight of blood on us, angel? Turns you on?"

"Yes," I whisper, my eyes dropping to the sheen of blood that coats their skin. "It makes you even hotter."

A feral grin spreads across his face, and he lifts me, my body pressed against his. The hard planes of his chest press against my nipples, and I moan. My arms wrap around his neck, holding on as he settles me against him, his cock nestled between my legs, straining toward me.

Nash is behind me, his chest pressing against my back. I feel his lips on my shoulder, and then his hands glide down my spine, hitching my breath.

"You're so wet for us, baby," Colt murmurs, his dick teasing my core. "I can't wait to feel you around my cock." His mouth slants over mine in a hungry kiss. His tongue tangles with mine, dueling for dominance. One of his hands cups my ass, tilting my hips to meet the insistent press of his cock.

Nash's finger circles my ass, slick with lube. "Fuck," he growls. "I want to feel her tight ass around my cock, Colt."

Colt growls while Nash's finger pushes inside me, and I tilt my hips to grant him better access.

His finger thrusts, preparing me as I surrender to the sensations. I bury my face in Colt's neck, inhaling his scent, my body trembling with anticipation.

"That's it, baby," Nash murmurs, adding a second finger. "Relax for me; let me in."

Nash's fingers work inside me, stretching my ass. I rock my hips gently, my body instinctively seeking more.

"That's my good girl," Colt rasps, his lips against my ear. "Take it all, angel. Take what he's giving you."

Nash's fingers continue to work inside me, my body yielding to his touch.

Colt's hands squeeze my ass, encouraging me. "You're doing so good."

Nash's fingers slip out, and I whimper, my body yearning for more. But the sensation is quickly replaced by the broad head of a well-lubed dildo.

"Let's get you suitably stretched exactly how we did yesterday. Then, we'll see if you can take my cock," Nash instructs.

Colt holds me close, his strong arms wrapping around me, providing the comfort I didn't know I needed. I bury my face in his neck, breathing in his familiar scent, calming. He rests his chin on my head, and I feel his hands gently trace circles on my back, soothing away the lingering tension. Colt's hard cock pushes against my clit, and he makes slow movements as he rubs it against me, making me moan.

Behind me, Nash works the dildo, slick with lube, into my ass. I gasp at the stretch, but it's not as uncomfortable as the first time. My body relaxes around the intrusion, remembering the feeling. I tilt my hips, silently asking for more, needing it. "You're taking it so well, baby," Nash murmurs. "So perfect for us."

Colt shifts, his hands moving down to cup my ass,

gently spreading my cheeks, allowing more access as Nash guides the dildo deeper. Their touches are gentle, even as they prepare to claim me. I feel cherished and safe in their arms.

The dildo slips deeper, stretching me, filling me. I rock my hips back, seeking more, my body eager. Nash groans, the sound vibrating through me. "Fuck, she's so responsive. She's gonna take my cock so damn well."

Colt nuzzles my hair, his lips close to my ear. "I know. She's perfect. Just like this."

The dildo is slowly withdrawn, leaving me wanting more. I feel empty for a moment, and then Nash is behind me again, his hands gentle as he aligns himself with my entrance. He teases my opening with the head of his cock, and I whimper, needing him inside me.

"You're so ready for me, baby," he says, his breath hot on my neck. "But we're going to take this slow."

The broad head of his cock pushes inside, stretching me further. My breath hitches as I feel the burn, but it's a delicious discomfort that signifies the pleasure that will come.

Nash groans. "So tight… So. Fucking. Tight."

Colt's lips brush my ear. "You take him so perfectly, angel."

I nod, my body relaxing. Nash's hands squeeze my hips, holding me in place as his cock sinks deeper with each thrust. "You like that, little bird?" he demands. "My cock invading that tight ass of yours, stretching you wide?"

He bottoms out, his hips flush against my ass, and he groans, holding still.

I moan, the sound trapped against Colt's neck as he holds me through it.

"That's right, baby, feel it," Nash rasps, his hips beginning to move in a slow, steady rhythm. "Feel how deep inside you I am."

Colt looks into my eyes, his face a mask of pure desire. I can see the hunger burning in his eyes, mirroring the longing in my soul. He reaches down, his fingers dipping between my folds, his touch eliciting a gasp from my lips. I'm so sensitive from the intensity of the night, that the merest touch has me trembling.

"You're so wet, angel. So ready for me. I plan to make you even wetter."

My breath comes in short gasps. "Yes, please. I need you."

"Look at her, Colt. She's so fucking beautiful like this, begging for our cocks," Nash murmurs.

Colt's eyes never leave mine. "She's perfect, isn't she? Made for us to take." He kisses me, his tongue tangling with mine. When he breaks away, his eyes are so dilated it takes my breath away. "Are you ready to see if you can take me, too? We'll go slow. If you need to stop, just shout the word stop, and we will."

I nod in reply, desperate to feel my two men inside me at the same time.

"Good girl," he breathes, lining himself up with my pussy.

I brace myself, knowing the stretch that's about to come.

Slowly, he pushes inside, filling me inch by torturous

inch. The sensation is incredible, his thickness spreading me wide as he works his way deeper.

Nash's hands squeeze my hips. I'm sandwiched between their solid forms, suspended by them both in the air.

The blood is everywhere, splattered on their skin, coating the floors, and yet, in that moment, it's beautiful. A reminder of the power we hold, of the lives we've taken. Colt's hands are on my hips, Nash's around my waist, and they lift me up and down on their cocks. My body stretches to accommodate them. The sensation is overwhelming.

"I want to hear you, angel," Colt growls, his eyes burning into mine. "Both of us stretching you, filling you up. Let me hear those moans."

And I do as I'm told, moaning as they fuck into me in the most maddening rhythm.

Nash's lips ghost along the shell of my ear. "Our cocks are buried so deep inside you. This is where you belong, bouncing on our dicks like a good girl."

Up and down, their strong arms lift my body, impaling me on their cocks over and over. My back is pressed against Nash's chest. Colt's hands squeeze my hips, his lips pressing against my neck as he kisses me there.

"Fuck, yes," Colt hisses against my skin. "You take us both so well, baby."

Nash nuzzles the back of my neck. "Your body was made for us. It craves the feel of two cocks, the stretch, the burn. Doesn't it?"

"Yes," I gasp, my head falling against his shoulder. "Please, don't stop."

Colt's hands leave my hips, trailing up my body until they cup my breasts. "You like that? Being played with like our little toy?"

"Yes," I moan. "More."

Nash's teeth scrape my shoulder.

The pressure builds inside me, coiling tighter with each thrust. I can feel the pleasure radiating out from my core, spreading through my body like wildfire.

"Fuck, I'm close," Colt grunts, his hips snapping forward, driving his cock deeper. "Gonna come, angel. Gonna breed that perfect little cunt."

Nash's fingers move faster against my clit, his breath hot against my skin. "Me too, little bird. Gonna fill this beautiful ass."

The pleasure spirals out of control, and I cry out, my body shaking as my climax overtakes me. My back arches, pressing me closer to Nash. I can feel the hot rush of his release inside me. Colt comes a moment later, his cock pulsing inside me, his breath hot against my neck as he growls.

They hold me, our bodies still joined, their hearts pounding against my back. I feel Nash's lips press against my shoulder, his arms wrapped tightly around me, possessive even in the afterglow. Colt's arms are around me as well, his breath evening out as he holds me close.

I seek Colt's lips, needing to feel our connection. Our mouths collide, a passionate tangle of tongues and teeth, urgency still burning within us.

Nash's hands slide up my body, his palms caressing my skin. "You're beautiful, Flora. Wild and untameable."

Colt pulls back, his eyes searching mine. "You're ours. Never forget that."

I shake my head, my hands sliding up his chest to cup his face. "I won't. I'm yours. No matter where we go, the two of you are my home."

Nash nuzzles my neck, his lips pressing kisses along my jawline. "Ours to take, ours to keep."

I close my eyes, savoring the feel of them surrounding me, their warmth, their strength. I rest between them, their warmth cocooning me as my thoughts drift to how perfectly we fit together. It's more than just how our bodies connect—something deeper defies explanation.

From that first moment at the masquerade, when Nash called me "beautiful," I felt it. A pull, like gravity itself, was drawing us together. And Colt, with those knowing eyes that seemed to see straight through my defenses, understood me without a word.

They're so different, yet they complete each other. Colt's fierce protectiveness balances Nash's calculated control. Together, they make me feel whole in a way I never thought possible. My soul recognizes theirs, like puzzle pieces clicking into place after being scattered for too long. I'm home; we are home.

This isn't just love. Love feels too simple, too ordinary for what we share. This is primal, ancient—like we've danced together in past lives, always searching until we find each other again. They fill the broken spaces inside me, not by fixing them but by showing me that my edges match theirs.

34

NASH

Flora moves with practiced grace, perfectly synchronizing with Colt's as we clean the lockup. There's something beautiful about how she handles the bleach and rags—no hesitation or fear. Just pure focus.

Today felt cathartic for me, too. I know all too well the demons Flora has carried around. Even if I don't think about it very often. I experienced similar abuse at the hands of an older kid at a foster home for three years.

I wring out the cloth, watching crimson-tinged water swirl down the drain. Flora pauses her scrubbing, tucking a loose strand of hair behind her ear with the back of her wrist to avoid leaving marks.

"Well, I guess Santa won't stop by tomorrow night." She gives a hollow laugh. "Pretty sure I made the naughty list."

"No need to be good this year, angel," Colt says, his

voice carrying that dangerous edge that makes my skin tingle.

"We prefer you naughty," I add, catching her eye across the room.

Flora's cheeks flush pink, and she ducks her head to hide her smile. "Lucky me."

"Very lucky," Colt agrees, moving behind her to kiss her neck.

I watch them together, my chest tight with emotion. Even covered in bleach and wearing latex gloves, Flora looks ethereal. Her laughter echoes off the concrete walls, transforming this grim space into something lighter.

"You two are terrible influences," she says.

"Guilty as charged," I respond, tossing her a fresh rag.

I focus on methodically cleaning each surface, appreciating our comfortable silence. There's something intimate about working together like this—no words needed.

We've fallen into a natural rhythm, passing supplies back and forth without asking. The harsh chemical smell of bleach fills the air, but it can't diminish the warmth I feel watching them work.

Flora's ponytail swings as she scrubs, and Colt's muscles flex as he hauls another bucket. The tension from earlier has melted away, replaced by this strange peace.

Flora hums softly under her breath—some Christmas carol that seems oddly fitting despite our macabre activity. Colt shoots her an amused look but doesn't comment; he just keeps working with that hint of a smile on his lips.

"Pass me that bag," Colt murmurs, and Flora hands it over without breaking her rhythm. We've done this cleanup routine countless times before, Colt and me, but having Flora here feels right. Natural. She was always meant to be part of this, too.

I gather the tools while Colt handles the heavier items. As we finish our work, the floor gleams under the harsh lights. Not a spot is missed, and not a trace is left behind.

Flora stands between us, her shoulders relaxed, her head held high. Pride swells in my chest as I watch her. She's transformed from the scared girl who first came to us into someone stronger and darker, making us more complete.

I catch Colt's eye as Flora notices the metal hooks embedded in the wall. Her curiosity was bound to surface eventually.

"Why does the carnival have a place like this?" Flora asks, examining the drain in the center of the concrete floor. "It's pretty... specific."

"Sometimes the carnival needs private spaces," I say, keeping my tone casual while I wrap the last of our tools in plastic.

Colt snorts. "That's one way to put it." He tosses me a fresh rag, and I catch it without looking.

Flora raises an eyebrow, her hands on her hips. "Private spaces with industrial-grade cleaning supplies and reinforced doors?"

"Observant little bird," I say, impressed by her attention to detail. She's sharp—maybe too sharp for her own good.

"Just part of carnival life." Colt steps behind her, wrapping his arms around her waist. His deflection technique needs work, but Flora melts into his embrace anyway. "Speaking of which, we should get back. You've got silk practice in the morning."

"Nice try." Flora turns in his arms, poking his chest. "You two are hiding something. This place isn't just for... personal revenge."

I exchange a look with Colt over Flora's head. His jaw tightens.

"She'll figure it out anyway," I say to him, ignoring Flora's narrowed eyes. "You know how she is."

"Ty won't like it." Colt's arms tighten around Flora's waist. "We're not supposed to—"

"I'm right here," Flora cuts in, jabbing his chest. "Stop talking about me like I'm not in the room."

I step closer, running my fingers down her arm. "You're right. No more secrets between us."

"Nash—" Colt starts, but I shake my head.

"Fuck it. Ty can deal with it." I cup Flora's face, making her look at me. "We move product and use the carnival as a facade. Drugs, mainly cocaine. This lockup? It's one of many in all the areas where we deal. It's reserved in case we need to handle problems during deals."

Colt sighs. "Way to ease her into it."

"Would you rather I sugar-coated it?" I keep my eyes on Flora's face, watching for any sign of fear or disgust.

"We can't keep things from each other. Not anymore. Not after everything."

I study Flora's face, searching for any hint of revulsion or judgment. But there's only determination in those hazel eyes as they meet mine.

"I want in," she says. "Not just watching from the sidelines. I want to be part of everything you and Colt do."

Colt's arms tighten around her waist. "Angel, this isn't—"

"Don't." Flora cuts him off. "Don't tell me it's too dangerous. I've proven I can handle myself."

She's right. How she dealt with Tommy and Jake showed us exactly what she's capable of.

The way she handled those barrels of acid without hesitation still amazes me. Most people would have balked at the task, but not our girl.

She'd helped us roll the heavy containers into position, her delicate features set with determination. When I explained that burial wasn't an option due to the frozen ground, she simply nodded and asked for thick gloves. There were no questions, no squeamish reactions—just pure acceptance and efficiency.

The memory of her methodically helping to dismember the bodies and put them into the corrosive liquid makes my chest tighten with pride. She didn't flinch at the sizzling sounds or the acrid fumes. Just stood there, steady and focused, as what remained of her tormentors dissolved into nothing.

Colt was worried she might break down, but Flora proved stronger than we expected. She watched the process with an almost clinical detachment, those hazel eyes clear and unwavering. When the job was done, she simply peeled off her protective gear and asked what needed cleaning next.

That's what strikes me most about her practical approach to the whole thing. There were no dramatic reactions, no hysteria, just calm, collected movements as she helped us erase all evidence of Tommy and Jake's existence. It was as if she was born for this life, this darkness we share.

Those moments remind me why we chose her and knew she belonged with us. She may look delicate, but there's steel in her spine and ice in her veins when needed. The way she handled disposal proved that beyond any doubt.

Still, this is different. The carnival's operations are complex and dangerous, and one wrong move could bring everything down.

"I'll talk to Ty," I say, earning a sharp look from Colt. "What? She's already involved. Better to bring her in properly than have her stumbling around the edges."

Flora beams at me, that rare, genuine smile that makes her whole face light up. "Really?"

"Really." I brush my thumb across her cheek. "But we do this my way. You learn everything from the ground up. No shortcuts."

"Anything you want," she says. "I just... I need to be part of this. Part of you. Both of you. All of it."

I glance at Colt, who's watching us with apprehension. He knows as well as I do that once Flora sets her mind to something, there's no stopping her.

"I'll speak with Ty tomorrow," I tell them both. "For now, let's get out of here."

My hands shake slightly as I gather the cleaning supplies. This depth of emotion terrifies me. I've spent years keeping people at arm's length, letting no one except Colt get close. Even with him, I've kept certain walls up.

But Flora crashed through every defense we had, and now I'm standing here, watching the two people I love most in this world, feeling more exposed than I ever have.

The thought of losing either of them sends ice through my veins. I've never been this vulnerable, this dependent on others for my happiness. It should make me want to run. Instead, I move closer, drawn to their orbit like I always am.

Colt catches my eye over Flora's head, and I see the same emotions reflected in his gaze. He understands—he's always understood me better than anyone. Now we share this terror of losing what we've found, this precious thing between us that defies explanation.

I love them. Both of them. The realization isn't new, but it hits me fresh every time I see them together. The depth of it scares me more than anything I've ever faced.

35

COLT

I pace in our trailer, my jaw clenched tight as Nash lounges on the couch like he doesn't care. The rage I've been holding back finally boils over as Flora sleeps in my bedroom.

"You had no right to tell her everything about the operation," I snap, running my fingers through my hair. "She wasn't ready."

Nash raises an eyebrow. "Wasn't ready? Did you see her back there? She handled it better than most."

"That's what worries me." I stop pacing and face him. "No one should take to this life that easily. It's not normal."

"Nothing about our girl is normal," Nash says with a shrug. "She's special. You know that."

"Don't try to deflect. This is serious. You overstepped. We should have eased her in slowly and talked to Ty first."

"Lighten up, Colt. What's done is done. She knows now, and she wants to be part of it. All of it."

I slam my hand against the wall, making the whole trailer shake. It's not just that Nash told her. I'm pissed because he kept the entire shady operation a fucking secret from me for countless years. With Flora, he's suddenly an open book. "That's not your call to make! Ty needs to know what you've done. I have to tell him."

"Then we tell him." Nash stands up, his calm demeanor only fueling my anger. "He'll see what I see—that Flora is exactly where she belongs, doing exactly what she was meant to do."

"You better hope you're right," I growl. "Because if this blows back on us, it's your head on the line."

Nash smiles that infuriating smile of his. "Trust me, partner. When has my judgment ever steered us wrong?"

I turn away, grabbing my jacket.

Nash places a hand on my shoulder. "Is this really just about me telling Flora?" He demands.

I freeze. "What else would it be about?"

"You seem unusually angry about it. What's up?"

I growl and turn to him. "What's up?" I shake my head. "You kept this side of the carnival secret from me since we joined the carnival."

Nash's expression drops, and he runs a hand through his hair. "Not quite. Ty didn't bring me into that side of the operation until I was twenty-two. That was four years ago."

"Right, but you had no fucking qualms lying about it for years to your best friend."

Nash clenches his jaw. "Ty made the rules. He told me it had to remain between the four of us. Lars, him, and Phoenix."

"And yet, you tell Flora at the drop of a hat?"

Nash's lips quirk into a slight smile. "Are you jealous?"

I glare at Nash, my fists clenched at my sides. "Jealous? You think this is about jealousy?"

"I think you're hurt that I kept secrets from you," Nash says softly, stepping closer. "And you're right. I should have told you years ago."

"Damn right, you should have." The anger deflates from me slightly at his admission. "We're supposed to trust each other with everything."

Nash reaches out, his fingers brushing my arm. "I do trust you, Colt. More than anyone. Keeping this from you was the hardest thing I've ever done."

I shake my head but don't pull away from his touch. "Then why did you?"

"Because Ty ordered it. And because..." He pauses, looking uncertain for the first time tonight. "Because I feared losing you if you knew the truth about me. About what I'm capable of."

"You really think I'd judge you?" I step closer, closing the distance between us. "After everything we've been through?"

Nash's eyes meet mine, dark and intense. "No. I was being a coward."

The last of my anger melts away at the vulnerability in his voice. Without thinking, I reach up and cup his face in my hands. Nash's breath catches, his pupils dilating as I lean in.

Our lips meet hesitantly at first, then with growing intensity. Years of feelings pour into that kiss, making my head spin. Nash's hands grip my waist, pulling me closer as he deepens the kiss.

When we finally break apart, we're both breathing hard. Nash rests his forehead against mine, a small smile on his lips.

"No more secrets," I whisper against his mouth.

"No more secrets," he agrees, stealing another quick kiss. "I promise."

"Now, let's go and fix this mess," I say, turning and walking out the door. Ty needs to know what's happened. I hope he sees it Nash's way because we're all in trouble if he doesn't.

I follow Nash into Ty's office, still fuming about last night's revelations. The morning sun streams through the dusty windows, casting long shadows across Ty's desk, where he's reviewing paperwork.

"Well, if it isn't my star performers," Ty says, looking up with a grin. "That Christmas show was something else. The crowd couldn't take their eyes off Flora and Nash."

"She's a natural," Nash replies, settling into one of the chairs.

I remain standing, my shoulders tense.

"More than natural," Ty continues. "You two have done an incredible job training her. The way she moved on those silks... I haven't seen anything like it in years. And the chemistry between her and Nash? Perfect."

I shift uncomfortably, thinking of Flora sleeping back in our trailer, exhausted from everything last night. I want to tell Ty everything, but something holds me back.

"The ticket sales were through the roof," Ty says, shuffling through some papers. "We might need to add another show next week if this keeps up. You've really struck gold with her."

Nash shoots me a knowing look. "We told you she was special."

"That you did." Ty leans back in his chair. "I must admit, I had doubts when we brought her in. But she's proven me wrong. Whatever you're doing with her training, keep it up."

If he only knew what kind of "training" Nash had initiated her into last night. But watching Ty's genuine enthusiasm about the show's success makes me reconsider my earlier anger. Maybe Nash was right about Flora being ready for all of this.

I clear my throat, the words feeling like rocks in my mouth. "There's something else you need to know, Ty. About Flora."

Nash shifts in his chair but doesn't interrupt. Good. He got us into this mess—he can sweat it out while I clean it up.

"Nash told her everything last night. About the operation. The drugs. All of it."

Ty's expression hardens, his earlier warmth vanishing. He sets down his papers. "He did what?"

"She knows we use the carnival as a front for moving cocaine," I continue, forcing myself to hold Ty's gaze. "And before you ask—yes, she took it well. Too well, actually."

"That wasn't your call to make," Ty says, his voice deadly quiet. "Either of you."

"She deserves to know what she is getting into," Nash replies, unfazed. "Especially after what we did to those boys last night."

Ty's eyes narrow. "What boys?"

Shit. I shoot Nash a warning look, but he's already leaning forward in his chair. "Her foster brothers. The ones who hurt her. We took care of them."

The temperature in the room drops ten degrees. Ty's jaw works as he processes this new information. I brace myself for the explosion, but his voice is controlled when he speaks.

"So not only did you reveal our operation to an outsider, but you also committed murder without consulting me first?"

Nash growls. "Flora isn't an outsider. She's one of us."

"I told you I needed the lockup for something personal," I counter.

Ty's jaw clenches. "Right, but not *why* you needed it."

I lean forward, meeting Ty's gaze head-on. "Flora isn't just some outsider we brought in. She's with us. Both of us. Nash and me."

His expression shifts, but I press on before he can speak.

"And let me ask you something, Ty. What if it was Sofia?" I watch his face darken at the mention of his woman. "What if you found out that two men had been raping her for two years? That they'd invited their friends over to gang rape her?"

Nash tenses but stays quiet. Ty's knuckles turn white where they grip his desk.

"What would you do?" I continue. "Would you wait to get permission? Would you think twice about using that lockup? Or would you make them suffer like we did?"

Ty stands up slowly, his chair scraping against the floor. For a moment, the only sound in the office is his measured breathing.

"You're right," he finally says. "I'd have torn them apart with my bare hands."

"That's what we did," Nash adds. "For Flora. Because she's ours, just like Sofia is yours."

"I can't blame you for dealing with those bastards," Ty sighs, rubbing his temples. "But telling her about the drug ring?"

I shift my weight, feeling the tension in my shoulder. "How were we supposed to explain the lockup? The tools? Why did we even have access to that kind of setup?"

"We couldn't lie to her," Nash adds. "Not after everything she's been through. She deserves the truth."

"Look," I say, bracing my hands on Ty's desk. "Flora saw things in that lockup that needed context. The restraints, the soundproofing—she's smart. She would have figured it out eventually."

"Plus," Nash interjects, "she handled the whole situation like a pro. Didn't even flinch when we explained what we really do here."

I nod. "We can't keep lying to her, Ty. Not when she's part of our life now. Every aspect of it."

Ty sinks back into his chair. "And you're sure she can be trusted?"

"With our lives," Nash and I say in unison.

"She's been through hell," I continue. "Survived things that would break most people. And instead of running from the darkness, she embraces it. Just like we do."

"The way she worked that hammer last night?" Nash's voice holds a note of pride. "That wasn't just revenge. That was a natural talent."

"She's one of us," I insist. "Whether you like it or not. And we won't lie to her about who we are or what we do."

Ty leans back in his chair, running a hand over his face. "Fine," he says after a long pause. "If she's in, she's in. But I need to brief her myself. Soon. We'll determine where her talents lie and how she can help the operation."

Relief floods through me. Nash shoots me a knowing look—that infuriating "I told you so" expression I both hate and love.

"She'll work with us," I say quickly before Ty can start planning anything else. "On our side of things."

Nash nods. "We've already seen what she can do. She's perfect for our specialty work."

"The enforcement side?" Ty raises an eyebrow. "You sure about that? It's not exactly..."

"She has a natural talent for it," Nash interrupts. "You should have seen her last night."

"And she's already proven she can handle extreme

situations," I add. "Plus, she's got the acrobatic skills to back it up. Makes for a deadly combination."

Ty drums his fingers on his desk, considering our words. "Alright. She stays with you. But I still need to brief her on the overall operation. Make sure she understands exactly what she's getting into."

I nod at Ty's words, relieved this went better than expected. "Just let us know when you want to do the briefing. We'll make sure she's ready."

Nash echoes my agreement. "She'll take it seriously, Ty. You can count on that."

Ty leans back in his chair, a puzzled expression crossing his face. "There's something else I don't get." He runs a hand through his hair, hesitating. "How the fuck does it work, sharing a girl? I mean, if anyone even looks at Sofia the wrong way, I want to murder them. Can't wrap my head around it."

I exchange a glance with Nash, understanding Ty's confusion. It's not something we've really explained to anyone before.

"It's different with us," I say carefully. "We've been partners for years. There's trust there that goes beyond normal friendship."

Nash nods. "Flora isn't being shared—she's ours. Together. It's not about taking turns or splitting her attention. The three of us just... fit."

I shift uncomfortably as Ty's eyes narrow with interest. "Like what—you two play with each other too?"

The question hangs in the air. I glance at Nash, who meets my gaze with quiet understanding. We've never discussed this part of our relationship with anyone, but if there's someone who won't judge us, it's Ty.

"Yes," I admit, my voice steady despite the heat creeping up my neck. "All three of us are together. Intimately."

Nash's hand brushes against mine, a subtle gesture of support.

"But we'd appreciate it if you kept that information to yourself," I add quickly. "It's not something we want to advertise."

Nash nods. "We know what the guys are like. Two men fucking each other isn't exactly something they'll be comfortable with."

My stomach tightens at Nash's blunt words, but I keep my face neutral. I've hidden this part of myself for so long. It's strange hearing it discussed so openly.

Ty shakes his head, surprising me with a small smile. "I'm not so sure that's true. Look, we're not exactly your typical carnival crew, are we? These guys have seen and done things most people couldn't imagine."

"It's different," I argue.

"Is it? Sure, they'll probably give you shit for it. There'll be jokes and banter—that's just how they are. But real hate?" He shrugs. "I don't see it. Not from this group."

Nash shifts beside me, and I feel some tension leave his shoulders. "You really think they'd be that accepting?"

"We're a family of misfits," Ty says. "Each one of us has something others might consider strange or wrong. But that's why we work. We accept each other."

His words hit home, making me reconsider everything I thought I knew about our carnival family. Maybe we're hiding for nothing.

Ty leans back in his chair, processing this new revelation. The silence stretches between us, but there's no disgust or judgment in his expression—just genuine curiosity.

"But your secret's safe with me," he says, a small smile on his lips. "Not my business anyway."

"Thanks, Ty," I say, feeling the weight lift from my shoulders.

"You two are something else," Ty chuckles, shaking his head. "Never thought I'd see the day when my best enforcers turned into lovesick puppies."

"Watch it," I growl, but there's no real heat behind it.

"Hey, I'm not judging." Ty raises his hands in mock surrender. "Just never seen either of you like this before. It... makes sense, though."

Nash stands, stretching his long frame. "We should get back. Flora will be wondering where we are."

"Can't keep the lady waiting," Ty smirks. "Go on, get out of here. And try not to murder anyone else without telling me first, yeah?"

I smirk as we head for the door. "No promises."

"That's what I'm afraid of," Ty calls after us, laughing.

Walking back to the trailer with Nash, my steps feel lighter than they have in years. The morning sun warms my face, and I can't help but smile at Ty's easy acceptance of our relationship.

Ten years. I've kept the fact I'm bisexual hidden, scared of what people would think. Scared of what Nash would think, considering I was attracted to him. How different things might have been if I'd been braver.

But then I think of Flora, probably still curled up in our bed, and realize it wouldn't have worked without her. The way she fits between us and completes us...

My chest tightens with emotion: I love Nash and Flora. With his quiet strength and calculating mind, Nash has been by my side through everything. And Flora, our beautiful, broken angel who proved to be stronger than either of us imagined.

Together, we make sense in a way I can't explain. Maybe that's why it never worked—Nash and I were waiting for her, even if we didn't know it.

36

FLORA

I stretch lazily in bed, savoring the warmth of the blankets on this Christmas Eve morning. The space beside me feels empty. Nash and Colt must have gotten up already. The carnival's usual bustle is absent today since we're on break until after Christmas.

Sitting up, I notice their pillows are cold. They've been gone a while. The trailer feels different in the morning stillness without their presence. I've grown so used to waking up between them, feeling their protective warmth.

I wrap myself in my soft purple robe and pad across the bedroom floor. The wooden boards creak slightly under my feet as I approach the kitchen. The living area is empty, too, though I spot coffee mugs in the sink.

The kitchen is unusually tidy for them. Colt usually leaves some evidence of his morning routine, and Nash typically has papers spread across the counter from reviewing show notes. But everything is put away, not a thing out of place.

Fresh snow has fallen overnight, coating the carnival grounds in white. The other trailers, with their frosted roofs, look like gingerbread houses. Somewhere in the distance, I hear faint Christmas music playing.

I step into the kitchen, the linoleum floor cold against my bare feet. The coffee pot is still warm, so they couldn't have left long ago. I wonder what my two men are up to on this peaceful Christmas Eve morning.

I curl up on the couch with my coffee, pulling my favorite blanket around me. The warmth seeps into my bones as I inhale the rich aroma. The door swings open as I settle, and my boys stride in, bringing a gust of cold air.

"Where were you two?" I ask, taking in their flushed cheeks and serious expressions.

Nash shrugs off his jacket while Colt stomps snow from his boots. "Had to talk to Ty," Nash says, running a hand through his dark hair.

"About what?" I ask.

"About you knowing the truth about the carnival's darker operations," Colt says, sitting beside me. "

My stomach tightens. I'd wondered when this conversation would happen. "How did he take it?"

"Better than we expected, actually," Nash says, claiming the spot on my other side. His body heat radiates through my blanket. "He understands why we told you."

"Really?" I look between them, searching their faces for any sign of trouble.

"Really," Colt confirms, wrapping an arm around

my shoulders. "He knows you're part of us now. That means you're part of everything."

Nash nods. "Ty gets it."

The tension drains from my body, and I sink deeper into their embrace. I hadn't realized how worried I'd been about Ty's reaction until now.

I curl deeper into the couch between Nash and Colt. "So we have a week off now?"

"That's right," Nash confirms, his fingers playing with my hair.

"Yes, a whole week to spend together, all day and all night long," Colt adds, squeezing my shoulder.

We all groan contentedly at the thought. No training schedule means we can really explore our relationship without interruption. The carnival's winter break gives us precious time to figure out our unique dynamic.

"And what about Tommy and Jake's disappearance?" I sink my teeth into my bottom lip, the image of their bodies broken and battered bringing me a sick satisfaction.

Colt shrugs. "What about it?"

My brow furrows. "We killed them. Surely they'll be reported as missing?"

Nash shakes his head. "Phoenix is covering all bases. I asked him to get onto it. We'll know if there's any trouble or whisper of them being reported missing. Tommy and Jake were adults. It will be assumed they've just taken off together or something. And after their cell phones landed their location here last, Phoenix changed the cell data to make it look like they left here and went straight to New York."

A heaviness lifts from my shoulders hearing that. "Wow, you guys think of everything, don't you?"

Colt smirks. "Of course, we're professionals, angel."

Nash moves a little closer to me. "Anyway, enough about those assholes. About the fact we've got all week to spend together." He raises a brow. "How about we get started with a Christmas movie and you naked on my dick?"

I feel an ache ignite deep at the idea, but I shake my head. "While that does sound perfect, first, I need to run to the store for some Christmas shopping."

Nash and Colt share a look over my head. I know they're still protective after everything, but I need to buy them presents without them hovering.

"I won't be gone long," I promise. "And the store is just in town. I'll take my phone."

"We could come with you," Colt suggests.

I shake my head. "How am I supposed to buy your presents if you're right there?"

Nash chuckles. "She has a point."

"Fine," Colt relents. "But straight there and back."

"Yes, sir," I tease, earning another squeeze from both.

I step into the shower, letting the hot water wash over me. After washing my hair and body, I dry off quickly, eager to do my Christmas shopping. The mirror is foggy as I brush my long blonde hair and apply minimal makeup.

Wrapping my threadbare coat around myself, I grimace at how thin it feels. The zipper sticks halfway up, reminding me why I usually layer sweaters underneath it.

"Wait," Colt calls from the bedroom. "Nash and I were going to save this for Christmas, but..." He disappears into the closet and returns with a large box.

"You need it now," Nash finishes, standing beside Colt.

Colt holds out the box to me. Inside, nestled in tissue paper, lies the most beautiful winter coat I've ever seen. The material is thick and plush, deep purple, with silver buttons down the front.

"It's perfect," I breathe, my fingers gliding over the soft fabric.

"Try it on," Nash encourages.

I slip my arms into the sleeves, marveling at how perfectly it fits. The coat hugs my curves while allowing room for movement, and the length falls past my knees. The inside is lined with the softest material I've ever felt.

"You both got this for me?" I ask, touched by their thoughtfulness.

"We couldn't have our girl freezing," Colt says.

I kiss him deeply, then turn to give Nash the same treatment. "Thank you both. I love it."

"Stay warm out there," Nash says as I approach the door.

My new coat staves off the cold as I walk down the steps and onto the snow-covered ground.

I pull it tighter around me as I walk through the snow-covered carnival grounds. For the first time in forever, I feel... lighter. Free. The weight of my past doesn't press down quite as hard anymore.

I don't remember much about my real parents. Just fragments, really—a woman's perfume maybe, or the sound of a deep laugh. The social workers told me my parents dropped me off at a care center when I was four. They didn't explain, no goodbye, just left me there like an unwanted package.

The foster homes that followed blur together in my memory. Some were better than others, but none felt like home. The worst foster home was here in Easthollow with the Lowleys.

A snowflake lands on my nose, and I smile, tilting my face up to catch more. The carnival is quiet this morning, peaceful under its blanket of white. No one around to see me act childish, spinning in slow circles with my arms spread wide.

The memories that used to haunt me daily are still there, but they no longer have the same power over me. My new coat wraps me in warmth, a physical reminder that I'm cared for now, protected, and loved.

For the first time since my abandonment, I feel like I have a real family. Not the kind that leaves, hurts, or ignores. The kind that stays, fights for you, and loves you exactly as you are.

I head into town, my first stop being a small boutique. For Alice, I find a quirky coffee mug with a sassy saying—perfect for her bold personality. Lily would love this delicate silver bracelet with tiny stars.

Moving to the bookstore next door, I spot a leatherbound journal that screams Tilly's name. She's always scribbling code and game ideas. For Aurora, I pick up the latest thriller novel she's been talking about.

Sofia's gift is trickier, but I find a beautiful burgundy scarf that perfectly complements her hair.

For my boys... I want something special. Something that shows how much they mean to me. In an antique shop, I discover two matching vintage pocket watches. The shopkeeper tells me they're from the same set—meant to be together, just like Nash and Colt. They're beautiful, with intricate engravings and heavy silver cases. They cost most of my savings, but they're worth it.

I also pick up some leather cords so they can wear the watches around their necks. The thought of them wearing matching pieces makes me smile.

As I gather my bags, warmth spreads through my chest. These aren't just gifts—they're tangible proof that I have people in my life worth celebrating—people who care about me and people I care about in return.

37

NASH

Colt's face lights up as we spot the perfect tree at the lot—not too tall to fit in our trailer, but full and green with that classic Christmas shape. We haven't bothered with a tree in years, but this year feels different. Flora deserves a proper Christmas.

"This one," we say in unison, making us both laugh. The lot owner helps us secure it to the top of the van while Colt loads boxes of ornaments and lights into the back. I insisted on getting everything new—shiny balls in red and gold, tinsel, a proper tree skirt, and a delicate angel for the top.

The drive back is tense with anticipation. I keep checking my phone, making sure Flora hasn't returned early from her shopping trip with Aurora. Colt drums his fingers on the steering wheel, probably as anxious as I am to set everything up before she returns.

When we arrive, our trailer is mercifully empty. We maneuver the tree through the door, knocking over a lamp. Colt rights it while I adjust the tree stand, ensuring it's perfectly straight. The fresh pine scent fills our small space, returning memories of childhood Christmases I thought I'd forgotten.

"Should we start decorating?" Colt asks, already opening one of the ornament boxes.

I shake my head. "Let's wait for our little bird. She should help with that part."

While Colt arranges the boxes of decorations around the tree, I head to the kitchen. Something is comforting about the ritual of baking—measuring flour, creaming butter, and sugar, the familiar motions grounding me as I prepare a batch of sugar cookies. I found my grandmother's recipe tucked away in an old notebook, and somehow, it feels right to share this piece of my past with my new family.

The cookie dough chills in the fridge while I start on some hot chocolate—the real kind, with melted chocolate and cream, not that powdered stuff. The trailer fills with warmth and sweet smells as we wait for Flora to return home.

I'm stirring the hot chocolate when I hear the door open, followed by Flora's gasp of surprise. Colt immediately moves to help her with the shopping bags weighing her down.

"Let me take those," he says, gathering them from her arms.

I watch from the kitchen as they disappear into the bedroom with her purchases. When they return, Flora's eyes fix on the tree in the corner.

"You two have been busy," she says, moving closer to inspect it. Her fingers brush against one of the branches.

"We wanted to wait for you before decorating," I tell her, pouring the hot chocolate into three mugs. "Thought you might want to help with that part."

The way her face lights up makes my chest tight. It's such a simple thing—a Christmas tree—but the joy in her expression tells me we made the right choice. I never knew creating holiday memories could mean so much until I saw that look on her face.

"I didn't think you two were the Christmas tree type," Flora says.

I set down the mugs of hot chocolate and move closer. "We aren't. But this year is different."

"We wanted to give you something special," Colt adds, his hand finding the small of her back. "The Christmas you deserve."

Her eyes well up with tears, and before I can react, she launches herself into my arms. I catch her, holding her tight against my chest as she trembles. Her tears soak into my shirt, but I don't care. I stroke her hair, breathing in her scent, while Colt wraps his arms around us from behind her.

"You both..." she chokes out between sobs. "I never had... nobody ever..."

I press my lips to the top of her head, unable to find the right words to express how much she means to us and how desperately we want to give her everything she's been denied.

I pull back slightly, keeping one arm around Flora while reaching for Colt's hand with my other. Her tears have slowed, but the raw emotion in her voice makes my chest ache.

"I love you both so fucking much," she whispers.

Colt's hand tightens around mine. "You saved us, angel," he says, his voice rough. "Before you, we were just going through the motions. Living half-lives."

"You brought light into our darkness, little bird." I press my lips to her temple. "You made us whole in ways we didn't know we were broken."

Flora turns her face up to look at us both, her eyes shining. "You're my home," she says. "My family. My everything."

"And you're our miracle," Colt murmurs, brushing away a stray tear from her cheek.

I draw them closer, overwhelmed by my feelings for them. "You healed parts of us we thought were beyond repair, Flora. You gave us permission to love each other and you, to be who we truly are."

I watch as Colt cups Flora's face in his hands. "I love you, Flora," he says, pressing his lips to hers in a tender kiss that makes my heart clench.

When he pulls back, his eyes find mine. Something shifts in his expression—vulnerability and determination. "And I love you, Nash," he breathes before capturing my mouth with his. The kiss differs from our previous ones—less desperate, more meaningful. My chest tightens with emotions.

Flora watches us tearfully, and I'm struck by how much I feel for them both. The words I never thought I'd say rise, demanding to be spoken.

"Little bird," I whisper, drawing her close. "I didn't think I was capable of love. Didn't think I deserved it.

But you changed everything." I kiss her softly, pouring all my feelings into the contact. "I love you."

Turning to Colt, I see the same overwhelming emotion in his eyes. "And you—you've been my anchor for so long. I love you, Colt. Have for years."

Flora's eyes glint with understanding as she reaches for one of the scattered boxes, removing a shiny gold ornament. "I think it's time we started decorating." Her voice is steady, but I sense the undercurrent of emotion.

"Let's get to it." I move to take my mug of hot chocolate but stop, needing to feel connected to Colt right now, especially as the implications of what we've just confessed hang heavy between us.

I need to feel his skin and remind myself that we're still here, still okay, together after revealing our deepest truths. I walk over to him, reaching out to touch his chest, and he immediately tangles his fingers in my hair, pulling me closer.

"I love you," he whispers against my lips before kissing me deeply. My body reacts instantly, every nerve ending igniting as it always does when his mouth is on mine. This kiss is different, too—not fevered and desperate like before, but slow and deep, conveying everything we can't say. My hands roam his chest and back as our tongues tangle, reveling in the taste and feel of each other.

Flora's soft voice interrupts us. "Can I...?"

I pull back from Colt, reaching for her as she steps forward, pressing a soft kiss to Colt's lips, then mine. My arms find their way around her, kissing her back, pouring all the love I feel for her into it.

Colt clears his throat, breaking the spell. "Why don't you hang that up?" He suggests signaling to the ornament she's still clutching.

Flora pulls back and nods, walking over to the tree. Watching her hang the first ornament—a symbol of our new beginning.

Colt's hand on my shoulder snaps me out of my thoughts. "I think we should be doing this naked."

A rush of want runs through me as I meet his gaze. "I think you're right."

Flora turns as I start unbuttoning her shirt. Her cheeks are flushed, but her eyes shine with need. "You two," she breathes, stepping closer and touching our chests.

Colt's hands tangle in her hair, guiding her toward him, and she moves willingly. I reach out, touching her bare shoulder, and she makes a soft sound, turning to kiss my palm.

My heart races as I start to unbutton her jeans. Colt pulls her tank top off, baring her breasts, and her breath catches as we both caress and worship her body, marking her as ours.

Flora arches into our touch, moaning softly as Colt traces patterns on her skin with his tongue while I kiss a trail down her neck, nipping at her sensitive skin. She's perfect, offering herself to us, trusting us with her pleasure.

Colt moves to kiss me. Our tongues tangle in a desperate kiss as Flora's hands roam our bodies, touching and exploring.

I pull away from Colt, needing more. His shirt is

already open, revealing his toned chest, and I push it off his shoulders, tracing the lines of his tattoos with my fingertips. His breath hitches as I lean down, my tongue swiping his nipple before I take it into my mouth, sucking gently.

"Fuck," he groans, tangling a hand in my hair, keeping me close.

Flora's fingers work the button of Colt's jeans, revealing his straining erection beneath.

I slip behind her, kissing her bare shoulder while she wraps her hand around Colt's cock. Her fingers pump him in a steady rhythm, her thumb sweeping over the sensitive tip, drawing a deep groan from his lips. I suck lightly on her earlobe, tasting the salt of her skin, savoring the way she moves.

Colt reaches between her legs, his fingers teasing her folds, making her gasp. "Fuck, she's so wet," he murmurs.

I mouth my way down her neck, nipping at her pulse point while my hands settle on her hips. She's moving with the rhythm of Colt's hand, pushing back into my touch.

"Too many clothes," Colt growls, his voice laced with desperation. "Bedroom."

Flora moans her agreement, her head falling back against my shoulder as Colt's fingers slide deeper.

Somehow, we reach the bedroom, a tangle of limbs and hunger. We sink onto the bed, and Colt rolls so Flora is beneath him, pinned by his gaze. "So fucking beautiful," he murmurs, his fingers tracing the curves of her body, his mouth following the path.

I move to the edge of the bed, wanting to see everything—to burn this image into my memory forever. Colt's head dips, his tongue swirling over Flora's clit, making her cry out. Her hips buck, seeking more pressure, and Colt obliges, devouring her with eager strokes of his tongue.

The sexual tension in the room is almost suffocating, but I can't look away. Flora's fingers twist in Colt's hair as he feasts on her, his hands gripping her thighs. "Yes," she gasps, her body arching. "Please, don't stop."

The way Flora moves against his mouth—soft, pleading sounds escaping her throat—has me rock hard.

Colt pulls back, his lips swollen and glistening, a testament to his devotion to Flora's pleasure. "Get over here," he says, voice thick with desire. "Show me what that tongue can do."

My cock twitches at the sultry tone in his voice, the filthy command he offers so effortlessly. I groan in response, moving to position myself behind Colt.

He's on his hands and knees, his ass presented to me, waiting. I sink to my knees behind him, my breath catching at the sight before me. His cheeks are clenched, his muscled back rippling as he leans forward, holding himself up with one arm while he eats Flora's pussy.

I lean in, my nose nuzzling the crack of his ass, inhaling the musky scent of him, the taste of his skin. My tongue teases the sensitive pucker, lapping at him, eliciting a soft moan from Colt. I press my mouth to the tight ring of muscle, circling the tip of my tongue around it before pressing forward, breaching him with a slow, torturous motion that makes us both groan.

Colt shifts, lifting his hips slightly to grant me better access. "That's it, such a good boy. Eat my ass."

The filthy words spill from his lips so naturally, so perfectly in tune with the decadent scene before us.

I swirl my tongue around his rim, teasing the sensitive flesh before plunging deeper, fucking him with my tongue while my hands grip his hips, holding him steady. He moans around Flora's clit, his shoulders tensing as he struggles to remain focused on her pleasure.

Beneath me, Colt is thrusting back onto my tongue, meeting each swirl and flick of my tongue with his impatient movements. The sounds of our pleasure fill the room—wet, sloppy noises of oral sex blending with our harsh breaths.

Flora's hands tangle in Colt's hair, holding him close, her hips moving with the rhythm he sets.

This Christmas marks the beginning of something extraordinary. Our first real holiday as a family— because that's what we are now. A dirty family who love each other so fucking much.

Love.

The word used to feel foreign, dangerous even. Now, it feels like coming home.

38

COLT

Flora writhes beneath me, her slender body arching as my tongue dances over her clit. A groan escapes my throat as Nash fucks my ass with his tongue, driving me wild.

Flora's hips buck against my mouth as I suck, her thighs squeezing my head. Her fingers twist in my hair, holding me there as if afraid I might stop. Fuck, she's so sweet. Her sharp intake of breath spurs me on, and I lick faster, savoring the way her body responds.

Nash's tongue is skilled, knowing exactly how to make me crazy. I bite down on Flora's inner thigh to stifle a moan as my cock leaks.

Flora's moans grow louder, her knees widening as she surrenders to me.

I pull back slightly, teasing her swollen clit with gentle flicks of my tongue. Her body trembles, teetering on the edge of no return. I want to draw this out, make it last, but her eyes plead me, and damn, I can't deny her anything. I dive back in, my tongue relentless, and she shatters.

"Fuck, you make such a beautiful mess when you squirt like that," I growl, lapping up every drop of her release.

My cock pulses at the sight, starving for attention.

I smile as I look over my shoulder at Nash, seeing his eager expression, his eyes dark with desire. "You ready to surrender that sexy ass so I can pop that cherry?"

A shudder runs through him. I've been stretching him for a week now, teasing his hole with my fingers and toys when we're all intimate. He's taken to it naturally, and I know he's craving more. "Yeah," he breathes, his voice husky.

I pat the bed beside me. "Get between her legs, then. Give our beautiful angel your cock while I fuck your ass." I watch as he maneuvers himself between Flora's spread thighs.

"She's ours. Take our girl and make her scream." I reach over, running my hand through his hair.

He nods, his hands gripping Flora's hips as he presses his leaking cock to her soaking entrance. His breath hitches as he pushes into her, her body welcoming him home the same way it does me. He closes his eyes at the feeling of being embedded in her heat.

"Fuck, so tight." His hips begin to move, his eyes sliding shut as he savors the sensation. "Such a good girl," he breathes. "Taking it all like you were created just for us."

Flora arches her back, lifting her hips to meet his thrusts. "Fuck, Nash," she groans, fisting her hands through his hair.

Nash's hips stutter, his eyes falling shut. He's always been the more controlled one, the calm to my chaos, but right now, he's that battle, and it's fucking hot.

I lean over, pressing a kiss to the back of his neck as my hand slips between the muscular cheeks of his ass. He moans, his hands tightening on her hips. I grab the lube from the nightstand, coating my fingers before teasing his tight hole.

He groans, his body clenching around me. "Fuck, Colt."

"You like that, huh?" I whisper, stretching him and finding his prostate, massaging it, and feeling him relax as pleasure overwhelms him.

I smirk, withdrawing my fingers. "Your turn to be ruined." I reach for the toy box under the bed, pulling out a couple of our favorites. The biggest one is a challenge, but he's so turned on that I think he can take it. It's the only one I haven't used with him yet.

I coat the toy with lube, positioning it at his entrance. Slowly, I apply steady pressure, watching hungrily as it glides inside him. I focus on his back for any signs of tension or discomfort. But he takes it, his body welcoming the invasion.

I tease it in and out, slowly at first, then more fervently as he relaxes. He's stunning like this, his control gone; nothing left but surrender.

"More," he begs, his voice strained. "Please, Colt."

"Greedy boy," I groan. Fuck. I'll never get enough of hearing him beg. "You think you're ready for the real thing?"

He glances over his shoulder and is eager, but I can see the trepidation in his eyes. "Yeah," he breathes.

His eyes flick back to Flora, who's moaning beneath him, her body moving in perfect rhythm with his thrusts.

I slick up my cock, my breath catching at the sight of him before me, open and willing. I brush my thumb over the smooth rides of his hole. Fuck. The number of times I've thought about fucking Nash. Flora's slim thighs frame his perfect ass, her hands gripping his shoulders as he moves within her. I have to remind myself to breathe as I slowly push into him, inch by inch, feeling that sweet tightness as he stretches to accommodate me.

His back arches, and he lets out a low groan, his head dropping forward. I pause, giving him a moment to adjust. "You okay, baby?"

He nods, his breath hitching. "Move, Colt. I need you to move."

I chuckle, my body on fire as I begin to thrust, finding a steady rhythm. I look down at him, loving the way he takes me. "So fucking tight. Such a good boy. Taking my cock like a champ."

Flora watches us, her eyes shining with desire. "Fill our boy up, Colt. Give it to him."

I obey, my movements becoming more urgent. "Your ass fits me like a tight glove, one made to sheath my cock, to milk me dry," I grit out, my hands digging into his hips. "Gonna breed our boy."

Nash groans, his fingers digging into Flora's thighs as he moves again, his body working to accommodate both of us. "Fuck, yes, Colt. Breed my hole while I fuck our girl."

Nash plunges into Flora again, his pace frantic now. His body works between us, his face buried in the curve of Flora's neck. She moans, her arms wrapping around him as he thrusts, her nails raking down his back.

I grip his hips, guiding my cock into him with forceful thrusts. He groans, his body clenching around me. I lean over, my mouth finding his ear. "Does that feel good, baby?"

"Yeah." His voice is strangled, his hips moving back to meet my thrusts.

Flora's hands move between them, her fingers seeking out her clit. "Feels so good, Nash. Harder, please."

He growls, his body tensing as he drives into her. "Take it, baby. Take my cock."

I lean forward, my lips brushing his ear. "Wish I could see your face."

Nash grunts, his head lifting as he looks back at me over his shoulder, his eyes dark with lust. "Like this?" he asks.

"Perfect," I murmur before leaning closer and kissing him messily.

Flora's breathing comes in sharp pants. Her eyes are half-closed, her lips swollen. "I'm close," she gasps. "Please, don't stop."

Nash's hips move faster, his body slick with sweat as he pounds into her. "Come for us, baby."

She bites her lip, her hips arching off the bed as she comes.

"That's it, baby. So fucking beautiful," Nash groans.

I thrust into Nash, my hands gripping his slender hips as I mark my territory. "You like watching her come, Nash? I want you to join her. Breed her cunt while I breed this tight ass."

He groans, his back arching as he fucks her through her climax. "I don't want it to end."

Flora's eyes shine as she looks up at him. "Me either."

He growls, his hips stuttering as he buries himself in her heat. He reaches between their bodies, his thumb finding her clit. "Then we'll do it again. I want to feel you come all over my cock a second time."

She whimpers, her head tossing back and forth as her hips move with his hand. "Yes, Nash. Please."

I grin, my pace matching his. Our skin slaps together, the sounds filling the room, mixing with our grunts and moans. Nash's body is slick with sweat now, his muscles gleaming in the dim light.

I reach around, my hand finding his cock where it slides in and out of Flora's wetness. He groans, his head dropping as I palm his balls. "Such a good boy. I want to feel you come while you get your ass fucked hard."

His back arches as he loses control. His balls pulse in my hand, his cum painting Flora's insides. That alone makes Flora fall apart again, her cries filling the room.

I grin, my pace becoming more urgent. "You want my cum, Nash? Bet that tight ass of yours craves it, fucking needs it."

"Yes, I crave your cum," Nash groans. "I need it dripping out of me, marking my ass as yours and yours alone."

I can't hold back any longer, my hips moving frantically as I lose myself in the feel of him. I bury myself deep, my cum filling him as I grit out, "Fuck! Nash!"

He groans, his body shaking.

I finish with a final, deep thrust. I come hard, my body pulsing as I fill his ass. Groaning, I pull out, my body utterly spent.

Flora's eyes are huge, a smile spreading across her lips. "Fuck, that was so hot."

I grin, feeling a surge of pride. I love this—the three of us together. It's not something I ever thought could work. You always expect some kind of jealousy, but I don't feel anything but love for them.

Nash rolls onto his side, reaching for Flora's hand. "I've never felt anything so good," he breathes, his eyes half-closed. "Your pussy clenching around my cock while Colt fucks my ass... It's my new favorite way of fucking."

Flora's cheeks are flushed, but she bites her lip with a playful smile. "You boys have ruined me for anyone else."

"Of course, we have." Nash's voice is a soft contrast to the harsh words. "You're ours, little bird. No one else will touch you in this lifetime."

I take her hand, pressing a kiss to her palm. "We love you, Flora. You're our girl."

Her eyes shine with tears, and her lips tremble as she whispers, "I love you, too."

Nash pulls her into a hug, and I join them, wrapping my arms around them. We stay like that for a long moment, relishing being together and whole.

39

FLORA

Winter sunlight streams through the trailer window, casting a golden glow across our bed. I wake cocooned in warmth between Nash and Colt. My heart flutters with anticipation—their wrapped presents, carefully chosen, are waiting under our small tree.

As I shift, Nash's arm tightens around my waist, and Colt's breath tickles my neck. They both stir at my movement, their bodies pressing against me, cocooning me in warmth and safety.

"Merry Christmas," I whisper, pressing a soft kiss to Nash's lips. His brown eyes crinkle at the corners as he smiles.

"Merry Christmas, little bird," he murmurs back.

Colt's hand slides up my arm, and I twist to face him. "Merry Christmas," he says, kissing my lips gently.

The two men exchange a tender kiss over my head, making my heart swell. This is everything I never dared dream of—safety, belonging, unconditional love. The carnival trailer may be small, but it's more of a home than any foster house ever was.

"I have presents for you both," I say, unable to contain my excitement.

Nash chuckles at my enthusiasm. "Eager to get up already?"

"The presents can wait," Colt adds, pulling me closer.

But I'm too excited to stay still. This is my first real Christmas and a chance to give gifts to people I love. "Please? I want to see your faces when you open them."

Their mock resistance crumbles at my pleading tone. They've never been able to deny me anything, not when it brings me joy, and I will wield that new-found superpower every chance I get.

"Alright," Colt concedes with a smile. "Lead the way."

I slip from between them, shivering slightly in just my matching crimson bra and panties. The trailer's living area is chilly despite the small space heater humming in the corner. Nash and Colt follow in their briefs, their muscled forms casting long shadows in the early morning light.

Our Christmas tree sparkles with its ornaments. I drop beside it, reaching for the two carefully wrapped boxes I've hidden toward the back. My heart races as I hold them—these matching antique pocket watches are perfect.

"These are for you both," I say, turning to present one to each of them. The boxes are wrapped in deep blue paper with silver ribbons—Nash's favorite colors. My hands tremble slightly as I hold them out.

I watch them unwrap their gifts, my fingers twisting in my lap. The silver watches gleam in the morning light as they lift them from their boxes. My heart skips when I see their expressions soften.

"Turn them over," I whisper.

They flip the watches in perfect sync. On the back of each, I had the shop engrave their initials intertwined with mine—a permanent token of our connection.

"Flora..." Nash's voice is thick with emotion as he traces the delicate script.

"I saw them in this little antique shop," I explain. "They're a matched set, and I just knew they were meant for you."

Colt's ice-blue eyes meet mine, filled with a tenderness that takes my breath away. "They're perfect, angel."

"Like you," Nash adds, pulling me into his arms.

I nestle against his chest as Colt moves behind me, surrounding me in their warmth. The watches catch the light between us, their synchronized ticking a steady rhythm like three hearts beating as one.

"I wanted something that showed how we belong together," I say softly. "How you two were always meant to be together, and somehow, I was blessed to fit between you."

Nash's lips brush my temple. "You didn't just fit, little bird. You completed us."

"These must have cost a fortune," Colt murmurs, his hand sliding down my arm.

I shake my head. "Don't worry about that. They were worth every penny to see your faces right now."

I watch Nash reach under the tree, pulling out a small velvet box. My heart skips—after the beautiful coat they gave me yesterday, I hadn't expected anything else.

"This is something special, little bird," Nash says, his eyes warm as he hands me the box. "Something to show you'll always be ours."

Colt's hand rests on my lower back as I carefully open the lid. Inside, nestled on black velvet, lies a delicate silver chain with three interlinked circles. The middle circle holds a small diamond that catches the morning light.

"The three circles represent us," Colt explains softly. "Forever linked, forever protecting each other."

My vision blurs with tears as I lift the necklace. It's the most beautiful thing I've ever owned, but more than that, it's a symbol of everything they mean to me—of how they saved, loved, and helped make me whole.

"We had it custom-made," Nash adds, taking the necklace from my fingers. He moves behind me, brushing my hair to fasten it around my neck. The silver circles rest just below my collarbone, cool against my skin.

"It's perfect," I whisper, touching the circles with reverent fingers. "I love it so much."

"Like we love you," Colt says, pulling me into his arms. Nash wraps his arms around us, and I'm enveloped in their warmth, strength, and devotion.

The necklace represents everything we are—three

pieces forming something unbreakable when joined together. As I stand between them, wearing their gift against my heart, I know I'll never be alone again.

I rest my head against Nash's chest, still overwhelmed by the beauty of their gift when my stomach growls loudly. Nash's chest rumbles with laughter.

"Sounds like someone needs breakfast," he says, kissing my temple.

"The Christmas feast isn't until later," Colt adds, his hand sliding down my back. "And Ty always goes all out in the main tent."

"Really?" I lift my head, curiosity piqued. Despite living at the carnival for a few weeks, I still need to learn more about their traditions.

"It's quite the sight," Nash says. "Ty sets up this massive table down the center of the main tent. Everyone comes together—all the performers, vendors, crew. It's like..."

"A big misfit family dinner," Colt finishes, smiling. "No one here has a normal family background, so we've made our own."

My heart swells at the thought. After years of painful Christmases with my foster families, the idea of sharing a meal with people who truly care about each other feels magical.

"Come on," Nash says, tugging me toward our small kitchen area. "Let's get some food in you first. Can't have you fainting from hunger before your first carnival Christmas dinner."

I follow him willingly, watching as he and Colt move around each other with practiced ease, pulling out eggs and bacon. The necklace rests cool against my skin, a beautiful reminder that I belong with them in this unconventionally perfect family.

"My first of many," I say softly, touching the three circles at my throat.

Both men pause their breakfast preparations to look at me, their eyes full of love and promise.

"Many, many more," Colt agrees, pulling me into a quick kiss before returning to the stove.

I move to the coffee maker, knowing exactly how they both take their morning brew. It's funny how quickly these little details become second nature. Nash likes his with just a splash of cream, while Colt takes his black with two sugars.

My hands work on autopilot, measuring the grounds into the filter. The familiar scent fills our small kitchen as it begins to percolate. Behind me, the sizzle of bacon and quiet domestic sounds of my men moving around the cramped space make my chest tight with emotion.

The coffee maker gurgles its last drops as I pour cream into Nash's mug. It seems like a simple task, but it means everything. These aren't cruel masters I'm serving out of fear—they're my partners, my protectors, my loves. I drop two sugar cubes into Colt's cup, watching them dissolve in the dark liquid.

Steam rises from the mugs, and I can't help but smile at how even a simple domestic act brings such joy; who knew? Who would have thought I'd find such peace in a carnival trailer between two men who most people consider dangerous? But they've never been gentle with me, even when I ask them not to be.

40

FLORA

I sit between Aurora and Nash, still playing with the three interlocked circles at my throat. The main tent has been transformed into a winter wonderland, with twinkling lights strung across the ceiling and garland wrapped around the support poles. The long table stretches before us, laden with more food than I've ever seen.

"Stop messing with your necklace and eat something," Nash murmurs, placing a roll on my plate.

Aurora leans over, admiring the silver circles. "That's gorgeous. Christmas gift?"

I nod, unable to contain my smile. "From my boys."

"Boys?" Alice calls from across the table, practically sitting in Lars's lap. "More like possessive giants."

Lars tugs her closer. "You're one to talk, princess. No one beats me when it comes to being possessive."

"I think it's sweet," Lily chimes in beside Cade. "They take good care of you."

"Unlike some people," Tilly teases, elbowing Phoenix. "All I got was a new gaming console."

"Which you love," Phoenix protests, but a smile plays at his lips.

Sofia, elegant as always, raises her glass. "To found families and unconventional love."

"Here, here," Ty agrees, pressing a kiss to her temple.

Gage remains silent beside Aurora, but I catch the way his hand squeezes hers under the table. She beams at him.

"Pass the potatoes," Remy calls from the end of the table. "Some of us are starving here."

Colt reaches across Nash to squeeze my thigh. "Eat up, angel. You'll need your strength later."

"Gross," Alice declares. "Some of us are trying to enjoy our dinner."

"You're being a prude, Alice. I'm sure you'll need your strength later, too. I've got lots of plans to make you sweat," Lars says, making me almost choke on my roll.

Alice's cheeks flush pink as she squirms beside him. I hide my smile behind my glass, grateful the attention has shifted away from us. But then Cade pipes up, his eyes glinting with mischief.

"Will Nash need his strength too, Colt?"

The table goes quiet. I feel Nash and Colt stiffen beside me, their bodies radiating tension. My heart pounds as I wait for their response. We've never openly acknowledged this aspect of our relationship publicly.

Colt's jaw clenches, and he meets Cade's gaze with determination. "Yes, he will." His voice carries across the sudden silence. "And if anyone has a problem with Nash and me being intimate, speak up now. It won't change anything, but you may as well get it done with."

I hold my breath, my fingers instinctively finding Nash's hand under the table. His grip is tight, betraying his anxiety despite his calm exterior.

Cade's face splits into that unnerving grin that makes my skin crawl. His eyes dance with a manic light as he leans forward, still keeping Lily tucked possessively against his side.

"Hey, if you two like dick as much as pussy, have at it. More power to you." He licks his lips, that predatory gleam intensifying. "Though I gotta say, watching you two perform has a new meaning. All that... gripping and holding."

Nash's hand tightens around mine under the table. I feel Colt's entire body go rigid beside me.

"Careful," Nash warns, his voice carrying that dangerous edge I rarely hear.

But Cade just laughs, the sound sharp and unhinged. "What? I'm being supportive! Though Flora must be one hell of a woman to turn you both. Or maybe you were always curious about each other's equipment, and she just gave you the excuse you needed."

"Cade," Lily hisses, jabbing him with her elbow. "We all deserve to be happy."

He ignores her, his grin widening. "Come on, tell us

—who tops? My money's on Nash. Colt seems like he'd make such pretty sounds taking it."

I feel the tension coiling in both men beside me, but Colt's shoulders suddenly relax. He lets out a low chuckle that vibrates through his chest.

"We take turns," he drawls, fixing Cade with an amused look. "Nash has the most magnificent ass. It would be a shame not to enjoy it. And I'm man enough to admit I love it when he bends me over, too."

The table erupts in startled laughter. Nash's grip on my hand loosens as he shakes his head, a reluctant smile tugging at his lips.

Lars raises his glass. "Here's to versatility."

Ty clears his throat, commanding attention without raising his voice. "Listen up, you nosy bastards. Who fucks who in this carnival is nobody's business but their own so long as it's consensual. We're family here. We don't judge or shame and sure don't make anyone feel ashamed for who they love."

"Or how many they love," Sofia adds softly.

I feel tears prick at my eyes as warmth floods my chest. Nash kisses my temple while Colt's hand moves to Nash's thigh. At this moment, surrounded by our misfit family, I've never felt more accepted.

I lean closer to Aurora as the conversation around the table shifts to lighter topics. Her eyes sparkle with warmth as she turns toward me.

"I'm so glad you joined us," she says. "The carnival needed another voice of reason among all this testosterone."

"Says the woman dating the scariest man here," I tease, nodding toward Gage, who, for once, isn't wearing a mask. And Aurora's right, he's shockingly handsome. It's natural to assume someone constantly wears a mask to hide something. However, he radiates the same unnerving aura without it.

Aurora's laugh rings clear. "He's a teddy bear underneath it all. Just like your two giants."

"They are, aren't they?" I glance at Nash and Colt, who are deeply conversing with Ty. "I never thought I'd find this kind of acceptance, you know? Let alone love."

"The carnival has a way of collecting broken pieces and making them whole again." Aurora's hand finds mine on the table. "When I first came here, I was running from my demons. Now I'm surrounded by family on Christmas."

I squeeze her hand, understanding what she means. In just a few weeks, Aurora has become the sister I never had. She doesn't judge my unconventional relationship or my dark past. Instead, she offers unwavering support and friendship.

"Thank you," I whisper. "For being there that day in the bathroom. For inviting me to movie night. For everything."

"That's what friends are for." Aurora's eyes soften. "Plus, someone needs to tell you when your boys are being overprotective idiots."

I snort into my wine glass. "Like Gage isn't just as bad?"

"Touché," she grins.

I watch the faces around the table, my heart full to bursting. In my darkest moments, I never would have believed I'd ever find this. Not just Nash and Colt's love, but this entire misfit family who accepts us exactly as we are.

41

NASH

I reach into the box beneath our small Christmas tree and pull out two packages, catching Colt's knowing smile. Flora watches with curiosity as we each unwrap our new masks—mine a sleek black skull, his the familiar white but reimagined with more sinister details.

"Remember our first night together, little bird?" I ask, running my fingers along the mask's smooth surface.

Flora's breath catches, her eyes widening with recognition. The memory of chasing her through the forest sparks something within her.

"Want to play tonight?" Colt asks, his voice low and teasing as he holds up his mask.

She nods eagerly, already backing toward the door.

I shake my head at Colt's suggestion of the forest. "Too cold out there tonight, but..." I tap my fingers against the mask. "The training tent's been heated all day. That's your destination, little bird."

Flora's eyes light up with understanding. The tent will give us privacy, warmth, and ample equipment to make things interesting.

"Twenty seconds," Colt declares, sliding his white mask into place. "Start running."

Flora lets out an excited squeal and bolts through the door, giggling. We step outside and begin the count as her footsteps crunch in the snow, her beautiful silhouette racing toward the training tent.

I secure my skull mask, sharing a look with Colt. The familiar thrill of the hunt courses through me. Flora wants to be caught. She's chosen this game, chosen us.

"Think she'll make it to the tent before we catch her?" Colt asks, his voice muffled behind his mask.

"Let's find out." I check my new pocket watch. "Time's up."

We enter the cold night air, following Flora's tracks in the fresh snow. Her laughter echoes ahead of us, carried on the winter wind, drawing us toward our bounty.

I race after Flora, Colt at my side, our boots crunching through the fresh snow. Her laughter carries on the wind, urging us forward. We're close, so close to catching her before she reaches the tent, but she puts on a burst of speed at the last moment and slips inside.

Colt curses under his breath, but I can hear the excitement in his voice.

We enter the tent, its warmth contrasting with the biting cold outside. The space is filled with training equipment—silks, trapezes, and mats—providing ample hiding spots for our clever little bird.

"Where do you think she's hiding?" Colt asks, his eyes scanning the tent.

I take a deep breath, trying to calm my racing heart. "Spread out. She's here somewhere."

We move through the tent, checking behind equipment and under mats. Each empty hiding spot only fuels my anticipation. I can almost feel Flora's presence, her barely contained excitement and fear.

A soft rustle draws my attention to a stack of mats in the corner. I motion to Colt, and we approach slowly, stalking our prey.

"Come out, come out, little bird," I call, my voice low and teasing. "We know you're here."

Another rustle, a stifled giggle. She's close.

I crouch down, peering into the small space between the mats and the wall. In the shadows, I glimpse her wide, excited eyes.

"Got you," I whisper, reaching for her.

She lets out a delighted shriek and tries to scramble away, but Colt is there, blocking her escape. We converge on her, pulling her out from her hiding spot and into our arms.

"Caught you," Colt growls, his hands roaming over her body.

Flora squirms in our grasp, her breath coming in quick gasps.

I tighten my grip on Flora's wrists, pressing her into the mats as she squirms against us. She bites down on my gloved hand, her eyes flashing with feral determination. The sensation sends a jolt through me, igniting something primal.

"Fight all you want," Colt says, his voice dark with desire. "You're not going to stop us."

I nod, stepping back as he produces a length of silk rope. With practiced ease, he secures Flora's wrists, her struggle only fueling our mounting need to possess her.

She continues to kick and struggle as Colt ties each of her ankles to her thighs, keeping her restrained and open to us. Our girl's eyes flashed with fury. "Stop it! I don't want this!"

Colt tears open Flora's shirt, exposing her breasts to the cool air and making her skin pebble with goosebumps. She arches her back in a silent plea for more.

"Please, no," she whimpers, attempting to cover herself.

"We know what you want," Colt says.

I reach for the waistband of her leggings, my fingers curling around the elastic to yank them off.

"Stop fighting," I murmur, trailing kisses along her spine. "Let us give you what you crave."

Her breath comes in short gasps as I nip at her earlobe, my hand sliding between her thighs. She's so wet, ready for us, even as she struggles against her restraints.

Colt pushes her thighs apart to expose her to my touch. I stroke her gently, feeling her tremble. Flora's eyes squeeze shut, her lips parting as she succumbs to the pleasure.

I lean in. "You like that, don't you, little bird?"

She whimpers, her body arching into my touch. "No, please stop."

I step back, observing as Colt strips his clothes and settles onto the mats, his powerful body relaxed. He's lying in wait, ready to claim her as I deliver her to him. Our little bird is squirming in my grasp, but it's all part of the game. Colt's dark eyes shine with anticipation, fixated on her. She'll submit to him, but first, she'll struggle.

"Give her to me," he growls, his voice filled with an urgency that matches mine.

This moment, the anticipation, the chase, the surrender—it's what we've been craving. I lower Flora over Colt, feeling her fight against her bonds as she hangs suspended above him, my hands tucked under her upper arms to position her easily. Slowly, I lower her, her core aligning with his eager cock.

"Do it, damn it," he snarls, reaching up to grasp her hips.

I let go, and she is impaled in a single act onto his length, taking him deep inside her. A soft whimper escapes her lips, and her eyes widen. A frustrated cry escapes her, ever the fucking wildcat.

Colt's hands slide up her thighs, gripping her ass as he holds her still. "Scream all you want, baby. No one's coming to save you."

She bucks against him, her breath coming in short gasps. "No, please, let me go!"

Even as she pleads, her body betrays her; judging by Colt's expression, her tight pussy is clenching around him as he fills her, thighs held wide open by the ropes binding them to her ankles. Her muscles strain around him, fighting against the ropes, keeping her immobile and at our mercy. It's a dance we've performed before, a ballet of seduction and control.

Colt's hands slide up her body, claiming her breasts as he moves beneath her. Her cries of protest continue, but beneath them, I hear the soft moans of pleasure.

"Time to shut this dirty little bird up." My voice is rough with need.

Her eyes widen at the declaration, and she presses her lips together defiantly. I smirk, stepping closer and reaching for my waistband. I can feel her gaze on me as I strip, my arousal thick and heavy in my hand.

I stroke my rock-hard cock, pressing it to her lips.

"Open wide, little bird," I murmur. "Surrender that pretty mouth of yours."

Flora's eyes flash defiantly, and she pinches her lips together.

"We're playing that game, are we?" I ask, pinching her nose to force her mouth open.

A frustrated growl escapes her lips which I silence with a thrust of my hips, choking her with my dick. A groan tears from me at the feel of her mouth and the subtle caress of her tongue. Using my free hand, I take a fistful of her hair and take control.

"Those gorgeous lips of yours belong wrapped around my cock. Deep-throating me while Colt fucks you."

Flora moans around me, and I hold her hair back, giving her a clear path to worship me. Thrusting gently into the back of her throat, Colt pounds into her.

Colt's not going to last much longer from the sounds he's making, meaning it's time to test Flora's capacity for pleasure.

As I pull out, Flora's lips are connected to me by a string of saliva.

"Lie back on Colt's chest like a good girl," I order.

Colt steads her as she complies, her eyes alight with curiosity as she rests on Colt's chest.

"Why?" she asks, her voice laced with anticipation.

"No questions," I respond, a hint of authority in my tone.

Her breath hitches as I kneel before her, grabbing her thighs and forcing them wider.

Slowly, I rub the head of my cock against her clit, feeling her body's instinctive response.

Colt continues his assault on Flora, fucking her hard and rough. Her breath comes in short gasps as he takes her in a reclined reverse cowgirl position, her body moving in perfect harmony with his thrusts.

Leaning down, I trace Flora's clit with my tongue, teasing her. Colt's hands grip her hips, his fingers digging into her soft flesh as he guides her motions. I reach down, palming Colt's balls while my tongue edges Flora, feeling their weight in my hand. A groan escapes him when I massage them. And suddenly, Flora's flying apart. Her body shudders violently, and her cunt floods his dick with her release. I drag my tongue from her clit, tracing lazy patterns on her inner thigh.

Colt's hand tightens on her hip, his cock still buried deep inside her. His breath comes in harsh gasps, his body stiffening as he fights for control.

He tenses as my mouth hovers over his balls, hesitating for just a moment before I take one into my mouth, sucking gently.

"Fuck," he groans.

I hum against him, savoring the way his hands tighten on Flora, holding her still as he fights for release. I take his other ball into my mouth, swirling my tongue.

"Nash, stop fucking about," he pants.

"Fine, let me in her cunt while you take her tight little ass."

Colt groans, and Flora lets out a whimper of protest as he withdraws.

I rock her bound, helpless form back toward his shoulders, just enough to release his length from her pussy. Making eye contact with him, I smirk, knowing what he's thinking by his nod. My cock is throbbing, aching for release, and I stroke it gently as I position his head at her tight hole until his pierced cock slips in, easily coated with her release.

"Come on, little bird," I murmur, meeting her gaze. "Take it all like our good girl."

Her eyes spark with desire as I ease him inside her until he is buried fully into her ass. Giving her only a moment to adjust, I press my cock to her soaked cunt and slowly fill her until we have both fully disappeared into her depths.

A groan escapes me as her head rocks back against Colt's chest, her lips parted as she savors the sensation.

"Fuck yes," she moans, lips parting. "Please fuck me, both of you."

Setting a torturous pace, we fuck her in deep, slow

thrusts allowing her to adjust to the fullness. I use her thighs for leverage as Colt grasps both breasts firmly in his hands to do the same, giving us complete dominion over her.

Colt groans. "Such a good girl. Take his beautiful dick, every inch."

We pick up the pace, bouncing her between us.

I palm her breasts as she moves, my thumbs flicking her right nipple as Colt's hand grips her left breast to anchor her in place.

Her gaze falls to where our bodies join, her eyes dark with lust as she watches herself take me. Colt takes hold of her throat with his other hand, squeezing gently.

"Look at you, taking it like you were made for this," he whispers, his thumb caressing her jaw. "Damn, you're perfect."

"More," she pants. "Please."

Colt chuckles, his thumb rubbing circles around her left nipple as he bites her shoulder. He releases his grip on Flora's throat. "Ready to take it to the next level?"

Flora whimpers, her body tensing. "Yes," she breathes.

"Relax, angel." His voice is gentle but firm. "Let it happen."

Flora bites her lip. She knows what to expect, and I can see the determination in her eyes.

Her inner walls flutter around my cock. Her eyes squeeze shut as we fuck her harder. "Good girl."

Colt's fingers dance over the sensitive flesh, teasing her nipples with pinches and strokes. I watch her face, her eyes squeezed shut, her mouth open in a silent cry as we take her body. Her pussy clenches around me, her cries growing louder as her pleasure mounts.

"Feel good, baby?" I murmur, reaching up to play with her nipples.

She whimpers, her hips jerking.

She bites her lip, nodding slowly. "Please," she begs.

Colt slicks up his cock and moves closer, his eyes fixed on Flora's ass.

I hold my breath, savoring the feel of his dick sliding against mine.

The hot, tight squeeze of her body around both of us makes me groan. Flora cries out, her body tensing at the enormity of the sensations. Her cries of pleasure join Colt's guttural groans.

The slide of Colt's cock between the thin membrane against mine makes Flora's pussy feel so damn tight. Colt's teeth grit as he fights for control.

"Fuck, yes," Colt grits out, his fingers digging into Flora's soft flesh.

I lean forward, my lips close to her ear. "How does it feel, little bird?"

"Full," she moans, tossing her head back. "Tight."

Colt grunts in response, his cock pounding into her ass harder with our increased rhythm. As I rock into her, it slides her up his chest and his cock a few inches out of her. With each thrust forward, he grips her breast and throat, using that leverage to impale her onto him again.

Colt and I always find a perfect rhythm, slamming into her holes in tandem. We find our rhythm, moving as one. Her strangled moans fill the tent, echoing off the canvas, spurring us on.

Our thrusts become more urgent, our need building to a crescendo. Flora feels amazing, Colt's cock rubbing against mine, making it almost impossible not to come apart.

"Fuck, she's tight," Colt grunts, his hands sliding up her body to reclaim her breasts. "So fucking tight."

I groan in agreement, leaning over her to find her mouth in a kiss. Her tongue duels with mine as I thrust into her. The slide of her body against mine is exquisite, torture and bliss all at once.

Colt bites the back of her neck, marking her like a fucking animal. My hands move to her ass, kneading the firm flesh, spreading her wide for him. She's so fucking beautiful, so responsive, and her cries grow louder as we take her harder.

"You like being stuffed so full, don't you?" Colt growls, his hips pistoning into her. "Bet you never thought two cocks inside you would feel so damn good."

Fuck. It feels so good. My balls slap against Colt's with each thrust. Her walls flutter around me, contracting and releasing, warning me she's close.

"Come for us, little bird," I groan, biting my lip as my orgasm threatens to overpower me.

"Let it take you," Colt commands. "Give in to the fire we spark inside you."

Flora's breath catches, and her body stiffens. "I—I can't," she whimpers, her eyes squeezed shut. "It's too much."

Colt's hand releases one of her thighs. Finding her clit he begins to rub. I watch him tease her with his fingers. Her skin gleams with sweat, and her muscles quiver with the effort of holding back, her chest heaving as she tries to catch her breath.

Her lack of obedience forces Colt to wrap his hand gently but firmly around Flora's throat, leaving him nothing else to concentrate on. "When you come for us, baby, you breathe," he growls.

Colt doesn't let up, fingers dancing over her clit relentlessly. "That's it, baby," he whispers. "Come on. Let go."

Flora arches her back. "Fuck. Nash! Colt!" she cries both our names as she shatters violently into the first breath he allows her. It feels like I fucking died and went to heaven. Her muscles flutter and contract around me, making her already tight cunt strangle my cock so fucking good I nearly see stars. My hips stutter, and Colt growls as he loses control. The pulse of his cock throbbing against mine as he reaches his climax drives me insane.

"Fuck," he grunts, his hips snapping forward one last time.

I keep thrusting into Flora, not wanting this moment to end, wanting to stay forever connected to her and Colt in this way, but my body betrays me, and I fly apart moments after Colt, filling her with my release as I bury myself deep.

For a moment, we stay in the same position with our bodies connected, breathing heavily. Colt's hand finds my shoulder, his touch electric. In the dim light of the lanterns in the tent, his striking blue eyes glow as if on fire.

Colt breaks eye contact first and slides out of Flora

slowly, and I follow suit, aware of her soft whimpers of protest. We shift into our preferred side-by-side cuddle with Flora between us.

I stretch out next to her, pulling her into my arms as she nuzzles into my chest. She mumbles something about needing tissues, and I chuckle, kissing her mussed hair. "I've got you, little bird."

Colt hands me a box of tissues, and I wipe her gently, aware of her sensitive state. We remain quiet, our hearts slowing.

"That was..." Flora trails off, searching for the right words. "Incredible," she finishes. "Really incredible."

Colt nods. "Yeah. It was."

I thread my fingers through her hair, brushing it away from her face. "It was perfect."

Flora's eyes shine with love as she pulls back to look at both of us on the training mats.

"I love you both so much," she whispers. A playful smile crosses her face. "And I was thinking... I'd like to do more of this chasing in the future."

Colt's eyes darken, and my spent dick twitches.

"You know what would be hot?" Flora's voice holds a note of mischief. "If you two chased each other and tried to overpower each other."

I look at Colt, seeing my hunger reflected in his gaze. The idea of him hunting me, of fighting for dominance, sends a thrill through me. There's no awkwardness now, no holding back. We're all together, completely and openly.

"What do you think?" I ask Colt, though I already

know his answer from how his body has tensed with anticipation.

"I think our little bird has excellent ideas," he replies, his voice rough with desire.

Flora beams, clearly pleased with herself for suggesting it. The dynamic between us has shifted into something deeper, more complete. No more pretending, no more denial. Just the three of us, exactly as we're meant to be.

42

COLT

I lean against the bar, nursing my whiskey, watching Flora dance with Aurora on the crowded floor. Her golden hair catches the pulsing lights, and her smile tightens my chest. Nash's shoulder brushes mine as he orders another drink.

"She's different," I say, not taking my eyes off Flora as she throws her head back, laughing at something Aurora whispers in her ear.

"Stronger." Nash's voice carries a note of pride. "Though she always was. Just needed to believe it herself."

The club thrums with energy as the carnival crew celebrates leaving Easthollow behind. Ty holds court at a corner table with Cade and Lars while Phoenix lurks near the DJ booth, probably critiquing the sound system. But my focus keeps returning to Flora. I watch how she moves without fear now, how she owns her space instead of trying to shrink into shadows.

"Remember how she used to flinch when anyone got

too close?" I take another sip, the whiskey burning pleasantly. "Now look at her."

Flora catches my eye across the dance floor and grins, beckoning us over with a crook of her finger. Nash chuckles beside me.

"Our girl's getting bold," he says, setting down his glass.

"About fucking time." I push off from the bar, drawn to her like always. The crowd parts as Nash and I approach her, and I catch more than a few envious glances. Let them look. They can see who she belongs to.

Flora slides between us, her skin glowing with sweat from dancing. She reaches up to touch my jaw, then Nash's, claiming us both in front of everyone. No more hiding. No more shame.

"Happy New Year," she says, pulling us closer as the music shifts to something slower and darker.

I hold Flora close as she moves against me, her back pressed to my chest while Nash faces her. The bass thrums through us, matching my heartbeat. Her fingers thread through Nash's hair as he dips his head to her neck, and my chest tightens, not with jealousy but with fierce pride that we've found this balance.

We dance until Flora's cheeks flush and her breath comes quick. She tugs us toward our table, where three fresh drinks wait.

"Aurora's got good taste in music," Flora says, sliding into the booth between us. She takes a long sip of her cocktail, then settles against my shoulder.

Nash reaches across the table to brush a strand of hair from her face. "Good taste in friends, too."

"Smooth talker," I say, smirking at him over Flora's head.

"You love it." Nash winks, and Flora giggles.

"Both of you are ridiculous." She traces the rim of her glass. "But you're mine."

The simple possessiveness in her voice hits me hard. I kiss her temple while Nash captures her free hand, threading their fingers together.

"Wouldn't want it any other way, little bird," Nash says.

We sit in comfortable silence, watching the crowd, sharing occasional touches and private smiles. There is no need to fill the space with words. We've moved past the uncertainty that used to plague us. Now, we just are.

Flora hums along to the music, perfectly content between us. Nash catches my eye, and I see my feelings reflected there—this bone-deep satisfaction, this sense of rightness, of home.

I pull Flora closer to the booth, unable to resist her any longer. My lips find hers, soft and tender, savoring the sweet taste of her cocktail. She melts into me, her fingers trailing up my chest as we share this gentle moment.

Nash watches us with dark eyes before claiming Flora's mouth next. Where my kiss had been gentle, his is fire—passionate, all-consuming. Flora whimpers against his lips, and the sound stirs something primal in me.

When they break apart, Nash's gaze locks with mine.

I cup his jaw, drawing him to me in front of Flora. Our lips meet, and it's different from kissing Flora—rougher, more demanding, but filled with just as much love. Nash sighs into my mouth, and I feel Flora's hands on our chests, holding us together.

"My beautiful men," she whispers, and I feel Nash smile against my lips.

We separate but stay close, foreheads touching as we catch our breath. Flora turns to press kisses along Nash's jaw, then mine.

"Fuck, you two are my world," Nash murmurs, his voice rough with emotion. "I never thought I'd have anything like this."

"Me either," I admit, threading my fingers through his hair while my other hand finds Flora's. "But here we are."

Flora nuzzles into my neck. "Wouldn't want to be anywhere else."

I pull Nash and Flora closer, the club's chaos fading into white noise. Flora's fingers trace lazy patterns on my chest while Nash's hand rests warm and solid on my thigh. The familiar scents of Flora's vanilla perfume and Nash's woodsy cologne blend and ground me in this perfect moment.

"Let's get out of here," I murmur against Flora's hair. She nods, already sliding out of the booth.

Nash takes her hand while I wrap my arm around her waist, and we weave through the crowd toward the exit. The winter air hits us like a kiss, crisp and clean after the heated club atmosphere. Snow falls in fat, lazy flakes, catching in Flora's golden hair and on Nash's dark lashes.

Flora tilts her face to the sky, letting the snowflakes melt on her cheeks. Her pure joy radiates from her, making my chest ache. Nash watches her, too; his tender expression steals my breath.

"I love you both," Flora whispers, her words creating little clouds in the cold air. "So much it terrifies me sometimes."

Nash pulls her close, pressing his lips to her temple. "You're ours, little bird. Always."

I step behind her, boxing her between us as I kiss the nape of her neck. "No more fear. We've got you."

The world narrows to just us three, standing in the gently falling snow. The distant thump of bass from the club, the occasional passing car, the sounds of the city fade away until I can only hear our synchronized breathing and the quiet crunch of snow beneath our feet.

Flora turns in our arms, rising to kiss Nash, then me, her lips warm despite the cold. Nash's hand finds mine around her waist, our fingers interlocking. The simple touch sends electricity through my veins. When Nash's dark eyes meet mine over Flora's head, I see everything I feel reflected there.

This is what home feels like. Not a place, but these two people who complete me in ways I never knew I needed.

43

FLORA

Two months later...

Colt and Nash tear down the wall between their bedrooms while I sip coffee, leaning against the far wall. Dust fills the air, but neither notice as they work in sync. Nash's muscles flex with each swing of the sledgehammer while Colt carefully removes debris, mindful of his now-healed shoulder.

"The delivery guys said they'll be here by noon," I call out, checking my phone.

The Alaskan king bed we ordered is massive—perfect for three people who can't keep their hands off each other but want space when we're sleeping. These past months sharing Colt's regular king has been cozy but cramped. More than once, I've woken up practically hanging off the edge.

Nash pauses, wiping sweat from his brow. His shirt clings to his chest in all the right places. "I guess we didn't need to start so early. This is going faster than expected."

Colt stacks another piece of drywall against the wall. "Though I'll miss having my own space sometimes." He winks at me, and I know he's teasing.

None of us have slept apart since Christmas.

The bedroom transformation represents something bigger—we're creating a space designed for the three of us.

I set down my coffee on the nightstand, grabbing a garbage bag to help collect smaller pieces of debris. The sooner we finish, the sooner we can christen our new bed. From Nash's heated glance, I can tell he's thinking the same thing.

"Better finish your coffee, little bird," Nash says. "We've got a lot more work ahead."

I work alongside Nash and Colt as we clear away the last of the debris. My muscles ache from hauling pieces of drywall, but I'm satisfied watching our shared space take shape. The wall that once divided the bedrooms is gone, leaving a wide open area perfect for our new bed.

Colt dismantles his old bed frame with practiced efficiency. At the same time, Nash and I vacuum every corner, ensuring no dust or debris remains. The empty space feels full of possibility.

"Last piece," Colt announces, carrying out the headboard.

I've just finished wiping down the baseboards when a knock echoes through the trailer. Nash opens the door to two delivery men with our new bed.

"Right this way," he directs them to our newly opened room.

The delivery guys work quickly, bringing in pieces of the massive Alaskan king frame. I stand back with Colt, watching them assemble it with professional speed. The dark wood perfectly matches Nash's existing furniture, making the space cohesive.

When they bring the mattress, all four men have to maneuver it through the trailer and onto the frame. It's enormous and exactly what we need. The delivery guys quickly set everything up, and then we signed the paperwork.

"All set," the lead delivery man says, handing Nash the warranty information. "Enjoy your new bed."

I catch one of the delivery guys giving us a curious look as he glances between Nash, Colt, and me. His eyes dart from one to the other, clearly trying to piece together our dynamic. The slight furrow in his brow and how his lips purse tell me he's figured out we're more than roommates.

He opens his mouth to say something, then thinks better of it. Instead, he busies himself with gathering their tools while his partner folds up the moving blankets.

Nash hands them each a tip, maintaining his professional demeanor despite the obvious judgment in the delivery guy's expression. Colt stands protectively close to me, his hand resting casually on my lower back.

The curious delivery guy's eyes linger on Colt's possessive gesture, then flick to Nash's matching stance on my other side. His cheeks flush slightly as understanding dawns. But to his credit, he keeps his thoughts to himself, simply nodding politely thanks for the tip.

I help Nash unfold the crisp new sheets, their deep burgundy color rich against the dark wood of the frame. The fabric feels impossibly soft between my fingers. Nash insisted on the highest thread count they had.

"Finally, room to stretch," Colt says, helping tuck in the corners of the fitted sheet. "No more elbows in my face at three a.m."

"That was one time," I protest, tossing a pillow at him. He catches it with a grin.

Nash spreads out the matching duvet, its weight settling perfectly across the massive expanse of mattress. "I still can't believe how big this thing is. Could fit half the carnival in here."

"Don't get any ideas," Colt warns playfully, arranging the decorative pillows I picked against the headboard.

Once everything's perfectly arranged, I can't resist anymore. I take a running leap onto the bed, landing in the middle with a bounce. The mattress is heavenly—firm but with just enough give.

"Come on!" I pat the spaces beside me. Nash and Colt exchange amused looks before joining me, one on each side. We lay there staring up at the ceiling, the bed so wide we could all spread our arms without touching.

"This is weird," Colt declares after a moment. "I'm too used to being squished together."

Nash rolls onto his side, propping his head on his hand. "We'll just have to get creative about filling all this space."

I stretch luxuriously, enjoying the room to move. "At least now, when one of you steals all the covers, there's enough left for the rest of us."

"I do not steal covers," they protest in unison, making me laugh.

"Sure you don't." I burrow into the plush duvet, sighing contentedly. "This is perfect."

Nash wastes no time turning to more enticing prospects, saying, "We have to christen this new bed properly."

Colt's smile widens as he shifts closer to me, his eyes sparkling with mischief. "Any suggestions for how we should do that?"

Nash's answer comes without hesitation. "A train, of course." He reaches out to brush a strand of hair behind my ear, his touch gentle. "Colt's dick in my ass, my dick in you, Flora. Like we've done so many times before."

My cheeks heat at the memory. It's true—the three of us have become intimately familiar with the pleasures of this arrangement. As Nash calls it, the train has become our new favorite way to connect, a physical manifestation of the bond we've formed. I nod my agreement, my voice hoarse as I say, "Sounds good."

Colt gets up, making no secret of his growing arousal, tenting his grey sweats. "You know I'm always up for that."

I'm already well aware of his enthusiasm. Our late-night training sessions often end together in a train of lust, hunger, and love.

I eagerly tear off my sweats and tank top, throwing them off the bed. Nash is quick to get naked, throwing his clothes in a pile on top of mine. And then we both glance at Colt, who is still dressed.

He slowly pulls off his tight t-shirt, revealing his corded muscles covered in dark ink. My stomach flutters every time I see him like this. Both of them are so fucking beautiful. And then he slowly peels away his grey sweats, his huge dick bobbing up and slapping his abs.

"Fuck, I never get enough of seeing you," Nash murmurs, dick in his hand already. And then he glances at me. "Or you, little bird. Turn over."

I turn onto my side, pressing my back to Nash's chest and feeling his hand caress my hip. His fingers leave a trail of fire as they slide down my body, slipping between my thighs and gently parting them. He probes at my core with his fingers, already knowing how wet and ready I am for him.

The bed dips beside us as Colt settles behind Nash. The telltale signs of the lubricant bottle cap clicking open, followed by Colt squeezing it out, tells me he's ready to prepare Nash.

Nash's cock nudges at my core, and he pushes into me with a slow, deliberate stroke. My breath quickens as he fills me, my body clinging to his length as he pulls out, only to thrust back in. I rock back to meet his rhythm, the pace slow and sensual as he works to claim me once more.

The slick sound of Colt's fingers moving in Nash's channel reaches my ears, and my hips stutter. The knowledge of what's about to happen, of Colt's dick entering Nash, pushes me closer to the edge.

Every time Nash gets fucked, his dick swells and gets so fucking hard inside me that it's insane.

"You feel so damn good, little bird," Nash growls against my ear. His thumb finds my clit, and he strokes in time with his thrusts. "I'm gonna make you come all over my cock."

My head falls back against his shoulder, exposing my throat. His lips curve into a smile against my skin as he nips gently at my neck.

"Colt, it's time for you to fuck our boy," I urge, wanting nothing more than to feel them both lose control. "Take his ass."

"Damn right, I will." Colt's voice is rough with desire as he lines up with Nash's entrance. "His ass is so fucking greedy for it."

Nash bites out a curse as Colt pushes inside him, his fingers digging into my hips, his grip tight as he battles through the stretch. I can feel his cock throbbing inside me, the erratic pulse of it a testament to his need.

"Fuck, yes, Colt. Give it to me." Nash's voice breaks as Colt slides deeper, the sound of his pleasure filling the room.

Colt's filthy commentary adds fuel to the fire already raging inside me. "That's it, Nash. Take that thick cock like a good boy."

Nash answers him with a broken groan, his hips stuttering as he fights for control. Colt knows exactly how to push his buttons, when to be gentle, and when to be rough. With a final, deep thrust, he seats himself fully inside Nash.

"Ah, fuck," Nash breathes, his voice wrecked. "Always forget how damn good that feels."

My breath comes in shallow pants. The combined sensations of Nash filling me and the wet sounds of Colt fucking Nash's lubed asshole push me to the brink.

"Nothing better than feeling your tight pussy clenching around my cock." Nash's voice is gravelly as he continues rubbing my clit while pounding into me. "Having my ass wrapped around Colt's thick dick while I do it..." His sentence hangs, and he groans loudly. "Fuck, I love knowing it's getting Colt off too."

His words paint a picture in my mind, one I've witnessed in videos we've taken of ourselves. The image of Nash buried deep in my pussy, while Colt thrusts into him—it's more than enough to push me over the edge. My orgasm hits in crashing waves, overwhelming me with pleasure. My inner walls flutter around Nash's cock, milking every last drop of pleasure as he continues to thrust through my peak.

Nash hits that spot inside me that never fails to make my vision blur and my breath catch. Everything becomes hypersensitive. Every touch, every sound, amplified. My inner walls flutter around him as he pushes deep, and he knows exactly how to prolong the pleasure, just how to drag out my orgasm.

His hand moves faster, his fingers circling my clit relentlessly as he continues to thrust. Colt's rhythm changes behind him, a counterpoint to Nash's pace. It's a dance they know well, perfectly matching each other's needs.

"Ah, fuck," Nash groans, his voice tight. "Your pussy

is milking my cock so fucking good, Flora. Gonna make me—"

Nash's growl fills the room, his hips stuttering as he spurts inside me. My inner muscles clench greedily, milking every last drop from him as he shudders. Colt keeps up his relentless pace, his need clearly building.

"Fuck my ass," Nash grunts. "Breed me while I'm still pulsing inside your angel."

I glance over my shoulder, catching a glimpse of Colt's face twisted in pleasure as he fucks into him. His hands grip Nash's hips hard enough to leave bruises, his expression fierce as he finds his own release. They're both so utterly beautiful.

"Yeah, that's it. Gonna breed that perfect ass, just like you want." His words are rough, each one punctuated with a deep thrust. "Bet you love the idea of my cum dripping out of that well-fucked hole."

Nash lets out a strangled cry, his body bowing under the force of Colt's thrusts. The sound of skin slapping against skin fills my ears as their bodies collide. I press my lips to Nash's shoulder, kissing him softly as they both succumb to the pleasure.

I hear Colt's guttural cry of completion. Their bodies still for a moment, spent and sated. Then Colt pulls out slowly, his softening length slipping from Nash. Nash is still inside me, his dick still semi-hard. I'm surrounded by the scent of sex, of our combined pleasure, and my inner muscles clench instinctively, hungry for more.

Nash pulls out and draws me close, nuzzling against my neck. "Turn around, little bird."

I shift to face him, and he kisses me softly.

"Love you," I whisper, my lips against Nash's. There was a time when those words would have terrified me, but now they roll off my tongue with ease, needing to be said.

"Love you too, little bird," Nash replies, his breath warm against my hair. It still feels new when he says it, but right in a way I never expected.

"You two are sappy as hell." Colt's voice holds a hint of amusement. "Couldn't you wait till after the afterglow to make googly eyes at each other?"

I watch Nash turn his head to look at Colt over his shoulder, a playful smirk tugging at his lips. "Feeling left out back there?"

The teasing lilt in Nash's voice makes my heart flutter. I love seeing them like this–the casual banter.

Colt rolls his eyes, but I catch the way his gaze lingers on Nash's mouth. "Shut up," he mutters.

Before saying anything else, Nash reaches back and threads his fingers through Colt's hair, pulling him forward. Their lips meet in a heated kiss that steals my breath. The sight of them together never fails to amaze me.

I trace my fingers along Nash's chest as I watch them, feeling how his heart races beneath my touch. The kiss deepens, and I hear Colt's soft groan as Nash's tongue slides against his.

The intensity between Nash and Colt breaks as Colt's hand reaches across Nash's body, gripping my arm firmly. He pulls me up and over Nash in one swift motion, who shifts to accommodate my new position. I find myself on my knees, straddling Nash's torso as Colt captures my lips with his.

His kiss differs from Nash's—more demanding, rougher around the edges. Where Nash tends to be calculated and precise, Colt pours raw emotion into every movement. His hand cradles the back of my head, fingers tangling in my hair as he deepens the kiss.

Nash's hands steady my hips, keeping me balanced as I melt into Colt's embrace.

I feel cherished between them, safe in a way I never thought possible. Colt breaks the kiss just long enough to look into my eyes, his gaze filled with an intensity that still takes my breath away. Below me, Nash's thumb traces soothing circles on my hip, grounding me in the moment.

44

NASH

One month later...

Flora's graceful form cuts through the glittering afternoon light as she executes a perfect aerial split. Her movements flow like water, each transition smoother than the last. Three months of living together has deepened our connection, making our performances seamless.

Colt spots from below, his strong hands ready, though we all know Flora won't fall. His shoulder has healed completely, and the way he moves now shows no trace of the old injury. My chest swells with pride, seeing them work together.

"Perfect form, little bird," I call up to Flora as she transitions into a drop sequence. The silk wraps around her legs, and she descends in a controlled spiral that takes my breath away.

The routine we're practicing isn't particularly challenging anymore since we've performed it dozens of times. But there's something magical about watching the two people I love most move in perfect synchronization.

Colt catches Flora as she dismounts, and I can't help but smile at the tender kiss he places on her forehead. When they look at me, their eyes shine with love.

We don't need words anymore. With a simple glance or a slight touch, we understand each other. What started as a complex dance of desire and protection has evolved into something pure and unshakeable.

"What are you thinking about?" Flora interrupts my thoughts, her eyes searching mine with her beautiful hazel gaze.

I shake my head, unable to meet her eyes now. Colt's gaze is on me, curious, but he stays silent.

"You've been quiet lately. Distant, almost." Flora sits beside me, her hand brushing mine where it rests on my thigh. "What's on your mind, Nash?"

My heart hammers in my chest. I've imagined this conversation a hundred times, but now that it's here, my tongue feels thick and clumsy.

"Something... I want," I begin, searching for the right words. I think of the night she suggested we chase her, had my mind spinning with the possibilities. How could I have known that it would lead me here? "It's... a fantasy."

Flora's eyes widen, and she leans forward, suddenly intrigued. She knows how much our fantasies have driven this unconventional relationship of ours.

"I want to be chased." My voice is hoarse. "I want to be the one running like you were that night."

Flora's eyes darken with desire, but she waits for me to continue.

"And I want Colt to chase me." I pause. "I want him to force me. To take me while he wears that mask of his."

Her eyes flicker to Colt, then back to me. "What else?"

I swallow, my mouth dry as I say the words I've never voiced before. "And I want you there, too. Watching, touching... sucking my dick too. Even riding me while I'll tell you to stop."

There, it's out. The deepest, darkest desire that's been gnawing at my insides for a while. I wait, breath held, for her reaction.

Flora's eyes burn with an intense heat, and her voice is a husky whisper. "Tell me more."

Relief washes over me, swiftly followed by desire. "It's a power play," I begin. I want to feel pursued, hunted even, and taken by force."

"Goddamn, it's hot," Flora remarks, wiping a strand of hair from her face. Her eyes shine with a mischievous light, reminding me of the first night. That night changed everything—it unlocked something within me.

Colt interrupts my fantasy. "Why this sudden urge to be chased?" His eyes are unreadable.

But he senses the weight behind my request, I can tell. He knows me too well.

I sigh, running a hand through my hair. "It's not so sudden. It's been building for a while." I hesitate, struggling to find the words to explain something deeply personal and buried. "When I was a kid, in one of my foster homes..."

I trail off, the memories swirling in my mind like dark clouds. They wait patiently, offering silent encouragement.

"I was... abused," I whisper. "By one of the older boys in the home."

Colt's eyes narrow, his protective instincts no doubt kicking in. I hold up a hand to ward off his questions, needing to get it all out in my own time. "It went on for a few years. I was only ten when it started."

Flora makes a small noise beside me, reaching for my hand. I squeeze her tightly, grateful for her presence.

"I felt your need for vengeance so strongly, Flora. I knew what you were going through, though my experience wasn't exactly the same." I pause, the old wounds aching. "I knew the pain, the powerlessness, the shame."

Colt's eyes glow with a fierce intensity. "I'm sorry, Nash. I never knew. Do you know if that bastard ever got what was coming to him?"

I shake my head. "He ran away. But it doesn't matter now. It's over, in the past."

"When I watched Flora that night, how free she became after we chased her..." I squeeze her hand tighter, drawing strength from her presence. "I saw something change in her. Like she took back control by giving it up willingly."

My throat tightens. "I need that, too. To heal the wounds and take back power. Making memories where I give up control and trust the person taking it."

Flora's fingers trace patterns on my palm as I

continue. "I've spent years building walls, staying in control. But seeing how Flora healed, how she found freedom in submission—it made me realize I'm still carrying chains from my past. I long to submit, too."

Colt moves closer, his presence solid and reassuring. "I want you to be the one to chase me," I tell him. "I trust you completely. I know you'll understand what this means."

"And I want Flora there," I add, turning to her. "Because she knows. She understands what it's like to reclaim yourself through surrender."

The weight of years lifts from my shoulders as I speak. For so long, I've hidden this part of myself, buried it under layers of control and the drive to be a perfectionist. Here, with these two people who love me, I can finally let it surface.

"I need to heal," I whisper. "And I think this might be the way."

Colt steps closer to me. His eyes burn with the same intensity I feel simmering inside. His thumb brushes my lower lip, sending a spark of electricity through me. "Okay. I'd do anything for you," he mutters before glancing at Flora. "Both of you. You sure you want this, Nash?"

I nod. "Yes."

"Then get on your hands and knees."

Without hesitation, I sink to my knees, desire coursing through my veins. My heart hammers as I lean forward, bracing myself on my hands and bending low, offering myself to him.

"That's my good boy." Colt's voice is thick with

arousal as he yanks down my shorts and then rips a hole in my leotard. "You look fucking perfect like that."

My cock throbs as I wait, my entire body on edge.

"Flora, come help me get him relaxed while I prep his ass." Colt's voice cuts through the charged silence. "If we're gonna do this, he must be lubed up before the chase."

Her soft footsteps pad closer, and she drops onto her knees beside me, rubbing my dick that strains against my leotard. "Relax, baby. Just let go for us."

I inhale sharply through my nose. My heart pounds as Colt steps behind me, his strong hands caressing my hips. Without warning, he spreads my cheeks and presses the tip of a cold, lubed dildo against my hole.

My eyes squeeze shut at the slight burn, even though I've gotten used to having my ass stretched. "Fuck," I hiss through gritted teeth.

"Shh, just breathe through it," Flora coos, her fingers threading through my hair, tugging slightly. Her lips press against the sensitive skin of my neck, her free hand rubbing my cock.

Colt's thick finger circles my rim, adding more lube as he slowly pushes the toy inside me. "That's it, bear down and let it slip inside you," he whispers, his hot breath fanning the nape of my neck.

"Yes, sir," I breathe.

"That's our good boy," Flora praises, her lips ghosting the shell of my ear, her touch teasing. Damn, she knows exactly how to play this game.

Colt thrusts the dildo all the way inside, adding more

lube to get me ready and stretched. "Christ," I pant, the pleasure overwhelming. "Feels so good."

The dildo presses deeper, and I cry out, my elbows collapsing as I let my forehead rest on the mat. Colt's fingers grip my hips, holding me in place as he moves the toy in and out. "You like that dildo in your tight ass, baby?"

"Yes," I manage, my voice hoarse with need. "More, please."

The pressure on my prostate sends sparks of pleasure through me, and I moan, my whole body trembling. Precum leaks through my leotard and onto Flora's hand.

Colt pulls the dildo out, and the sudden emptiness has me gritting my teeth. My entire body tingles with need, and the cool air on my exposed skin sends goosebumps across my flesh.

"You ready, baby?" Colt asks, his eyes dark with desire. "This is your fantasy, so you set the rules. Bubblegum work as your safe word, same as Flora?"

I nod, my voice a hoarse whisper. "Bubblegum. And I'm ready."

Colt pulls my shorts back into place to hide the hole in my leotard for the chase.

"All right, then run." Colt's voice is rough. "Run for your fucking life," he growls as he slides his mask over his face.

My pulse pounds in my ears as I get to my feet and tear out of the tent. As I sprint toward the forest, I hear Colt and Flora start the countdown. "Ten... nine... eight..."

I push harder, feeling the burn in my thighs and the

cold wind against my sweaty skin. Their distant voices echo through the carnival, counting down.

My footsteps eat up the ground, weaving through the carnival grounds. I quicken my pace, wanting to put some distance between us.

The adrenaline surges through my veins, spurring me on. I take a sharp left, veering off the path to cut through the supply tents. My heart races as I catch glimpses of Colt through the trees, his fast stride never wavering. His boots pound the ground, drawing relentlessly closer.

"Where are you, pretty boy?" His voice is rough. "Don't you wanna feel my cock inside you?"

My traitorous cock twitches in response to his words, making it difficult to focus on running. Even so, I move my limbs faster, the muscles in my thighs burning. Part of me wants to give in, to let him catch me, but another part wants to run forever, chasing this high.

His shouts grow louder, and I take another sharp turn, cutting between two huge tree trunks.

"You can't hide from me," Colt taunts, his voice frighteningly close now. "I'll find you, and when I do, I'm gonna fuck you so good."

His words drive me crazy, making me moan despite myself. I'm torn between wanting to escape and desperately wishing he'd catch me, take me, claim me.

I reach the main path again, but my legs feel like lead. Colt's footsteps echo behind me. Suddenly, his hand shoots out, wrapping around my bicep, and he pulls me to a halt.

Spinning me around, he slams me against a tree. The rough surface bites into my skin.

I struggle against Colt, my body humming with adrenaline as I try to break free.

"Stop fighting me," he growls, his hips grinding against mine. "You want this."

"Fuck off," I snarl, my hands balling into fists. I swing, my fist connecting with his jaw.

Colt grunts, but he doesn't let go. His lips find my pulse point, sucking and biting as he explores my neck, making my skin sing with sensation.

I try to shove him away, but it's like pushing against a wall. Colt's stronger than me, and when he wants something, he's relentless.

"Please," I manage to get out. "Don't."

Colt rips my shorts off and then tears apart my leotard entirely, leaving me completely exposed. His hand wraps around my hard cock, stroking. "So hard," he growls in my ear. "Does me chasing you make you hard? Bet you were imagining me tearing apart your ass once I caught you."

I grapple with Colt, fighting against his hold. My chest heaves with exertion, and I grunt, attempting to shove him away. But his grip is like steel, his eyes glittering with fierce determination.

My words fail me as he pins me against the tree, his mouth descending on mine, his tongue demanding entry. I twist my head to the side, evading his hungry kiss.

"Let me go," I snarl, struggling in earnest now.

Something about his dominant nature sparks my defiance, and I can't submit so easily. Not this time.

Colt grins, the icy blue of his eyes darkening with lust. "I don't think so." His hands move swiftly, and before I know it, my wrists are bound together with the thick rope he pulls from his back pocket. The rough fibers bite into my skin as he secures my hands in front of me.

"Let me go, damn it!" I strain against the bonds.

My rational mind knows I'm trapped, but something deep within me refuses to yield.

"Ask me nicely to fill that pretty ass," Colt challenges, his fingers stroking my aching erection. "Beg for it."

His touch sends shocks through me, and I buck my hips. "Fuck you!" I spit. I am at Colt's mercy, and I can't stop thinking about his cock plunging into me, taking what he wants with force.

Colt smirks, enjoying my struggle. "No, I'm going to fuck you."

He maneuvers me, his strong hands gripping my hips and positioning me on the forest floor on my back. I glare at him, my heart pounding.

"No," I whisper, my throat tight. "Don't."

Flora appears above me, watching as I'm wrestled into submission by Colt. "Fuck his ass, Colt. Make him scream," she demands.

My legs and hips are pushed up in the air. I'm completely at Colt's mercy. He groans, lining himself up with my prepared hole, his eyes trailing over my balls and landing on my rock-hard dick. Fuck. The way he looks at me undoes me.

"Tell me you don't want it."

"I don't," I lie, my breath catching as I feel the head of his cock.

"Liar," he growls, his eyes dark and intense as he slams forward. The burn elicits a strangled cry from me as he pushes deep, burying himself inside me in one smooth stroke.

"Fuck!" I scream, trying to adjust to the stretch, the burn, the sensation of being filled so suddenly. "Too much!"

Colt stills, his hands gripping my hips as he waits for me to relax around him. "Fuck, this ass is fucking tight." Colt moves inside me, my back sliding against the rough ground.

Flora kneels beside me and wraps her hand around my pulsing cock, stroking. I can't help but thrust my hips into Colt, lost in the slide of our bodies, the way he fills me. "You like that?" Flora's sweet voice cuts through the night. "Do you like him taking that tight ass of yours?"

I want this—to be taken, possessed, and marked by them both—but something inside me, some remaining fragment of control, makes me resist.

I shake my head, not wanting to put this into words.

Flora's giggle is light and wicked. "Bullshit. Your dick is so fucking hard."

"Fuck off," I grit out, even though I know she's right.

Colt thrusts into me, his hips snapping forward, and a groan escapes my lips.

Flora releases my cock and trails her fingers up my thigh, their path ending where our bodies join. "Look at you, taking that big cock so well."

I gasp, my vision blurring as Colt's pierced dick presses my prostate, making my dick leak. Flora laps at the tip, just tasting me. She knows how to push all my buttons.

The force of each thrust takes my breath away, but it's not enough. I want more. I crave Flora's touch, her beautiful body pressed against mine.

Her pretty eyes are locked on my cock, while Colt claims my ass. "It would be a shame to waste this beautiful hard cock," she purrs, her voice laced with need. "I'm going to ride it."

She sheds her clothes, revealing her stunning body. The sight of her sends even more blood pumping to my cock, making it ache for her.

Flora climbs onto me, breasts bouncing as she lines herself up with my dick. Her eyes glitter with desire as she sinks down, taking me inside her.

"Shit," I breathe, the sensation overwhelming.

Colt continues his relentless thrusts. Flora rides me fast, her hair a golden halo around her face.

They move in sync, their rhythm perfect. Each thrust from Colt sends me deeper into Flora.

I attempt to roll my hips to guide our rhythm, but Colt's grip is absolute. 'No,' he says, his voice strained. 'You follow our lead.'

Flora rides me hard, her walls squeezing me, milking me. "So good," she moans, her hands gripping my shoulders.

I want to thrust up into her, but Colt keeps me pinned in place, pounding into my ass.

Her eyes lock with mine, the hazel depths turning darker with arousal. "Ride my cock, baby," I hear myself say, my voice thick with desire. "Ride it hard."

Obeying my command, she sets a furious rhythm. "I love your cock," Flora moans before kissing me passionately, our tongues tangling.

All the while, Colt nails me with each thrust. "Yes," I breathe, my entire body on fire. "More, please. Both of you."

I buck my hips, Colt's dick sinking deeper than I believed possible as I plunge into Flora. "So fucking tight," he growls. "Gonna breed that ass, make you mine."

Flora's nails dig into my chest as she moves with fierce determination. "Come for me, Nash. I want to be filled with your cum."

Her words send me over the edge, and I shout her name as I explode inside her. White-hot pleasure courses through my veins, and my body convulses with each pulse.

Colt's thrusts become erratic, his grip on my hips tightening. "I'm gonna fuck you so good. Fill that ass up and mark you as mine," Colt growls, coming apart and shooting his cum into my ass.

The sensation pushes me higher, and I bite Flora's lip, finding sweet relief as her blood fills my mouth.

"Nash!" Flora cries out, her inner walls gripping me as she reaches her peak. Her breasts press against my chest as she collapses forward, her fingers digging into my chest. "Don't stop," she begs, her voice hoarse with need.

I thrust up into her, spurred on by her pleas. My cock pulses with aftershocks of pleasure, each one sending fresh spurts of cum deep inside her. I feel boneless, yet I continue to move, riding out our shared release.

Slowing to a stop, we pant, our chests heaving as we struggle to catch our breath. Colt's arms wrap around us, pulling us close, our sweaty bodies pressed together.

Colt's lips press against my temple, his kiss tender. "That was fucking incredible," he whispers. "I love you both so goddamn much."

Flora's fingers thread through my hair, her nails gently scraping my scalp. "I needed that," she breathes, her lips brushing my cheek as she grazes my ear with her teeth. "I love you both."

Colt and I share a look over her shoulder, our eyes locking in silent communication. The intensity of this moment hits me.

Sitting upright with Flora still in my lap, Colt leans down and kisses my lips fiercely.

Pulling back, I gaze at Flora, my heart feeling too big for my chest.

As if reading my mind, she says, "Don't overthink." She cups my cheek, her thumb brushing my stubble. "We're all here together. You're safe."

I turn my head, catching Colt's eye. He smiles, dimples flashing. That smile always undoes me, revealing the man's heart beneath the tough exterior.

"I love you both," I whisper. I'm not usually one for

sappy declarations, but what we did has obliterated my walls.

Colt pulls me in for another kiss, our lips and tongues tangling. Flora kisses my neck, and we slowly explore each other as if we've been doing this for years.

We're all connected, bound together by more than just sex or shared secrets. It's something deeper, an unbreakable link that defies explanation.

We continue, taking turns savoring each other, losing ourselves in the heady pleasure of skin-on-skin contact.

The forest floor is hard beneath me, but at this moment, I couldn't care less. I've never felt so at home.

We remain like that for some time, basking in each other.

As the cool night air caresses our sweat-dampened skin, I realize we'll have to move, even though I'm content to stay here forever, wrapped in them.

"I don't want to let you go," I murmur. "Ever."

Colt's hand squeezes my shoulder. "We're not going anywhere."

"We stick together," Flora says, her voice steady. "Forever."

I feel her lips press a kiss against my shoulder, and I tighten my arms around her. "Always," I agree. It's a promise, a vow among the three of us.

45

EPILOGUE

COLT

Eight months later…

I stand with Nash and Flora, our birthday girl, in an abandoned warehouse on the outskirts of town. It's the anniversary of the day we met. The first time, we all felt whole.

The muffled screams of Marcus, a dealer who tried to steal from Ty, echo through the empty space. His face is barely recognizable after what we've done.

"You should've known better than to cross us," I tell him, admiring Flora's handiwork with the blowtorch. She's learned well over the past month, her movements precise and calculated.

Nash circles behind Marcus, his fingers trailing along the chair. "I think he needs another reminder about loyalty."

Flora's eyes meet mine, that familiar darkness swirling in their depths. Her chest rises and falls rapidly, and I know she's feeling the same rush I am. This brings us together—not just love but our shared appreciation for justice.

Nash grabs Marcus's hair, yanking his head back. "Tell us where the money is." When Marcus stays silent, Nash nods to Flora.

She steps forward, her movements graceful even in this grim setting. The sound of another scream fills the space as she works. The way she handles the tools with such precision makes my heart race.

"I have to admit," Nash says, his voice low and heated, "watching you both work is incredible."

Flora smiles, that dangerous glint in her eye that I've come to love. "He's almost ready to talk. I can feel it."

I move behind her, touching her hip as she continues. Nash watches us intently, his breath quickening. The tension in the room shifts, becoming charged with something else entirely.

I watch as Marcus's resolve finally crumbles under Flora's expert touch. His body convulses with sobs, the chair creaking beneath him.

"Please... please stop," he chokes out. "The money's in a storage unit at Victory Storage. Unit 247. The key is taped under the dumpster behind Joe's Bar."

I catch Nash's eye and give him a subtle nod. He pulls out his phone, stepping away to contact Remy. We'll need verification before deciding what happens next.

Flora maintains pressure on Marcus's wounds, keeping him on edge. Her fingers dance across the tools before her, a silent threat of what's to come if his information proves false.

"How long until Remy can check?" I ask Nash.

"Twenty minutes," he replies, tucking his phone away. "He was already in the arca."

I slide my hand along Flora's back as she works. "Hear that, Marcus? Twenty minutes to pray you're telling the truth."

Marcus's whimpers fill the space between us. His eyes dart frantically between us, probably wondering which of us will hurt him next. My money's on Flora—she's been particularly creative today.

Nash picks up a pair of pliers and turns them over. "Shall we pass the time productively?"

I watch Flora's fingers trail across Marcus's chest, each touch precise and methodical. Her work sends shivers down my spine. Nash stands behind her, his eyes dark with appreciation for her technique.

Marcus screams again as Flora applies pressure to a particularly sensitive spot. The sound echoes through the warehouse, mixing with the hum of anticipation between us.

"You have such natural talent," Nash whispers to Flora, his voice thick with admiration. His hand finds her waist, steadying her as she works.

I step closer, drawn by the electricity crackling between us. The familiar darkness rises within me, matching the shadows in their eyes. We're broken in all the same ways, fitting together like jagged pieces of the same puzzle.

Flora looks up at me, her chest heaving with exertion. "Should we try something new?" she asks, gesturing to the array of tools before us.

Nash selects a particularly wicked-looking instrument. "I think this might elicit the response we're looking for."

The anticipation builds as we work in perfect synchronization. Each gasp and plea from Marcus only intensifies our connection. We move like dancers in a macabre ballet, our bodies gravitating toward each other as we circle our victim.

"Ten more minutes," Nash reminds us, his voice husky. His hand brushes mine as we reach for the same tool, sending electricity through my arm.

Flora's movements become more fluid and more confident. Her power transforms her, and I can't tear my eyes away. Nash watches her, too, his breathing shallow and quick.

Marcus's suffering becomes background noise to the symphony of our shared darkness. We're drawn together by something primal and dangerous that normal people would never understand.

But we understand each other perfectly.

I check my phone, which buzzes with Remy's message. "He was telling the truth. Money's all there."

Nash's hand tightens on Flora's waist. "Well, Marcus, it looks like you get to make a choice."

Marcus sags in relief, blood dripping from his various wounds. "Please... please just let me go. I won't say anything."

I crouch in front of him, gripping his chin. "That's not one of the options." His eyes widen as I continue.

"Here's what you get to choose from: we can drag this out, make it slow and painful until you're begging for death. Or we can make it quick."

Flora steps forward, her fingers trailing down my arm. "There is a third option."

I glance at her, seeing that familiar dark gleam in her eyes. Nash moves closer, understanding immediately what she's suggesting.

"You can watch us fuck each other while you bleed out," I tell Marcus. "Consider it a final show before the curtain falls."

Marcus's face contorts in confusion and terror. "You're all insane."

"That's not an answer," Nash says, his voice dropping to that dangerous register that makes my cock twitch. "Choose."

Marcus looks between the three of us, tears mixing with blood on his cheeks. "Just... just make it quick. Please."

"Let's give our guest what he wants," Flora says, stepping closer to Marcus. Her eyes shine with a mix of excitement and cruelty.

Nash asks, "You want the honors, little bird?"

She nods, a wild smile playing on her lips. The rush of anticipation hits me like a drug as I watch her step closer to Marcus. Her gaze meets mine, and I see the feral desire burning in her eyes. She takes the knife from Nash, positioning herself in front of Marcus.

In one smooth, graceful movement, she slashes the blade across Marcus's throat. Blood sprays across her face and chest, and her eyes close in ecstasy at the sensation.

That raw, primal display sends my own desire skyrocketing. "Time to reward our birthday girl," I growl, stepping forward and gripping her hips.

I tear her panties off in my haste. Lifting her off the ground, I sink my cock into her in one thrust, holding her suspended in the air as I pound into her. Her blood-spattered body arches against mine, her legs wrapping around my waist as she meets my rhythm.

Nash stands to the side, stroking his hard cock. "That's it, Colt. Fuck her hard. Give her a real good birthday gift she'll never forget."

My hands dig into Flora's skin as I pound into her, reveling in the feeling of her tight heat. "You like that, angel? You like being fucked while you're covered in blood?"

She moans, her head falling back. "Yes... Oh, yes."

I look over at Nash. "Think she can take both of us?"

He grins, stepping closer. "Let's find out."

I pull out of Flora, setting her down on her feet. Without hesitation, she turns and straddles Nash, sinking down on his cock with a gasp. I move behind her, gripping her hips as I guide my cock back into her pussy. It took a while to work her up to take us both in her cunt, but now she's a fucking pro. We fall into a rhythm, our movements in sync as we take her.

Flora's breath comes in sharp pants, her body caught between ours. "Yes... oh God, both of you... feels so good."

I lean forward, my lips brushing her ear. "That's it, angel. Take it all."

Nash's hands grip her hips, his fingers leaving marks on her skin. "Look at me, Flora. Watch me while we fuck you."

She lifts her head, meeting his gaze as I thrust into her from behind.

The hot, slick tightness of Flora envelops me, pulling me further into our shared frenzy. I close my eyes, surrendering to the sensations coursing through my body. Her pussy grips me like a velvet vise, milking my cock as I thrust into her. I feel the smooth, hard length of Nash rubbing against my shaft, then the head of my cock.

"Fuck, yeah," Nash grunts. "Ride that cock."

His cock slides against mine, making me shudder as we both plunge into her. The feeling of being buried balls-deep in Flora's pussy with my best friend and lover is better than any drug. I clench my jaw to hold back the roar that's building in my throat. Every nerve ending is on fire, and my skin feels too tight for my body.

"You feel that?" Nash murmurs. "The way our cocks rub together inside you? You like being filled up by both of us?"

Flora moans, her fingers digging into Nash's shoulders. "Yes... Fuck yes, I do."

My hands find her hips, guiding her as I thrust into her. The wet, slippery sounds of our fucking fill the air, mixing with our heavy breathing and moans. Nash fucks her in perfect sync with my rhythm, our cocks working in concert to bring her pleasure.

I bury my face in her neck, breathing in her scent as I pump my hips. "That's it, baby. Such a good girl taking us both in that perfect little cunt."

Flora's breaths come in short gasps, her body moving desperately between us. "It's too much... oh God, I can't..."

I tighten my grip on her hips, pulling her onto my cock harder. "Then come for us. Let us feel it, baby."

Nash's hands slide down to cup her ass, lifting her up and down on his shaft. "That's right, Flora. Let go. Let us see your beautiful face when you come."

The tension in Flora's body winds tighter and tighter, her muscles clenching around us. I feel the telltale ripple of her orgasm building, and I know she's close. I've never seen anything more beautiful than her face twisted in ecstasy as we take her.

"Fuck, Colt... Nash... I'm gonna..."

Her body spasms around us, her liquid heat pushes me to the edge. I can feel Nash's cock throbbing inside her, his own release nearing. Our rhythm becomes frantic as we both chase our peaks, spurred on by the sounds of Flora's pleasure.

"Come for us, angel," I growl, biting her shoulder. "Come all over our cocks."

Nash's fingers dig into her ass, and he groans, his hips stuttering as he fills her with his release. "Fuck, yes... come with me, Flora."

Flora screams, her pussy clamping down on us in waves as she comes. The sensation pushes me over the edge, and I bury my cock deep inside her, pumping her full of my release. Our tangled trio trembles as we ride out the storm of our shared ecstasy.

I kiss the curve of her neck, tasting the salt of her sweat, mingling with the coppery tang of blood that still clings to her skin. Her body is slick and warm between us, the sticky mess of our combined fluids coating our skins. After a few more strokes, Nash pulls out, leaving my cock buried inside her.

Flora's head falls back against my shoulder as she pants, riding out the aftershocks of her orgasm. I hold her close, my arms wrapping around her, and her hands cover mine, still on her hips. I bend my head to place soft kisses along her shoulder and neck, enjoying the feeling of her soft skin beneath my lips.

Nash runs his hands through his hair, his breath slowly returning to normal. "That was definitely one for the record books."

I chuckle, pressing a final kiss to the curve of Flora's neck. "You can say that again."

She shifts in our arms, turning her head to meet my eyes. Her cheeks are flushed, and her hair is sweaty, but she's never looked more beautiful. I brush a strand of hair behind her ear, unable to resist the pull I feel toward her.

"You okay, angel?" I ask softly.

"I'm definitely more than okay," she says, touching my cheek. Nash steps up behind her, his arms wrapping around her waist. Their blood-spattered bodies lean against each other, and for a moment, it's just us three, lost in the bubble of our shared passion.

But then reality creeps back in. I survey the room,

taking in the mangled body of our victim. We've all been here before—the adrenaline, the blood, the sex. Cleaning up and disposing of the body is routine, but that doesn't make it any less necessary.

With a soft sigh, Flora extricates herself from Nash's embrace and begins gathering her clothes. I hear the soft sounds of fabric rustling and zippers being pulled as she and Nash put their clothes back on.

"You're beautiful," Nash says softly, his voice laced with affection. Flora pauses, and I can almost feel the warmth of his words from across the room.

"Thanks," she replies, her voice sounding small. "I must be a sight, all covered in blood."

I turn back to see her reaching up to touch her cheek, her eyes reflecting the turmoil I feel inside. I've learned that conflict intimately—the desire and disgust that bubbles up after a kill. It's a product of our shared darkness, a strange shame that sits uncomfortably alongside the thrill of taking a life.

I cross the room to stand behind her, touching her shoulders. Together, we look in the mirror at our reflection—three killers covered in the blood of our most recent assignment.

"We're fucked up," Flora says softly, her eyes meeting mine in the reflection.

"Yeah, we are," I reply, stepping closer so our bodies are pressed together. Her warmth seeps into me, chasing away the chill that always follows a kill. "But you wouldn't have it any other way."

She turns in my arms, her eyes searching mine. "No, I wouldn't."

Nash steps up beside us, his eyes raking over us with heated intent. "You know we're just getting started, right?"

Flora's eyes widen, and she bites her lip, but the spark of desire I see there tells me everything I need to know.

We're fucked up, all right. Maybe even beyond saving, but in that moment, standing in a grimy warehouse, covered in blood and sweat, I wouldn't change a thing. Not as long as I have Nash and Flora by my side.

I lean down, capturing Flora's lips in a searing kiss. Nash joins us, his hands tangling in her hair as he pulls her closer. Our shared obsession consumes us once again, the memory of our kill only adding fuel to the fire.

The violence we just inflicted, the blood we wear like war paint, only serves to heighten our desire. We're monsters, through and through, and we crave this darkness together.

And in that warehouse, bathed in the afterglow of violence and debauchery, I know we're exactly where we're meant to be.

THANK you for reading *Carnival Mayhem!* Did you enjoy it? If so, check out my other Carnival Books:

Cade & Lily's Book - Carnival Nightmare: A Dark Stalker Romance

Lars & Alice's Book - Carnival Obsession: A Dark Romance

Gage & Aurora's Book - Carnival Monster: A Dark Serial Killer Romance

Phoenix & Tilly's book - Carnival Stalker: A Dark Stalker Romance

Tyson & Sofia's book - Carnival Master: A Dark Romance

I will release one more carnival book in this series, as I feel Remy deserves his HEA, too. That will be coming early next year.

More books by me:

Grave Intentions: A Dark Taboo Romance

Forbidden Harvest: A Dark Taboo Romance

Hunted: A Dark Romance

Welcome to Carnage: A Dark Romance Novella

Stranded: A Dark Romance novella

Salvation: A Dark Stalker Romance

Carjacked: A Dark Hitchhiker Romance

ABOUT THE AUTHOR

I've always been drawn to the dark side of fiction. My stories? They're an exploration of that darkness, filled with mysterious masked men, fearless heroines, and spice that'll set your Kindles ablaze.

Ever since I can remember, I've been captivated by the darker side of romance. It's necessary to add that I don't condone these kinds of relationships in real life. However, the intoxicating chase, the deadly dance, the heart-racing fear, and an irresistible attraction I adore writing.

I exclusively publish on Amazon, providing a thrilling escape for those who dare to venture into the dark side of love and lust. If you've read my book and found yourself wanting more, follow me on Amazon or social media for updates on my next dark novella release. Your adventure is only a page flip away.

Printed in Great Britain
by Amazon